THE
SCHOOL
FRIEND

BOOKS BY ALISON JAMES

THE
SCHOOL
FRIEND

ALISON JAMES

bookouture

Published by Bookouture in 2019

An imprint of StoryFire Ltd.

Carmelite House
50 Victoria Embankment
London EC4Y 0DZ

www.bookouture.com

ISBN: 978-1-78681-955-0
eBook ISBN: 978-1-78681-954-3

Previously published as *The Friendship Pact*

PROLOGUE

What frightens her most about the body is its unresponsiveness. The absolute inertia. It might as well be a piece of wood. That's what she remembers clearly from that last time, all those years ago when they were children. The instinctive holding of breath, waiting for some sort of reaction; a sigh, a twitch.

It lies there at their feet, and the absolute stillness starts to play tricks with her mind. Did she just see something – a slight upward movement of the chest, the flicker of a finger? In the dim light, she can't be sure and convinces herself that they could have got this all wrong. That he wasn't dead after all.

But before she can speak – or even articulate this thought – it has slipped away, out of reach, and for the second time in her life she watches that dark, cold water receive a body and swallow it up.

PART ONE

ONE

SEPTEMBER 1995

The movement is swift and vicious, like an assault. An arm hooked around her neck, half strangling her.

Lucinda Katherine Mary Gibson twists round to look at her assailant, who has hurtled up to her as she's innocently walking through the school gates at the end of the day. She knows this girl is in the same class, but Lucy has only been at Redgate High School for two weeks and so hasn't learned all her classmates' names. Even so, she recognises this particular girl. She has 'hard' written all over her. She's about the same height, but while Lucy still has the slight, knobbly body of a child, this girl is heavyset and well-developed. She has breasts. Her sandy-red hair is thick and straight, but instead of having the pinkish freckled skin of a redhead, her complexion is a sallow dark olive and her eyes slant in an unexpected way. There's a distinct gap between her two top teeth and she wears her socks extra-long so that they cover her knees and end at mid-thigh. In an as yet unexplored area of her brain, Lucy understands that this is a provocative gesture, designed to draw attention to the girl's body.

'You're the teacher's pet,' her assailant says accusingly.

In response, Lucy walks faster down the street, trying to get away. Wishing it was one of the days when her mother came to collect her in the car.

'Oi, four eyes,' the girl says, giving Lucy a slight shove with her elbow. The gesture is boisterous rather than malicious. 'I said: you're the teacher's pet. Miss Gresham's, I mean.'

'I'm not,' replies Lucy hotly. She can feel sweat breaking out along her hairline, underneath her straight, baby-fine blonde plait. It makes her glasses slip down her nose slightly, and she pushes them back up with a self-conscious little gesture. She reaches instinctively to fiddle with the end of her hair, which is something she does when she's nervous.

'You're rich too, though,' says the girl. She pronounces it 'dough'.

It occurs to Lucy that, in her own clumsy fashion, the girl is trying to spark up a conversation, but Lucy doesn't have any idea why or to what end, so she doesn't know how to respond. She dips her head. 'I'm not rich,' she mumbles.

'You are. I've seen your Mum's car.'

Lucy's heart sinks. Her mother drives an ostentatiously shiny 4x4 and is in the habit of parking it on the zigzag lines near the front gates, despite the school's ban on this practice.

'It's that big black one, isn't it?' the girl goes on, with a knowing smile. 'Must be nice being rich.'

Lucy opens her mouth to contradict her, but then shuts it again. Possibly, compared to some of the other pupils at Redgate, she is rich. Or at least well off. She is aware that she and her parents live in a large, comfortable house with a big garden, and that they have a cleaning lady, and go on foreign holidays at least twice a year.

'Where d'you live?' her tormentor goes on, with her uncanny ability to read Lucy's mind.

When Lucy fails to answer, she grabs Lucy's forearm and jostles her slightly. Lucy's satchel slips off her shoulder and her new pencil case drops onto the pavement, spilling its contents.

'Is that a protractor?' the girl asks, snatching it off the ground before Lucy can reply. Their class has just been told they need to use a protractor for their maths homework, which involves measuring line segments and angles. Her eyes gleam. 'Can I have a lend of it?'

'You mean can you borrow it?' Lucy corrects her primly.

'Yeah, can I have a borrow? I haven't got one.'

'Sure.' Anything to get her to go away. 'But I'll need it back.'

The fact is, Lucy isn't too worried about the protractor. She has more geometry equipment at home, and if she can't find a spare protractor her mother will be only too happy to pop out to the shops for one, or ask her father to get one on his way home from work.

'Ask me for it tomorrow,' the girl says. She turns on her heel to walk in the other direction, thrusting the protractor into her bag with the relish of an archaeologist discovering a rare treasure.

Is that all it took, Lucy wonders, taken aback. 'What's your name?' she calls.

'Adele.' The girl shouts over her shoulder. 'Adele Marie Watts.'

Adele homes in on Lucy during morning break the next day. She's chewing on a rubber band, twirling it between her gapped white teeth.

'Have you got my protractor?' Lucy asks, although she has already completed her geometry homework using one she found in her father's desk drawer.

'It's up my house,' says Adele casually. She's wearing a denim jacket over her uniform blouse, although the school rules are very clear that only blazers with the RHS badge are allowed. 'Why don't you come round to mine for your tea, then I can give it you back.'

'What – today?' Lucy's pale grey eyes widen. She is not used to social arrangements being treated so casually. In the Gibson household, these things are always scheduled in advance, with full parental consultation.

'Yeah, why not? You're not scared, are you?' Adele flicks her arm playfully.

Was Lucy scared? The truth was that she probably was, a bit. 'I can't really come today,' she says, trying to sound unavailable rather than anxious. Her mother is picking her up in the car and they're going straight to ballet, but she doesn't tell Adele that. Ballet classes will provide further evidence that she's rich. Even if today was a day when she was walking home, her mother would probably call the police if she didn't show up by 4.30 p.m. She can't just go round to someone else's house.

'Fine, tomorrow then,' says Adele.

What Adele refers to as her 'house' turns out to be a council flat on the eastern edge of Redgate. Lucy, on the other hand, lives in a detached Edwardian villa in Haverleigh Park, a slice of stockbroker belt to the north-west of Redgate that enjoys a speedy thirty-minute service direct to Waterloo from Haverleigh Holt station. She's never been inside a flat in her life, let alone a local authority one.

The Watts family are numerous, loud and frankly terrifying. In addition to Adele's mother, who is as wide as she is tall and has Adele's freckles, there's her older half-brother Jamil, her younger siblings Tyler and Chelsee and assorted cousins. There's also an older half-sister Janine, who has a baby and a flat of her own. Adele's father puts in an appearance, standing in the kitchen, arguing with Adele's mother and smoking a fat hand-rolled cigarette. He has dreadlocks and is, Adele informs Lucy proudly, 'mixed race'.

Nobody sits at the table for tea. In fact, there is no table. People perch on the edge of armchairs and the sofa with crisp sandwiches and – 'for afters' – Pop Tarts. Lucy, who has never eaten a Pop Tart before, would have been thrilled by this menu if she weren't so nervous. She discovers from the family's exchanges while they're eating – more argument than conversation – that Adele is twelve and a half, a whole year older than she is, but she has been held back at school and is repeating Year Seven.

'Shall we go into your room and play?' Lucy whispers, licking icing from her fingers in the absence of anything resembling a napkin. Adele looks at her blankly, then shows her the tiny room that she shares with Tyler and Chelsee. The two younger children sleep on bunk beds and Adele sleeps on a single mattress on the floor next to them, surrounded by a mess of toys and clothes.

'Sometimes I sleep on the couch,' she says, with a defensiveness that sounds almost like pride.

Jamil has the other single bedroom and her mother occupies the third bedroom.

There is no mention of the borrowed protractor or any offer to return it, and Lucy is reluctant to mention it, especially as she has no need of it. Whereas Adele clearly does.

Lucy's mother wanted to come to collect her from the Watts' flat, but Lucy persuaded her to agree to a less awkward compromise and meet her at the bus stop where Adele catches the bus to school. The two girls walk there together, and as they do so Adele slips her arm unselfconsciously through Lucy's. Lucy is surprised but oddly pleased by this gesture of intimacy. The car is already parked opposite the bus stop, and Lucy sees her mother studying the interaction in the rear-view mirror.

'Did you have a nice time, darling?' she asks as the car pulls out into traffic, with Adele waving from the pavement.

'Um, yes,' says Lucy uncertainly. She's still not entirely sure how she feels about the visit. 'We had Pop Tarts.'

'Goodness!' Mrs Gibson forces a smile. 'You'll need to make sure you brush your teeth when we get back. And this girl, Adele... you like her?'

'Yes,' says Lucy, more with confusion than conviction. 'I like her.'

'So when am I coming to yours, Luce?'

Adele barrels up to Lucy in the playground the next day, slinging an arm round her shoulder with such vigour that Lucy almost falls over. Her glasses bounce to the end of her nose and she has to put up a hand to stop them falling onto the tarmac.

'Coming to mine?' Lucy asks stupidly, rearranging her fair plaits.

'Yeah. You came to tea at mine, so now you need to invite me over to yours. That's how it works, dummy! You know; being friends.'

'I'll have to ask my mum when you can come,' Lucy prevaricates.

'Ask her tonight,' Adele instructs her impatiently. 'And don't forget, okay?'

Lucy knows that Adele certainly isn't going to forget, much as she secretly hopes for such amnesia, so has no choice but to broach the topic with her mother after school.

'I don't know, darling,' her mother says, stacking freshly ironed cotton sheets into the airing cupboard, 'I'm not sure she's the ideal friend for you.'

'Why not?' Now that her own reluctance is being mirrored, Lucy feels oddly defensive of Adele,

'Well, didn't you say that she's a year older than you? She's almost a teenager. So she's bound to be more... mature than you are. Maybe it would be better to concentrate on making friends with the girls who were in your intake.'

Lucy would be only too happy for this to happen, but all those girls seem to know each other from primary school and have expressed no interest in her. And the boys do nothing but shout and pull her plaits. At the very least, Adele is a useful buffer between her and bullies.

'But I want Adele to come,' she says mulishly and, to her mother's surprise, flounces out of the room.

Later that night she gets up to use the bathroom and pauses on the landing. She can hear her parents talking through the open kitchen door.

'I mean, we know this was how it would be if we sent her to the local comp,' her father says. 'That's why we did it, isn't it? To expose her to a breadth of social experiences. Vital, with her being an only, we decided.'

'I know, Jeffrey, but…' Her mother says something she can't quite catch, but it sounds as though it ends in 'rough'.

'It'll burn itself out,' her father says calmly. 'These types of friendships always do. It's just the thrill of the unfamiliar. Completely normal as developmental stages go.'

'What if it doesn't?'

'It will. Just try and be a bit forbearing, for now.'

So Adele is formally invited to tea at the Gibsons' house three days later, on a Friday. The table is set with a linen cloth, and there are napkins. They eat chicken casserole – 'Euh, what even is this?' Adele grumbles through a mouthful of food when Felicity is out of earshot – followed by apple crumble and custard. After the meal, the girls go up to the top floor of the house where Lucy has her bedroom, along with a playroom and her own bathroom.

'You have three rooms?' Adele is incredulous. 'Three whole rooms just for you?'

'Yes.' Lucy nods.

'What about your brother and sisters?'

'I don't have any.'

'What – none at all? Not even half ones?'

Lucy shakes her head, while Adele spins round on the spot, taking in the heavy lined curtains in pink and white chintz, the thick carpet, the built-in bookshelves. On the wall is a large framed sampler embroidered with 'Lucinda Katherine Mary, 13th March 1984'.

Adele points at it. 'Who's that?'

'That's me. I'm Lucy for short.'

'Three names?' scoffs Adele, as though this is sheer greed.

'Katherine and Mary are my two grandmothers. I'm named after them.'

'So what's your mum called?'

'Felicity.'

Adele scrunches her nose with distaste. 'My mum's called Dawn.' Her eyes alight on the camcorder that Lucy was given for her eleventh birthday. 'Oh wow… wicked! Shall we make a TV show with it?'

'Like what?' asks Lucy uncertainly. The sad fact is that she's never really used the camcorder, because making videos is no fun on your own. A lot of the things in the playroom are more or less useless when there's no one else to play with.

'Let's do something like *Noel's House Party*. Except we can call it Dell and Lu's House Party.'

'What's that?'

'You know, on telly. Mr Blobby. Everyone watches Mr Blobby!'

Lucy doesn't. Her parents think Saturday-night light entertainment shows rot the brain, and she reads a book or does a jigsaw puzzle instead.

'He's, like, a character. He's pink and covered in big blobs and he talks like this – "Blobby, blobby, blobby".' She makes her eyes go big and googly and adopts a strange robotic voice. Lucy starts giggling, and finds that once she has started it's difficult to stop. Adele giggles too, a hysterical yelping which just makes Lucy laugh harder. 'You film me being Blobby and then we'll make me go backwards,' Adele suggests, showing Lucy how to rewind the footage and play it in reverse.

Adele's Mr Blobby voice and the walk are even funnier this way, and they spend the rest of the evening falling around clutching their sides, until Felicity Gibson taps on the door and announces that it's time to drive Adele home.

'We're best friends now,' Adele announces, with an endearing mixture of solemnity and confidence, before they head downstairs. She crooks her little finger and links it through Lucy's. 'Pinky promise.'

'Pinky promise,' agrees Lucy happily. She's had so much fun that she's quite prepared to overlook the fact that she saw Adele taking one of the silver christening bracelets from her jewellery box and secreting it in her skirt pocket.

Later that evening, Lucy sits with the jewellery box on her lap, looking at the square tray of red velvet where the silver bracelet used to be. An empty space created by Adele taking something from her. She experiences a strange, haunting sense of premonition, although she has no idea what it could mean.

TWO

MARCH, 2018

'This is my wife, Lucinda.'

As Lucy has anticipated, necks crane discreetly to see exactly who has managed to bag the eminent Mr Marcus Wheedon FRCS, celebrated interventional cardiac surgeon. Saviour of at least one member of the cabinet and – it's rumoured – a senior member of the royal family. The frank scrutiny of the assembled diners towards her make her feel like the painfully shy eleven-year-old who arrived at Redgate High with no friends and who shrank from the stares that her glasses, her height and her pale blonde hair attracted. Next to her, Marcus is like her shield, his confidence wrapping her in a protective cloak.

They are at a dinner party at the home of Marcus's sister, Fiona, in her large detached house on the edge of Wandsworth Common. Lucy has known her sister-in-law since she and Marcus first married, and she remembers meeting one of the couples – Fiona's friend Jane Standish and her husband Robin – at a Christmas drinks party, but the other people round the table are all strangers. The women wear jeans and casual tops, rendering her instantly overdone in her black figure-hugging Roland Mouret and teetering heels. But Marcus likes her to wear a dress when they go out.

'Lord knows you slob around the house in your jeans and sweats far too much as it is,' he chides her. 'It's not too much to ask to see you in something feminine is it, Lucinda? Every once in a while?'

That's Marcus's refrain if he ever senses the possibility of not getting his way – 'Is it too much to ask?' In doing so, he makes himself seem the reasonable one and Lucy, in wanting to dress for comfort rather than show, unreasonable.

'Besides,' he adds, because Marcus knows how to charm better than anybody, 'You should show off your fabulous figure. I want everyone to know how lucky I am.'

He is such an admirer of Lucy's willowy but curvy form that he cites it as one of many reasons for them not to have children: 'Think what pregnancy and childbirth will do to your body. I know; I saw it on my obs and gynae rotation as a junior doctor. You don't want that,' he assures her, meaning *he* doesn't want that.

They're late arriving at the dinner, of course, because Marcus was operating. But Lucy has discovered that people are only too willing to forgive a late arrival if they think you're saving a life, and everyone round the table beams when Marcus announces that he's come straight from an emergency quadruple bypass.

'Sorry… sorry!' He holds his arms wide in exaggerated bonhomie.

'Poor you,' one woman with glossy dark hair murmurs. 'You must be exhausted.'

'Get that man a glass of champers, stat!' one of the male guest chimes in. The Wheedons have missed their starter of crab cakes and arrived just as the boeuf bourguignon is being served. Marcus is seated next to the woman with the dark hair, who cups her hand and stares at him in frank awe. Lucy is next to Robin Standish, a quiet, serious academic with a weak chin and glasses. He, at least, doesn't seem to be affected by the godlike aura of Marcus Wheedon.

'Shame you had to miss the crab,' he says equably, pouring her wine while everyone fusses over making sure Marcus is served the vegetables first. 'Must be a pain, being permanently on the on-call surgeon's diet.' He raises an eyebrow and Lucy smiles back at him. She catches sight of Marcus watching her, and smooths a loose lock of creamy blonde hair behind her ear, pretending to examine the silver mark on her knife. Robin's expression switches to one of combined pity and curiosity. She knows he's pigeonholed her as a trophy wife and, sadly, he's right. Mrs Lucinda Wheedon (Marcus never calls her Lucy) has always been pretty, stylish and elegant, and completely in the shadow of her overachieving husband.

As the plates are cleared and chocolate mousse is served, one of the women leans across the table to Lucy. 'Do you and your husband have children?'

Lucy is about to shake her head, but before she has a chance, Marcus cuts across her.

'Two,' he says. 'One of each.'

'They're my stepchildren,' Lucy adds, as always feeling the need to explain this.

The woman doesn't even try to hide her curiosity. 'How long have you two been married?'

'Five years,' Lucy murmurs, dipping her head.

'So… didn't you want any of your own?'

Marcus is watching her over the rim of his claret glass. She shakes her head at her inquisitor, as she is expected to do. Because having had two children with his first wife, Amber, Marcus was adamant that further offspring were quite unnecessary. Surplus to requirements. 'More than two will be too much work,' he had said firmly. 'Not to mention the expense.'

Lucy didn't point out that plenty of doctors on a similar salary managed to provide for three or even four children more than adequately.

'And, anyway, there isn't the space,' he had added. (This last reason despite their house having four bedrooms: one for them, one for each of his existing children and one for guests; rarely used).

As a result, alternate weekend visits from fourteen-year-old Tom and eleven-year-old Lydia are the extent of Lucy's parenting experience, and likely to remain so.

'You're free to work full-time then,' Robin says. 'What is it you do for a living?'

The dreaded 'What do you do?' question. Lucy's heart sinks. The truth is that her job is to make Marcus's extremely pressured working life easier. By anticipating and dealing with any minor problems that can't be allowed to disrupt his day.

'At the moment I'm studying part-time,' she tells him. 'Social Anthropology.' The part time structure of the course had been a compromise Marcus had insisted on: full time would have meant her being away from home too much in his opinion.

'Ah. That sounds very interesting,' he says kindly. 'What sort of career will it lead to when you've finished?'

Before she can stop herself, Lucy has let out a bitter little laugh. 'Sadly, there's only room for one career in our household. And, according to my husband, Humanities degrees are pointless and "arty-farty".'

Across the table, Marcus sets his wine glass down slowly. 'I'm afraid you'll have to excuse my wife.' Even though the remark is addressed at the assembled guests, his gaze is directed straight at Lucy. 'Jokes never were her forte.'

'But, actually, there are lots of careers you can do with a master's in Social Anthropology,' Lucy has turned back to Robin but raises her voice slightly so that her husband can still hear her. 'Human resources, charity work, NGOs, the criminal justice system…'

Fiona appears from the kitchen with a big tray of cups. 'Coffee in the sitting room, I think. It's a bit too chilly for the garden.'

Her husband, Jonathan, stands up and the other guests start to get to their feet too.

'A word please, darling,' Marcus says to Lucy, with a rictus smile. She follows him out into the hall, where he grabs her elbow and jerks it sharply upwards. 'Why are you always so intent on making a scene?'

'I was not making a scene!' Lucy feels suddenly cold, even though the skin on her neck and cheeks is burning. 'Robin asked me a question and I answered it.'

'Well, I'll thank you not to show me up like that,' he releases her arm abruptly, pulling her off balance so that she stumbles sideways into the wall. Fiona and Jane are watching mutely from the kitchen doorway, and from their silence Lucy knows that they are embarrassed to be witnessing this marital discord.

Fiona bustles forward with the jug of milk she has been to fetch. 'He's overworked, that's all,' she says quietly, her tone placatory. 'Under terrific strain, with all the NHS cutbacks in his department. Poor Marcus: his working life is intolerable at the moment.'

Lucy knows from past experience that Fiona, who worships her older brother, will always make excuses for him. And saving lives on a daily basis is the best excuse of all, every time. His family indulge him; his colleagues worship him or fear him, or both. A god at work and a dictator at home. She manages a weak smile, rubbing her elbow.

It's a relief when Marcus decides they need to leave before the port and brandy are produced.

No sooner have they got in through the front door of their house in Barnes, when the phone rings. Marcus answers.

'Marcus Wheedon... Oh, hello there, you! Yes, of course.' His tone is graciousness personified, but he covers the handset with a scowl and says, 'It's Fi's pet guard dog.'

Lucy takes the handset, frowning.

'Lucy, hi... it's Jane Standish. Listen, are you okay? Only I was a bit worried about you earlier.'

Marcus stands three feet away from her, his eyes on her face. A muscle twitches in his neck.

'Oh yes,' Lucy says as brightly as she can muster. 'Of course I am. I'm absolutely fine.'

THREE

A week later, Lucy receives a text from an unknown sender.

*Hi Lucy, I'm in the Barnes area today, and I wondered if you
fancied meeting for a coffee? It would be great to have a chat. Jane x*

It's obvious to her that Jane Standish is checking up on her,
having witnessed Marcus's behaviour at the dinner party. A tiny
part of her is relieved. Marcus is so charming when in company
that no one is ever willing to believe anything negative about him.
And here, now, is someone who has seen with her own eyes what
he can be like. Someone who is prepared to reach out. On the
other hand, if Marcus knew she was meeting with Jane Standish
behind his back, he would be furious. She starts to type.

Sorry, afraid I'm not free.—Then she pauses and deletes what
she's just typed. Marcus will be in the operating theatre all day: he
has no idea how his wife will be spending her morning. And she
would only be going in order to reassure Jane anyway. To show
her that she really is fine. She types again.

*Great. How about The Good Egg café on White Hart Lane?
11.30?*

As she sets off on foot in the direction of Mortlake, she wonders
how, or even if, she will be able explain her marriage to Jane. It

was never going to be easy taking on the role of a second wife, but at the time of their engagement, Lucy was still so infatuated with Marcus that she reassured herself – and everyone else – that it would be fine. Not that there was any vigorous opposition: her future husband won over both of her parents, especially her father. Her mother died from breast cancer three years ago, and although she liked Marcus, she was a little more wary. 'He is quite a bit older,' she had counselled. 'And taking on someone else's children isn't going to be easy, especially for an only child with no experience of younger siblings.'

Therein lies Lucy's problem, according to Marcus. Whenever they have a disagreement or Lucy shows any sign of doubt or weakness, he claims that her character defects are due to her mother being overprotective, mollycoddling her, insulating her from the realities of life. Perhaps there is some truth in that. But Lucy attended university a hundred and fifty miles from her parental home and loved every minute of it. She has had plenty of other boyfriends too. Because she went to a girls' school for GCSEs and A levels, she was a late starter on that front, but she had only been at university for days when she fell into her first proper relationship. Dan was a medical student that Lucy met at a freshers' week party. He was shy, serious and sweet-natured and they dated for over two years.

After she graduated, she had a few short flings and a couple of relationships that lasted nine months and eighteen months respectively. But none of these men had the impact on her that Marcus did. Compared to Marcus, they were just boys. Dan was an embryonic doctor, a doctor-in-waiting, but Marcus Wheedon was the finished article. He could crack open a chest cavity and get to the heart in under two minutes. Lucy's male contemporaries could barely do their own laundry. Marcus knew things too: if he couldn't fix a practical problem himself, he always knew someone who could. He got stuff done, and in the early days of their relationship, he seemed to delight in doing things for Lucy too. He took care of her. She passed seamlessly from the care of her parents to the care of this older, more worldly, man.

They met when she was hired to do some temporary work organising a research project in Marcus's department at St Mary's Hospital, six years after graduating from UAE. When she overheard him in the coffee room asking one of the junior doctors, 'Who's the pretty blonde with the fantastic legs?' her first reaction was astonishment that he meant her. That someone so powerful and charismatic had noticed her at all. From then on, every time she passed him in the corridor, her heat rate would speed up, something that she previously thought only happened in cheap romance novels. He was tall and extremely handsome, with piercing green eyes and a thick shock of chestnut brown hair so shiny that Lucy's fingers itched to reach out and touch it. Her discomfiture seemed to amuse him, and he made a point of smiling at her every time he saw her.

Then one day he saw her name written down on a piece of official paperwork and started saying, 'Morning, Lucinda' or 'Goodnight, Lucinda'. She had asked her other co-workers to call her Lucy, but somehow she didn't mind the more formal name from him. One day he even said, 'And how are you, Lucinda Katherine Mary?' and laughed when she blushed, unsettled at the intimacy of him having memorised her full name.

After a few weeks, Marcus asked her to help him with preparation of his research papers and started visiting her at her desk and leaving her flirtatious notes when she wasn't there. He would come in wearing blue scrubs that revealed a patch of dark chest hair and blood-spattered white clogs, surgical mask still knotted round his neck; attire that Lucy found both strangely glamorous and extremely sexy.

She was single at the time and renting a room from a friend in Battersea. As her infatuation with the dashing surgeon took hold, she all but abandoned her social life to spend most of her waking hours at work. She would rise early to wash her hair and plan her outfits, hurrying out of the house with her heart already pounding, and leave long after most people had gone home, dawdling in the hopes of snatching stolen moments with Marcus Wheedon. Within six months, she was hopelessly smitten. She overheard someone referring to her as 'Wheedon's latest acolyte', but this didn't trouble her. By definition, an acolyte was, after all, someone who provided help and devotion.

Even so, she could hardly avoid the knowledge that Marcus was married, though there were rumours that the marriage was troubled. She studiously avoided the subject of his wife and children, but one evening when he was leaning on her desk, and everyone else had gone home, he told her how unhappy he was with Amber, how impossible she was, how he wouldn't still be there if it wasn't for Tom and Lydia. These admissions were talismans of hope for Lucy, who would never have dared act on her infatuation otherwise. She told him she was sorry.

'I know you are, Lucinda; that's because you're lovely.'

He put a finger under her chin and tilted it slightly so that their eyes met. It was the first time there had been physical contact between them, but it was his words that thrilled Lucy as much as his touch.

A couple of weeks later, Marcus came round to her house to deliver a departmental laptop that she was borrowing. It was a flimsy excuse to visit, and they both knew it: there was no need for him to bring it round in person. For her part, Lucy suggested a time when her flatmate was out, and offered him wine. After a couple of drinks, Marcus told her that he and Amber were separating. That was all the encouragement Lucy needed, and they ended up in her single bed in her rented bedroom. The sex was as sensational as she had fantasised it would be. And so their affair began.

As an isolated only child who had grown up with her nose in a book, she had a rich fantasy life and a very romantic view of the world.

And here was a real-life romance, one that was happening to her, while her friends and contemporaries were still dating one disappointingly immature twenty-something after another. She felt special, chosen.

Six months later, by which time Marcus and Lucy were the chief topic of departmental gossip, he informed her that he was moving out of the house in Notting Hill Gate that he shared with Amber and into a flat of his own.

And then came the phone call.

'Is that Lucinda Wheedon?' The voice was cold, unfriendly.

'Yes; speaking.'

'This is Amber Wheedon.'

She never explained how she had got hold of Lucy's number, but by the time the call had finished, Lucy had a pretty good idea. Because what Amber had to say was that she and Marcus were not separated at all. He was still living under the same roof as Amber – and still sleeping in the same bed.

Marcus dismissed Lucy's attempt to end their relationship briskly and dispassionately. That was just Amber making trouble, he told her. He was in the process of moving out, and Amber was simply refusing to accept the inevitable.

'Could I visit you at the flat, then?' Lucy asked, still troubled. All their trysts were still in the bedroom of her shared house. This, and Amber's overt unhappiness, were not part of the romantic script she had written in her head.

'Not yet,' Marcus said firmly. 'When it's all settled.'

Confused and shocked, Lucy had taken the unprecedented step of not speaking to Marcus or returning his calls for three whole days. It was the tone of Amber's voice that disturbed her most. The fact was: Lucy believed her.

When she eventually admitted a rain-soaked Marcus to the Battersea house one dank, wet February evening, he handed her the keys to a newly-acquired flat. And then, to her shock, he dropped on one knee and said, 'Will you marry me, Lucinda?'

She hadn't answered for a few minutes, by which time Marcus had stood up again, frowning, as she brushed rain drops from his overcoat.

'I thought you were in love with me. I thought you'd be thrilled.'

'I am… it's just…' Lucy had been flustered. 'You're not even divorced yet… Maybe we should try living together in the flat for a while before we make any big decisions?'

And then she saw him angry for the first time.

'You little bitch,' he had said coldly, snatching the set of keys back from her hand so roughly that it left a weal on her palm. But it was his words that hurt her most, sending a jolt of ice down her spine. 'You tempt me away from my home and family and then have the nerve to suggest it's too trivial for us to get married? That it's less hassle just to shack up?'

Wrong-footed and a little frightened, Lucy assured Marcus that she did want to marry, but perhaps after a year or two. But he moved her possessions into the rented flat the following evening and they ended up marrying as soon as his divorce was finalised, in May 2013. It was a small affair at Chelsea Town Hall, with just Lucy's parents and a handful of friends. She wore a cream Chanel suit and a wide-brimmed hat rather than a long dress and veil, which seemed right, even if it was not how she had once pictured herself as a bride. It ended up being a happy day, happy enough to convince Lucy that getting married to Marcus was the right thing too. Because, after all, Lucy really did love him. She couldn't have loved anyone more. Or more blindly.

It starts to rain halfway through the fifteen-minute walk to the café, and Lucy has not brought an umbrella with her. By the time she arrives, her jacket is spotted with wet patches, her cheeks are damp and her pale hair is slicked darkly to her scalp. She feels flustered; more so knowing that she is not giving off the confident, reassuring air she had aimed for. At this moment in time, she does not look like someone who has their act – or their life – together.

The café is filled with sodden coats and umbrellas, steaming up the windows so much that Lucy doesn't see Jane coming in. Jane has remembered her umbrella, so her springy auburn curls look fresh and her make-up intact. She does look like a woman who has her act together. She's stylishly, if not fashionably, dressed in cowboy boots and a plaid dress that disguises her slightly matronly hips.

After they've ordered coffees, the two women exchange light chat about the terrible weather and discuss Jane's work at a chi-chi homewares shop in Clapham.

'It's not exactly an intellectual challenge,' she says with a rueful smile. 'And my dad would be turning in his grave at the thought of his brainy daughter working in a shop. But the hours are really flexible, so it's great for fitting in around the kids and their activities.'

'Sounds perfect then,' Lucy smiles over the rim of her coffee cup, hoping the entire conversation is not going to centre round children or the lack of them.

'So have you had any more thoughts about what you'll do once you've got your master's? You'll be finished with your studies in a few months, presumably?'

Lucy nods. 'I'm planning to take the summer off and then start looking around.' She hasn't run this past Marcus, of course, but it feels like the right thing to say.

'Any particular direction you're interested in?'

Lucy feels her cheeks colour slightly. Of course she has thought about this, quite a lot. She has discussed it with the other students on her course. But saying it out loud still feels strange, makes it disturbingly real. 'I'd really like to go down the charity route. Ideally something that involves working with asylum seekers.'

Jane nods, clearly thinking this sounds neither odd nor silly. But her warm brown eyes are fixed on Lucy's face as she says, 'I get the impression Marcus isn't keen. That he's not going to make that easy for you.'

Lucy makes a reflexive shrug. 'Well… I mean, obviously he's incredibly busy, and relies on me for support at home. And it's not as though we need a second income to make ends meet.'

'Of course not,' Jane says, with a slightly sardonic smile.

'But if there was something I really wanted to do then he wouldn't stand in my way.'

'I would bloody well hope not.'

'I mean, he'd support me.'

Lucy is aware of the guilty flush spreading up her neck. Would he? Does she really believe that? Jane clearly doesn't.

'It can't be easy, being married to Marcus,' she observes bluntly. He seems to take the expression "control freak" to a whole new level.'

'He's not that bad,' Lucy begins, then remembers that Jane saw with her own eyes that he was.

'And do you really not want children?' Jane goes on, before Lucy can steer the conversation onto something neutral. She glances desperately at her watch. 'You're… how old?'

'I've just had my thirty-fourth birthday.'

'Oh, so you're still young enough,' Jane exclaims. 'There's still plenty of time.' She is looking straight at Lucy, expecting an answer.

Lucy lowers her gaze. 'I did want children, yes. But Marcus is adamant that two is enough, so…' She picks up a paper packet of demerara sugar and twists it until the golden crystals scatter over the table. They have two children. Just not *her* children.

'He might change his mind. Men do, you know. Robin was one hundred per cent certain he never wanted three, but he relented.'

Lucy screws up the packet of sugar and tosses it onto her saucer. 'Unfortunately, Marcus can't really change his mind. He's had a vasectomy.'

Jane gives a sympathetic sigh, looking down into her own coffee as she stirs it. 'I suppose that's the risk of being the second wife. That he's already gone down that road with his first.'

'No…' Lucy bites her lip. 'He had the vasectomy a few weeks before we got married.'

Jane stops mid-stir, her eyes widening. 'What? And you knew about this?'

'He told me when we were on honeymoon.'

This time Jane makes no attempt to disguise her shock, allowing her mouth to fall open and shaking her head slowly.

'He didn't want there to be any accidents,' Lucy keeps her voice low. 'Any drunken mistakes.'

'You mean he doesn't trust you to use contraception correctly?' Jane says. 'Seriously, Lucy, that's so wrong! To do it without telling you. And for you to not find out until you're married and it's too late. Although…' She narrows her eyes slightly, adding darkly, 'of course, it never is too late.'

But it is too late, Lucy thinks grimly; *he's made sure of that.*

'Belt and braces: that's how Marcus does things at work,' Lucy explains. 'He can never afford to leave anything to chance: someone's life might depend on it. And I suppose that carries over into his private life as well.'

Jane gives her a long, steady look. There is kindness in it, but also resolve. 'What I saw at Fiona and Jonathan's the other night… that kind of behaviour isn't right, you know. Manhandling you like that constitutes…' Jane hesitates, moving her lips as though trying to pluck the right word from her mouth, '… abuse.'

Lucy pretends to be inspecting flaws in her manicure. She becomes aware that she's holding her breath.

'Lucy?' Jane's voice is gentle. 'I'm only bringing this up because I'm concerned for you. I know Fiona saw it too, but she's so blind to her brother's flaws there was no point in trying to discuss it with her.'

'What do you want me to say?' Lucy juts her chin slightly.

'Had he ever done that before?'

'Not really.'

This is not true, and she hopes Jane won't ask her to expand. She doesn't want to have to tell her that Marcus routinely asks where she's going and where she's been and with whom, has demanded to know her passcode so that he can access her phone at will. That he shouts and smashes things when he loses his temper. Instead she would like to tell Jane all about the day, when they were first working together, that she slipped into the back of the lecture theatre at St Mary's and watched Marcus explaining a procedure to medical students. She would like to describe the rapt attention on their faces, as he talked them through the intricacies of cardiac disease, infusing the talk with passion, humour and fascinating anecdotes. She'd love to tell Jane how attentive her husband can be, and about the surprise gifts that he brings home for her: expensive but personal pieces of jewellery, beautiful silk lingerie, exquisite scent. The impromptu trips he's planned for them: to Rome and the Swiss Alps. And Paris.

The trip to Paris, though, has stuck in her mind for other reasons too. Because that was when it all began to go wrong.

When they arrived in the city, Marcus was tired and stressed from operating, and rejected Lucy's suggestion of a moonlit wander along the Seine. They would eat in the hotel restaurant and then get an early night. But still, because it was Paris and the restaurant had a Michelin star, Lucy made an effort. She put on a sexy dress and very high heels, and plenty of scarlet lipstick. Over dinner, Marcus was tetchy and impatient with the waiters, who fawned over Lucy.

'More champagne for you, Madame?'

'Some dessert for you perhaps, Madame?'

As soon as they got to their room, he slammed the door and grabbed her by the arm. 'What the fuck was that about?'

'What? What was what about?'

'Flirting with the waiters like that. It was disgusting! Were you deliberately trying to humiliate me?'

'I wasn't flirting!' Lucy had protested. 'That's just what they're like in places like this. It's all part of their job.'

Marcus picked up a piece of brass sculpture from the antique side table and hurled it in her direction. It hit her temple, cutting it open. Lucy, shocked into silence, felt blood on her fingers. Then she started to cry, tears and mucous taking on the colour of the blood and making a rust-brown smear on her upper lip and chin. He came towards her, reaching out for her, but she shrank away, then darted to the door. He blocked her exit by placing his back against it, and shook his head.

'You're going nowhere, Lucinda. If you leave me, it will be the last thing you do.'

The memory of that night makes Lucy shiver.

'Are you okay?' Jane asks, peering into her eyes.

'I'm fine.'

Because she *is* fine, and therefore there's no need to tell Jane any of this. Instead of telling tales out of school about her marriage, she is going to embark on a campaign of positive public relations. She'll demonstrate that Marcus is no monster, that he can be reasonable. And she'll start by inviting the Standishes round to their house for supper.

'How about next Thursday?' she asks Jane, consulting the calendar app on her phone. Marcus doesn't usually operate on Thursdays, and so tends to get home at a more reasonable time. 'Just a kitchen supper: you and Robin and a couple of other friends.'

If Jane is taken aback by this development, she hides her doubts graciously. 'Of course, that would be lovely. Fiona says your house is fabulous. Can I bring anything?'

Lucy shakes her head as she pushes her arms into her damp jacket. She's already planning the menu: things Marcus particularly likes. 'Just yourselves.'

FOUR

Lucy decides she'll invite Helen to supper – one of the women on her university course – and Helen's partner Pete. She doesn't really know Pete, but he's an IT systems analyst so she calculates he should at least be intelligent enough to hold a decent conversation. Helen has a nose piercing and favours dungarees and boiler suits, so won't exactly be Marcus's cup of tea. But he's used to meeting people from very varied walks of life, and so there's nothing to stop him being at his affable best, even if he doesn't share Helen's politics. And Helen and Pete are childless, which is a big incentive for choosing them over her other friends. It will help steer Jane away from the vexed topic of parenthood. And Robin Standish is the easy-going sort who will get on with anyone.

First, and most importantly, she needs to get the occasion put in the diary. Almost every minute of Marcus's days are taken up with operating, outpatient clinics, private consultations, teaching commitments and committee work. Anything that Lucy and Marcus do together has to be tabled in his appointment diary at work, and in order to do this he insists that Lucy speaks to his PA, Beryl. 'Beryl's the only one who knows what I'm doing at any given time,' he tells her. 'Everything has to be run by her, or it's not happening.'

Lucy hates phoning Beryl. She tried arranging to text her instead, but Beryl, who is in her sixties, doesn't hold with this as a form of communication. In Marcus's presence, she's twinkly, smiley, almost flirtatious, but with everyone else she's a brisk, no-nonsense woman whose smile never reaches her eyes and who can signal disapproval with a single syllable.

'Isn't it time Beryl retired?' Lucy queried once.

'Nonsense, she's got as much energy as women twenty years her junior,' Marcus snapped back. 'And my life would grind to a halt without her: she's the only one who knows what's going on and where I'm supposed to be.'

His *life*, Lucy noted. Not his work life, but his entire life.

'And how are we?' Beryl trills when she picks up the phone on Lucy's fourth attempt.

She hates me, Lucy thinks. *She hates me because I get to sleep with her adored Marcus, and she never will. And she disapproves of me because I'm the flibbertigibbet he left his children for.* Lucy knows that Beryl is no fan of Amber either, but to her Tom and Lydia are mini deities.

'I'm fine, thank you,' Lucy says politely, inwardly furious that she has to defer to this woman before she can invite her own friends to her own home. 'I wonder if you could put something in the diary for next week: we're having people over for supper on Thursday, 7.30 for 8.'

'I'll double-check, but as far as I know, that should be fine.' Beryl speaks with vinegary politeness.

Lucy pauses a beat. 'So it's in the diary?'

'Yes,' says Beryl slowly and clearly, a parent being pestered by annoying child. 'I've just said it is.'

They're having a braised shoulder of lamb, because it's easy and because Marcus likes lamb. And they're start with some prawns, because he loves seafood, and finishing with lemon meringue pie, which is his favourite. She spreads a grey linen cloth over the long oak table in the breakfast room and sets it with floral plates, coloured glassware and a vase of bunched jonquils, creating an effect that's both pretty and informal, then sets about tidying the drawing room. Not that it needs very much doing, because her cleaner vacuumed and dusted in there a couple of days ago, and the room isn't used much. It's very much a grown-up room, with its tall shuttered windows, walls painted in Farrow & Ball's 'Down Pipe' and huge magenta velvet sofas. Tom and Lydia are discouraged from coming in here, and Marcus is insistent that their belongings stay in their own rooms. Lucy plumps up the sofa cushions and puts a vase of white tulips on the coffee table, then goes upstairs to change.

At seven twenty-five she hears Marcus unlocking the front door, slamming it behind him and flinging down his briefcase. The slamming and the flinging do not augur well. She has learned the signs over the years; the non-verbal clues to her husband's mood. When she comes downstairs, he doesn't compliment her on her red floral dress – which, like her supper table, is both pretty and informal – but instead scowls.

'I need a drink,' is all he says.

'I've just opened the wine,' Lucy says calmly, walking into the kitchen, where the air is filled with a deliciously garlicky aroma.

Marcus follows her then stops, stock-still, in the doorway. 'What the fuck is this?' he demands, gesturing towards the table.

'What d'you mean?' Lucy asks. Her fingers tremble, slipping on the neck of the chilled bottle of wine.

'All this? Why is the table set for six people?'

'Because we're having people over for supper,' Lucy says, keeping her tone even. 'Jane and Robin Standish, and Helen from college and her boyfriend Pete.'

'Why wasn't it in the diary?'

'It was,' Lucy insists, though, of course, she has no way of knowing this, because she is not the keeper of The Diary. She is just the wife. 'I phoned Beryl about it last week and asked her to put it in there.'

Marcus is shaking his head. 'No,' he says coldly. 'No, you didn't. It wasn't in there. If it was, Beryl would have told me. She never makes mistake about these things. It's her job, for fuck's sake.'

Lucy feels little currents of anger run down her spine, ending somewhere behind her knees, which start to shake. She grips the back of one of the chairs. 'I did. I told Beryl.' She forces the words out between her teeth. 'And she was supposed to let you know about it.' The wine in the glass she has just poured slops slightly as she lifts it to her mouth and takes a large gulp. 'Anyway, what does it matter? You're here now, and everyone else will be arriving in half an hour.'

'What does it matter?' Marcus's lips curl in a sneer. 'I'll tell you why it flaming well matters. I've been on my feet since six this morning. I've done a ward round, seen about twenty patients all with horrendously complex problems, had a meeting with hospital managers to try in vain to stop them axing the salary of our desperately needed second consultant, and I've done surgery to try and save a myocardial infarction case, who then went and died on the table.'

'But you don't operate on Thur—'

'It was an emergency case, you idiot! One that came in via A&E. And, in the middle of all this, nobody said anything about having to come home and entertain a bunch of strangers.'

Lucy is about to point out that Marcus already knows Fiona and Robin but thinks better of it. 'You'll feel better once you've had a drink and something to eat,' she soothes. 'I've made braised lamb.'

'I. Don't. Want. Fucking. Lamb,' Marcus roars. He stamps over to the oven, yanks open the door and pulls out the roasting tray, dropping it and its contents onto the floor. Boiling fat and roasting juices splash Lucy's bare shins and leave a crime scene smear on the floor.

'Marcus!' Lucy stares at the lump of half-cooked meat, which looks oddly human as it rests against a chair leg. 'What are you doing?' She ignores the sting of the hot liquid and tries to wipe the smears from her skirt.

He doesn't move. 'I would have thought that was bloody obvious. Even to you.'

Lucy squats down and tries to replace the lamb joint in the roasting tray. It's much hotter than she expected, and she burns the tips of her fingers. 'For heaven's sake, we've got people coming… please, let's just—'

But he's got the bit between his teeth now. She recognises the escalation of his mood only too well. 'How dare you hold a party without even telling me? I pay for all of this, you know!'

Marcus grabs the edge of the tablecloth and yanks it off the table. Lucy has seen people do that as a party trick and the objects on top of the cloth mysteriously stay where they are. But that is not what happens now. The vases of flowers and glassware topple onto the tiled floor and shatter; the silverware skitters against the skirting board. And Lucy's beloved Clarice Cliff butter dish, painted with a cheerful design of crocuses, smashes into several pieces, spilling out around the yellow splodge of butter. The dish belonged to her mother and was one of the few things in the house that pre-dated their marriage.

'Oh no!' Lucy drops to her knees and tries to rescue the dish, cutting her thumb on the sharp edge of the china.

'We're not having people for supper. Not if it's not been put in the diary.'

Marcus strolls to the fridge and opens a bottle of beer, tossing the cap in Lucy's direction with a careless lob.

'What am I supposed to tell people? They'll be on their way over here by now.' Lucy straightens up, still holding the debris of the broken butter dish in her hand. She extends the pieces to Marcus, her eyes swimming with tears. 'And this belonged to my mum.'

'Ah yes. Dear Felicity, the woman who made you into the overindulged child you are,' snaps Marcus. 'And I don't care what you tell them, just get rid of them.' He pushes roughly past his wife, and she loses her footing, knocking her hip painfully against the corner of the table.

Lucy phones Jane's mobile. She's driving, so Robin picks up. She's terribly sorry to cancel so late, Lucy mumbles, but she has just started vomiting. 'A gastric flu bug,' she lies. 'There's been a nasty one going round the hospital. Marcus must have brought it home with him.'

'Poor you,' Robin is all sympathy. 'Don't worry. We've got the babysitter anyway, so we'll probably pop along to the Picturehouse and catch a movie. Something we rarely get chance to do, so it'll be a bit of a treat to be honest.'

'I'm so sorry.'

'Don't worry at all. Another time. You just rest up.'

His kindness makes Lucy feel even worse, and the tears start to flow. In a croaky voice which probably makes her tale more plausible, she tells the same lie to Helen.

'We're just at the end of your road now actually,' says Helen, who sounds mildly irritated. She has driven all the way from Crouch End, crossing most of London, so it's hardly surprising. 'We could call in and check up on you? I've got flowers for you anyway: you may as well have them to cheer you up.'

Lucy closes her eyes, wondering if it is possible to feel any more wretched. 'No, don't do that; this bug is desperately contagious apparently. We'll rearrange, I promise.' She knows as she says this that it will never happen. She's not going to risk going through this again. This is the end of her trying to promote Marcus to her friends, to sell the idea of the perfect marriage. She'll just have to see them alone from now on. At least it means she won't have to humiliate herself by arranging social events via Beryl.

Beryl. Lucy wonders if she genuinely forgot to put the supper party in Marcus's diary, or if she accidentally-on-purpose forgot. She wouldn't put a spiteful act like that past the old shrew but resigns herself to the fact that she'll never know.

She can hear Marcus moving around in his study, putting on loud classical music. Shutting her out. Hobbling to the sink, she splashes cold water over her face and neck, attempting to wash away the tears. But they keep on coming. There's a bruise on her hipbone, and the patch of skin on her leg that was scalded by the meat fat is red and blistered. She presses a damp cloth against it for a few moments, then limps across the room and sets about clearing up the shattered remains of her kitchen supper.

FIVE

JULY 1996

It all begins to go wrong when Joanne Beckett's mother takes it on herself to befriend Felicity Gibson.

In the spring, Lucy's parents cave in to years of cajoling and wheedling and buy a cocker spaniel puppy for her twelfth birthday. When the days grow longer, and Kibble the puppy has had his jabs, Felicity falls into the habit of walking him to meet Lucy after school, thereby combining the need to exercise the dog with supervision of her daughter. And Sally Beckett, the mother of a girl in Lucy and Adele's class, makes a beeline for the creature, cooing loudly and petting him in an ostentatious manner.

Although Lucy lacks the vocabulary to define the phenomenon, she's a bright and sensitive child, and understands that by making a fuss of Kibble, Sally Beckett is social climbing; that she has taken in Felicity Gibson's designer clothes and expensive blonde highlights, seen her top-of-the-range car and labelled her someone important, someone to get to know. Sally Beckett works part-time in a travel agency in Redgate and has a sunbed in her spare room, which she uses too much. Her hair is also bleached blonde, but it's cheaply done, and her designer bag is a cheap copy from the market. She lives in a new executive home off the bypass but aspires to Haverleigh Park.

Of course, Adele notices this too. There was no chance she wouldn't. Her attitude to Lucy is entirely proprietorial.

'You friends with that loser Joanne now?' she asks huffily, after they've overheard Sally Beckett inviting Felicity to her house for 'a coffee morning' for at least the third time. Joanne Beckett is a drab, nondescript girl who wears her dull mousy hair pulled back into a ponytail. Like Lucy, she needs glasses, but hers have lenses so thick they make her look as though she's staring even when she isn't. She also has severe allergy problems, which give her an unfortunate tendency to breathe through her mouth.

'No,' says Lucy, truthfully. 'No way.' She has no interest whatsoever in Joanne, and is pretty sure her mother is only being polite when she chats to Sally Beckett. But despite these reassurances, Adele takes it on herself to start bullying Joanne with a thousand subtle cuts: directing mocking glances in her direction, muttering comments under her breath, excluding her from conversation. No doubt if they were in the thick of the school year, then the campaign would have had a chance to escalate, and parents or teachers might have stepped in to take action. And in turn maybe that would have prevented the disastrous events that followed. But the summer term is almost over and the year seven pupils are disbanding until September. The Gibsons will be spending the second half of August at an upmarket resort in Greece that provides a holiday club for pre-teens, while the Watts family are spending a week in a static caravan in Filey.

July that year is baking hot. Sultry. Lucy mooches around the house, bored and restless. Occasionally, she puts on her swimsuit and joins her mother on a sun lounger in the garden, lying there until her fair skin is turning pink. Most of the time, she reads or sketches in the draught from the electric fan, essential in the hot attic storey of the house.

After a week, Adele arrives at the house on her bike and is admitted by Felicity with a frosty smile. She won't go so far as to ban Adele from the house, but she never tries to encourage her.

'Aw right, Luce?' she says cheerfully. 'Fancy a bike ride?'

Sensing an outing, Kibble circles at her feet, yapping.

'In this heat?' Felicity frets. 'I'm not sure that's a good idea.'

Adele shrugs, as though the temperature is irrelevant. Her own olive skin has darkened since school broke up, suggesting she has spent most of her time outside, probably riding her bike.

'I want to go,' Lucy says stubbornly.

Shaking her head slightly, her mother fetches sunscreen from the kitchen table and rubs it onto Lucy's forehead and bare arms. She's still in her swimsuit, underneath her shorts and T-shirt. 'Where will you go?' Felicity asks. 'I need to have some idea.'

'Just around,' Adele says innocently, but Lucy can tell from her lopsided smirk that she already has a destination in mind. 'Have you ever been to Blackwater Pond?' she asks as soon as their bikes are clear of the house.

Lucy hasn't, but she knows all about it. She and her parents have driven past the reservoir on the edge of Redgate Heath several times on their way to the bypass and Lucy has always craned her neck at the glimpses of the glassy-smooth water, ringed with trees.

'Are we allowed?' she asks, letting her legs dangle over the pedals momentarily to slow her bike's progress. She's aware of how feeble she sounds.

'Course,' says Adele with her usual insouciance.

She seems quite happy to ignore the 'NO SWIMMING' sign on the fence at the edge of the water, as do all the other teenagers lured there by the siren call of cool water. Most of them splash carefully around the edges, with just one or two of the older boys striking out towards the centre of the reservoir. There's a patch of scrubby sand that passes for a beach on the southern edge, and on the eastern perimeter a gnarled oak branch growing over a flat, rocky promontory is providing the ballast for a makeshift rope swing. The boys take it in turn to hang off the rope and swing out over the rippling depths before letting go and splashing into the deepest reaches of the water with shrieks of triumph. They jostle one another and play at waggling the rope within reach before snatching it away, like a toy dangled in front of a kitten. Lucy is far too timid to take a turn on the rope swing, but, of course, Adele does it, stubbornly ignoring the catcalls and jeering.

The bottom of the reservoir is uneven and stony, and the water shockingly cold even with an air temperature of thirty degrees Celsius, but Lucy eventually swims gingerly around the edges. Adele abandons the rope swing to the adolescent boys and joins her in the shallows, splashing Lucy's face and shoulders by smacking the flat of her hand on the smooth surface of the water. Lucy splashes her back, and the two of them are soon engaged in a battle to see who can drench the other the most, shrieking with laughter. Still giggling, Lucy hauls herself out of the pond, flinging herself onto the grass and feeling rivulets of water course down her neck as she squints up at the blazing ball of the sun. Her chest is heaving, but she is quite sure she has never felt more alive than she does at this moment. Adele flops down beside her, pulling a can of Coke from her bag and cracking it open.

'Brilliant, isn't it?' she asks proudly.

'Yes,' Lucy nods. 'It's brilliant.'

'Only I wouldn't come here with just anyone. It's only because you and me are best friends.'

Lucy nods again. Despite their 'pinky promise' when Adele came to tea, she has been hesitant to give Adele that title in her own mind. But she supposes it's true. She can't imagine being here, doing this, with anyone else. She doesn't have any other friends she would do this with, and laugh so hard with. So it must be true. The two of them are best friends.

Adele takes the metal tab from the can and draws it swiftly against the inside of her left wrist, leaving a trail of tiny red dots. Before Lucy has time to react, she has done the same to Lucy's own left wrist.

'Owww!' protests Lucy. She tries to yank her hand away, but Adele grabs it and presses their wrists together, smearing the two red trails into one.

'It's a blood oath,' Adele says solemnly. 'You know, like a pact.' Then she holds the red drink can up against the scorching blue sky, as if in a toast. 'Best friends forever.'

After a couple of hours, hunger sends most of the swimmers off in search of food, and Adele announces that she has to go home and mind Tyler and Chelsee. Lucy cycles back to Haverleigh Park alone, her damp swimsuit making dark patches on her back and the seat of her shorts. She stashes her bike in the garage and tries to sneak upstairs unseen, but Kibble's delighted yapping acts as an alarm, and Felicity intercepts her.

'Goodness, darling, you're soaking wet!' She lifts a tendril of hair that clings to her daughter's nape, then spots the bloody abrasion on her inner arm. 'What on earth have you been up to?'

'Swimming,' says Lucy, lowering her eyes.

'Where?' Felicity demands and instantly narrows her eyes as a thought occurs to her. 'Please don't tell me you've been to the reservoir!'

Lucy considers denying it, but only briefly. Above anything, she does not want to risk her mother instigating an awkward confrontation with the Watts family. So she feigns wide-eyed innocence, which leads to one of her parents' earnest tag-team chats after supper that night; a tactic they employ when they're worried about her.

'Darling, there's a reason water utility companies ban swimming in reservoirs,' her father begins. 'Tempting though it must seem in this weather, it's very dangerous. The water's icy cold, you can't see what's going on beneath the surface and there's no lifeguard supervision.'

'A boy drowned swimming there a couple of years ago,' Felicity continues. 'It was in the local paper.'

'It's just not safe, quite apart from the potential for toxic substances in the water,' Jeffrey Gibson goes on. 'So Mummy and I want you to promise you won't go down there again.'

'But Adele's allowed to go,' Lucy is aware she sounds sulky. 'She can go where she likes.'

'Yes, well,' Felicity tightens her lips. 'Every family's different, and they would no doubt look on us as overprotective. But you're still only twelve. Adele's a teenager now, which is a big difference.'

'But—'

'You're not to go again, Lucy. That's the end of the matter.'

SIX

On the evening after the failed supper party, Lucy is alone in the bedroom, engrossed in a Netflix documentary about the FBI when '*Jane Standish calling*' appears on the screen of her mobile. She cuts the call, but thirty seconds later there it is again: *Jane Standish calling.*

If Jane rings again, I'll pick up, she decides. *Otherwise I'll text her tomorrow.* The phone does ring again as the thought is running through her mind, so reluctantly she presses 'Accept'.

'Just calling to see if you're any better.'

'Better?' Lucy momentarily forgets her excuse for the cancelled meal.

'The gastric flu.'

'Oh… yes. Much better, thanks. Still taking it easy, you know.'

There is a long pause, which manages to communicate wordlessly that Jane does not believe the stomach bug lie. Then she asks, 'Are you on your own now, Lucy?'

'Yes. I'm just watching some random Netflix real-life crime stuff. Marcus is out doing an emergency case.'

'I know it's a bit late, but if you felt like coming over for a glass of wine and a slice of Molly's leftover birthday cake, Robin and I would love to see you.'

She wants to ply me with wine and then grill me about my marriage, Lucy thinks. And there is definitely a real temptation to go over to Clapham and spill her guts. But then Jane is friends with

Fiona, and Fiona constantly has Marcus's ear. It would probably cause more problems than it would solve.

'That's a lovely offer, thank you, but I'm still a bit tired.'

'Of course,' Jane concedes. 'These bugs can take it out of you. Your university term must be over soon – are you going to get away anywhere?'

Lucy sighs. 'Marcus is just too busy. They've lost a consultant from the team recently due to funding cuts, so he's having to do the work of two surgeons.'

'Well, maybe you could think about going away somewhere on your own? Clear your head. Get a fresh perspective on things. Do you have any friends you've been dying to visit?'

'Maybe,' says Lucy cautiously. 'I'll definitely give it some thought.'

'Well, I just wanted to let you know that I'm here if you ever need someone to talk to.'

After she has hung up, Lucy can't settle. She goes down into the kitchen, makes a mug of tea and takes it out into the moonlit garden. Two fighting cats shatter the silence with their yowls and, somewhere nearby, a neighbour is holding a party. Faint bossa nova rhythms are punctuated by the rise and fall of laughter and animated conversation. Lucy thinks again of Marcus's sabotage of her planned evening. And something Jane said over coffee comes back too: 'You're still young.'

There is still time, she tells herself. There's time for her to start again, but to do so she has to admit to herself that in marrying Marcus she made a mistake. And she has to leave.

Back in the house, Lucy scrolls though her contacts until she reaches her father's number. She realises, guiltily, that it's at least a week since she's spoken to him. And she hasn't been down to Redgate for over a year. Marcus hates being a guest, preferring it if people visit them, so Jeffrey Gibson usually makes the trip to London. She's about to press 'Call', but notices the time, and decides against it: phone calls after nine thirty make him anxious.

A glance at her calendar also reminds her that Tom and Lydia are arriving for their regular bi-monthly visit in the morning. According to their normal routine, she will be devoting the weekend to her stepchildren. She is quite fond of them, even though Lydia can be entitled and Tom surly. But now that she has made her decision, she realises she can't face even one more weekend of being belittled in front of them. Marcus constantly reminds her, and the children, that she is not their mother and has no real parenting experience of her own. Which in turn is a reminder, as sharp as a knife blade in her flesh, that she will never be a mother. At least, as long as she's with Marcus she won't.

Hurrying upstairs, she pulls a weekend bag from the wardrobe, then swiftly rejects it in favour of a suitcase that will contain a whole week's worth of clothes. She packs it with jeans, sweatpants and trainers – all the clothes her husband disdains – then pushes it back into the corner of the dressing room. She climbs into bed, switches off the light and arranges her limbs in a way that will suggest sleep.

First thing the following morning, Marcus announces that he needs to see a couple of private patients in his Harley Street rooms.

'I'll pick the kids up after I'm done,' he says over his shoulder to Lucy, as he inserts gold links into the double cuffs of his bespoke striped poplin shirt. Paying customers expect a certain image, and Marcus knows how to play up to that. 'We should be back by midday though.'

Lucy nods but makes no comment.

'Have you thought about what you'll give the kids for lunch?'

She has not. Nor will she.

'Pizza?' she suggests, simply because it is the first word that comes into her brain.

Marcus frowns. 'I think you can do better than that, Lucinda. Is it really too much to ask that the children get something nutritious to eat? Not bloody junk food.'

Lucy doesn't point out that her home-made pizzas – which Tom and Lydia both love – are made with fresh tomatoes and the best quality mozzarella and olives. 'Fine,' she agrees, avoiding eye contact. 'I'll think of something else. And there's a chicken in the fridge to roast tomorrow. Tom's favourite.'

Mollified, Marcus grunts and pulls on his Oswald Boateng jacket. 'I'll see you later.'

Once he has gone, and there's no chance of him doubling back for something he's forgotten, Lucy drags her case out to the car and gets behind the wheel. She doesn't unload the dishwasher or make the bed before leaving: two small but satisfying acts of rebellion. Instead she pulls over at her favourite café on Church Road to buy a takeout coffee, then drives straight to Redgate.

Jeffrey Gibson looks confused as he opens the door. Since Felicity's death, the family home in Haverleigh Park has been sold, and he now lives in a characterless detached bungalow about half a mile away. The furniture from the old house looks all wrong in the smaller rooms, a reminder that there is no longer a Felicity to add homely touches.

'Have I forgotten something?' he asks, when he sees his only daughter. 'Did we make an arrangement?'

She shakes her head.

'Where's Marcus?' He instinctively looks into the front passenger seat. Jeffrey greatly admires his son-in-law, is even somewhat in awe of him. Like Fiona, Jeffrey believes that because Marcus is a doctor, he can do no wrong.

Lucy embraces her father, his hair now thin and completely white, his tall figure a little stooped. 'You'll have to make do with just me,' she says lightly.

When he sees her drag her large case from the boot of the car, his look turns to one of concern. 'Is there something wrong, darling? Something I need to know about?'

'Everything's fine, Dad. I just haven't visited for ages, and I thought it would be nice to spend a couple of days with you.'

'A couple of days?' He points at the suitcase.

Lucy gives him what she hopes is a convincing smile. 'Give or take? That's all right, isn't it? I can do some cooking: help you stock the freezer. Or we could take a run out to the South Downs, blow away the cobwebs with a bit of a walk.'

Her father may be slowing slightly now that he's seventy-seven, but his mental faculties are still perfectly sharp. 'Is everything all right between you and Marcus?' He examines her face for signs of distress.

'Yes, fine,' Lucy lies, wheeling her case into the small, cramped hall. 'I just felt like a few days away, that's all. A bit of a break from the big smoke. How about I put my stuff in the spare room, then rustle up some lunch for us both?'

In the bleak little guest bedroom, with its odd combination of heavy oak wardrobes from the Haverleigh house and cheap Ikea drawers and rug, Lucy checks her watch. Eleven thirty; Marcus won't be home yet. Sure enough, there are no messages on her phone. Lucy does what will irritate him most: switches it off. It's a relief, and yet anxiety gnaws away at her stomach, making her feel light-headed.

She prepares a salad with some boiled eggs, a tin of tuna and some wilting lettuce she finds at the bottom of the fridge, then leaves Jeffrey doing *The Times* crossword while she drives to the local hypermarket to stock up with groceries.

As she reaches over her shoulder to remotely engage the lock on the car doors, she catches sight of someone in her peripheral vision, pushing a filled trolley out of the store. It's only a glimpse, and the car park is busy with reversing cars and squabbling families, but it's enough to make Lucy stop in her tracks. She inhales so hard it's as though someone has winded her; and her heart pounds in her chest.

Adele Watts.

She's changed of course. She was always a stocky girl, but now she looks overweight, possibly even obese. Her sandy hair has been bleached and the tips dyed pale pink. But it's unmistakably her. Even from this distance, Lucy knows. It's the tilt of her head, the way she carries herself. It's Adele.

She turns and looks in Lucy's direction for a beat. Has she seen Lucy? It's hard to tell at this distance, and, anyway, would she even recognise her former best friend?

Her heart still pounding, and blushing furiously for reasons she doesn't quite understand, Lucy grabs a trolley and pushes it through the doors of the supermarket, using it for support in the way a pensioner relies on a wheeled walker.

You're being ridiculous, she tells herself. *If you're back in your home town, it's hardly a huge surprise to see someone you were at school with. It's to be expected really.* But Adele, of all people. Of course, it had to be her. Who else?

The rhythmic thunk-thunk of the trolley wheels soothe her, as do the vast, overstocked aisles full of Saturday shoppers. Her heart rate subsides sufficiently for her to concentrate on the task in hand and she buys enough groceries to feed two people for several days, with leftovers for freezing.

Back at the bungalow, she makes moussaka because it's one of her father's favourites, and the two of them sit through an awkward meal, where they both try and avoid discussing the real reason she's there. *If Mum were alive, this would be so much easier*, Lucy thinks sadly. She could confide in her mother, and whatever her misgivings, Felicity would understand.

Pleading a headache, she retreats to her bedroom as soon as the dishes have been done and switches on her phone. The handset vibrates fitfully as the messages land. Nine missed calls from Marcus, starting at 12.25 p.m., and two texts. The first, sent at 13.31 reads: *Where the hell are you?* and the second: *Lucinda: is this sort of childish and selfish behaviour really fair on the children? They're worrying about you.*

It's not her husband who's worrying, Lucy notes, it's his children. Though, in reality, they are almost certainly not. They're probably only too happy to have their father to themselves, without the spectre of their insecure, desperate-to-please stepmother. Of course, it's to her advantage that this is one of Marcus's access weekends. He can't really dump the children in order to go looking for her, which means he will be unable to do anything about her absence before Tom and Lydia are back with Amber on Sunday evening. And by then Lucy intends to be out of reach. She's already decided that she'll leave her father's home after Sunday lunch, drive down the A3 to Portsmouth and get on an overnight ferry to St Malo.

Ignoring the calls and texts, she opens up her web browser and types 'Adele Watts' into the search bar. The most recent results are both from local newspapers, dating back to 2015.

A local Redgate woman, Adele Watts, aged 32, was today found guilty of benefit fraud at Guildford Magistrates' Court, after being caught claiming unemployment benefit while in paid work. Watts, a mother of two, was sentenced to six months' imprisonment.

There is the obligatory tabloid-style shot of the accused arriving at court with her coat pulled over her head. Adele, who had her hair dyed brown at the time, was wearing a dark blue skirt suit and white shirt that looked as though they had been borrowed from someone else. The skirt cut into her hips and the shirt buttons strained over her chest. She had large breasts as a thirteen-year-old and now they're huge, like a bulky shelf.

Staring at the photo, Lucy recalls the last time she saw Adele in the flesh. It was the day she left Redgate to go to university, a long eighteen years ago.

So Adele ended up going to prison. From nowhere, Lucy conjures the sight of that drowned body being lifted from the water, and a shiver runs the length of her spine. She switches off her phone before it can ring again and tosses it into her bag.

SEVEN

Lucy is woken at eight by the door chime, followed by a loud hammering on the front door.

It must have been opened by her father, because the next thing she hears is Marcus's voice warmly exclaiming, 'Jeffrey! Wonderful to see you.' This is followed by the sound of manly back-clapping.

She tiptoes to the door and listens. Marcus has lowered his voice, but she catches snatches of what he's saying: 'Look, I'm really sorry about this... not right to involve you in this way... no idea what she's playing at.'

'I'll fetch her,' Jeffrey says. 'There's tea in the kitchen; help yourself.'

He appears at the doorway of the bedroom.

'Marcus is here.'

'I know,' says Lucy, more calmly than she's feeling. 'I heard.' She turns and heads towards the door of the en suite bathroom.

'Well come on then, darling, he obviously wants to talk to you.'

'I need a shower first.'

'Can't you do that later? I don't think you should keep him waiting.'

No, of course, not. Nobody's ever allowed to keep the great Marcus Wheedon waiting. Not for the first time, Lucy feels a rush of anger at her father for kowtowing to his son-in-law. For treating him as a superior. But she says nothing, simply closing the bathroom door firmly behind her and switching on the shower tap.

Fifteen minutes later, she comes into the kitchen dressed in T-shirt and jeans, her hair still wet. Jeffrey is hovering nervously with offers of toast and marmalade or boiled eggs.

'Finally,' says Marcus. He gives his wife a smile, purely for Jeffrey's benefit, but his eyes are cold. 'Good of you to join us.'

'Coffee, perhaps?' asks Jeffrey. He's addressing Marcus.

'No thank you; we really need to get going. I've asked my long-suffering PA to keep an eye on the kids for a couple of hours, but she has another commitment, so we need to go straight back to London.'

Beryl, of course. *I might have known she'd be involved in this somewhere.*

Lucy reaches for the cafetière and pours herself a mug. 'No,' she says calmly. 'You can go back to London, but I'm staying here.'

'Lucinda, for heaven's sake… what's this all about?' Marcus is moderating his tone, but it's only because his father-in-law is present. 'Come on, don't be silly. This isn't fair on your dad.'

Lucy turns to Jeffrey, inviting him to back her up, but he doesn't.

'Marcus is right, darling, whatever needs sorting out, it's better done at home,'

'No,' repeats Lucy, more loudly this time. Marcus reaches for her, but she sidesteps him and stands behind her father. 'I'm not coming.'

'For Christ's sake!' Lucy is aware of Marcus grabbing at her wrist, and at the same time, Jeffrey, who is sandwiched between them makes an odd sound and staggers back against the worktop.

'Dad? Dad, are you okay?'

Marcus helps his father-in-law into a chair. His body sags oddly. 'I can't… I can't…' His voice sounds strange, as though it's being projected from his body by somebody else. Only one side of his mouth is moving.

'He's having a bloody stroke,' says Marcus, reaching into his pocket for his phone and punching in three 999s. He glares at Lucy 'You happy now?'

*

The neurology consultant at the Royal Surrey says that Jeffrey Gibson's stroke was caught early enough for the damage to be limited, and he was one of the lucky ones who could be helped by clot-busting drugs. Marcus had marched around the A&E department pulling rank, demanding that Jeffrey be seen immediately, and for once Lucy was grateful.

'Malcolm Denehay is a good guy,' he pronounces as they sit at Jeffrey's bedside. Lucy is holding his hand, her eyes fixed on the bleeping heart monitor. 'You're in the right place in that respect. You should be up and around in no time.'

'You two go,' Jeffrey says drowsily. 'I need to sleep and you have things to sort out. I'll be fine here with all these lovely nurses.'

Marcus places a hand on Lucy's shoulder and steers her away from the cubicle. 'I sincerely hope you're coming with me this time. After what's just happened.'

'But Dad's just had a stroke. He needs me here with him.'

'You heard what he said,' Marcus hisses. 'And anyway, he's not going anywhere, not for a few days.' He grabs her elbow as she turns to go back to the cubicle. 'You realise that if you upset him further, he's at risk of a second stroke. And next time it could be fatal.'

So Lucy ends up collecting her case from the bungalow and driving up the A3 with Marcus's Range Rover close behind her rear bumper. He insists that she goes first and that he follows her, 'So that I can make sure you're not doing another disappearing act.'

And then she's compelled to prepare roast chicken for the children and behave in front of them as though nothing has happened. Their loud but self-absorbed company dissipates the tension, and she ends up being rather sorry when Marcus has to take them home. When he gets back, he finds her sitting on the drawing room floor, her back against her sofa.

'Is all this because of the other evening, when I lost my rag over your guests?'

He has remained standing up, so she is effectively conversing with his lower legs. She nods, focusing her gaze on his suede loafers and jeans. She stares at them, as though they belong to someone she has never met.

'Look, I'm sorry, okay? Maybe I went a bit over the top, but I'd had the day from hell at work. The number of patients we see has doubled in the last few years and the services we can offer have halved… the stress of it all gets a bit much.'

A bit over the top? Dear God.

Lucy lets out a harsh sigh. 'Our guests didn't believe I was ill, by the way. They know something's wrong. People aren't stupid.'

Marcus slumps down onto the sofa, but Lucy keeps her back to him.

'So is that your intention?' he asks. 'To communicate to people that something – in your view – is wrong? Is that what all this is about? This absurd running away? Scaring your poor father into having a stroke?'

'I wasn't running away,' Lucy responds instinctively, if not entirely candidly. 'I just needed some time out.' Even as she says the words, she knows this isn't true. She was running all right. And if Marcus hadn't shown up when he did, she would probably have kept running.

'Great. So you pissed off and left me high and dry, when you knew the kids were coming. What about them? Tom and Lydia? Do you ever think about their feelings? Their lives have been disrupted enough as it is.' His tone strongly implies that this is Lucy's fault.

Lucy stands up. 'I need to go and phone Dad.'

'I've told him I'll try and visit him sometime in the week,' Marcus calls after her, as she heads for the kitchen, 'Make sure you give him my best.'

Leaning against the kitchen door, Lucy closes her eyes and steadies her breathing. Then she pours herself a generous glass of wine before punching in the number for the stroke unit and asking to be connected to her father.

He is doing better, her father tells her. He certainly sounds brighter, his voice stronger.

'I'll come down again as soon as they discharge you. You'll need someone at home with you, at least to start with.'

There is a long pause. 'The thing is, darling, I've asked Rhea to come and stay when I'm discharged.'

Rhea is Lucy's first cousin, the daughter of Jeffrey's older brother.

'Rhea?'

'She seemed the obvious choice, given she's had nursing training.'

'I'm your daughter. Surely I'm the obvious choice?'

There's another awkward pause. 'I don't want there to be any more trouble between you and Marcus. I can't go through any more scenes like there were this morning; I'm sure you understand that. I need proper rest.'

So my husband can come and see you, but I can't, Lucy thinks. *That just about sums it up*.

Two weeks later, on a breezy Monday in April, Lucy makes a second attempt to take control of her life.

On Sunday morning, while Marcus is doing an emergency bypass, she goes online and trawls through listings for jobs in the charity sector. There are a couple of potential openings in central London, but neither of them particularly appeals. One job does catch her eye – at a refugee support NGO in Bristol.

> *We are looking for a mature self-starter to help run our advocacy and information unit and assist clients with all aspects of the asylum process.*

Lucy presses the link to the organisation's website and clicks through the gallery of photos. The premises are a little shabby, but the diverse group of people in the welcome centre are all smiling, and not in a posed way: genuine smiles. She finds herself smiling back at the screen. The ethos seems positive, creative even. In addition to a help desk, there's a crèche and initiatives for art and music. Lucy makes a note of the application process and starts working up her CV. Then she googles '*Live in Bristol*' and browses through pages that tell her how vibrant, community-minded and green (literally and politically) the city is. Lucy feels her pulse quicken with a burst of positivity. She even checks an estate agent's website and looks at properties to rent in Bristol. The decent ones seem quite pricey, but then again, nowhere near as expensive as Barnes. *I could live there*, she thinks. *I could actually do it.*

But that evening, after they've eaten supper and Marcus has retreated to his study, he calls downstairs ominously, 'Lucinda. I need a word with you.'

She trudges up to the first floor like a schoolgirl going to the headmaster's study.

He's sitting at his desk and has her iPad in his hand. 'What the hell is this?' he asks.

'What's what?'

He shows her own browser history. 'Let's see now, where shall we start? The vacancy you've bookmarked… in Bristol. Lots of pages about Bristol and what a great place it is…'

Lucy tries to take the iPad from him, but he snatches his arm away and holds it aloft so she can't reach it.

'And then, properties in Bristol. Is that what your master plan is, to move to Bristol?'

Lucy shakes her head. 'I was just looking. There's no law against it.'

He ignores this. 'Because that's what your aim is, isn't it? To humiliate me? To make me look like a fool in front of all my colleagues and friends? Oh dear, they'll say, no sooner had he left his wife and kids for that spoilt bit of a girl than she got bored and pissed off to another city.'

'No,' says Lucy. 'It's not about that.'

It's not about you, it's about me, about what I *want. You're making it all about yourself, as always.*

'Because, let me tell you now: it's not happening.' He waves around the room. 'This lovely home you live in – my hard work pays for it. Ditto the clothes you wear and the holidays you go on. Oh, and I also paid the fees for that expensive postgraduate degree, which it seems is just a springboard to moving on. So, you're not leaving me and buggering off to Bristol, or anywhere else come to that. Over my dead body.'

Lucy turns and runs out of his study, sitting alone in the kitchen until she hears Marcus going to bed. She waits until the faint vibration of his snores starts up, then brushes her teeth in the guest bathroom and goes to lie down in the spare bedroom. It's late but her mind is running at a mile a minute and she knows that sleep will be a long time coming. If it comes at all. She plucks at the tangle of duvet, turning first to lie on her left side, then her right. Since her mother's death, she has held frequent imaginary conversations with her. What would she say in this situation? she wonders.

Closing her eyes, she can hear Felicity's calm, measured and slightly plummy tones. It's not hard to imagine how the conversation would go on this occasion.

'But is this marriage ever going to change?' her mother is saying. *'Is this really how you want to live your life? If not, then you have to* do *something, darling.'*

Tomorrow – Monday – Marcus will be in the operating theatre all day, which will buy her a little time. She switches on the bedside lamp and sends a text to Jane Standish.

Can I come over? Need that talk. L x

EIGHT

'Please try and ignore the mess.' Jane steers Lucy through the clutter of their family room in Clapham. A bike leans up against the wall along with several micro-scooters, and play tables overflow with painting equipment and bowls of home-made slime. The floor is studded with Lego bricks and plastic action figures. 'Organised chaos is the norm here... actually, make that disorganised.' She shrugs, sweeping a sleeping cat off the seat of a chair. 'You know how it is with kids.'

Lucy doesn't really. Most of her stepchildren's clutter resides at their mother's house, and the small amount that has made its way to Barnes is rigidly controlled. But she nods sagely, anyway.

'Coffee?' Jane enquires. She takes clean mugs from a half-emptied dishwasher and rummages through packets in one of the cupboards until she finds some ginger biscuits, which she tosses onto the table.

Lucy doesn't normally eat biscuits, but then again she has skipped both dinner the night before and breakfast. Her insides are curdling with hunger. She takes one gratefully, along with the mug of instant coffee. 'I'll come straight to the point,' she says with her mouth full of crumbs. 'I wondered if I could stay here for a couple of nights. I've left Marcus.'

Jane sets down her mug. 'Wow.'

Lucy manages a rueful smile. 'I know.'

'Does he know you're here?' Jane asks. 'Did you tell him what you were planning?'

'No, and no. And I won't tell him I'm here either; don't worry. I just desperately need to buy some time. To get my head straight, think about next steps.'

Jane leans over and gives Lucy's shoulder a reassuring squeeze. 'Sure. Of course you can, though with the three kids it's not exactly going to be a haven of peace.' She pushes the biscuit packet back in Lucy's direction. 'And, for what it's worth, I absolutely think you're doing the right thing. I know it's not easy.'

Lucy nods slowly, feeling tears sting at the back of her eyes. Slowly, in a halting voice, she confesses to Jane exactly what happened the night of the supper party, then gives her a brief summary of the past forty-eight hours.

'I imagined it must have been something like that,' Jane says, nodding. 'But trashing the dinner table. Jesus, Lucy.'

'I don't want to dwell on it,' Lucy declares firmly. 'That's the past. I want to concentrate on the future. Look, I want you to tell me what you think of this.'

When she came to pack her things that morning, she couldn't find her iPad anywhere. The last sighting was when she had her row with Marcus in the study the previous evening, but in the morning it was no longer on his desk, or in any of its drawers, or on her bedside table where she usually kept it. He must have hidden it to spite her. So she has to show Jane the NGO in Bristol on her phone screen instead, which diminishes its appeal somewhat.

'Goodness,' Jane says, and Lucy can tell she's trying to be tactful. 'Looks really interesting, but Bristol? Do you really want to move away from London?'

'I'm going to have to. If this is ever going to work, I'm going to have to get right away from him. From Marcus.'

*

Jane has to call in at the shop where she works for a couple of hours to inventory some new stock, so Lucy volunteers to buy ingredients that she can cook for the family that evening.

'It's the least I can do,' she insists.

'Just keep it kid-friendly,' Jane advises. 'Nothing too exotic. They're fussy little buggers.'

Lucy decides on something her stepchildren enjoy: home-made burgers and chips, with optional salad for the grown-ups. After she has hauled the ingredients, plus a couple of bottles of decent wine, back from Northcote Road, Jane has returned from work. They go together to fetch four-year-old Barney from nursery, then to the school gates to collect Molly, who has just turned seven, and nine-year-old Oscar. Molly needs to be immediately ferried to her weekly ballet class, and Oscar dropped off at a friend's house en route, with this journey repeated in reverse once ballet is over. Barney has to be kept amused with books and toys, plied with snacks and drinks and taken to the loo at inopportune moments.

When they finally get back to the house at nearly six o'clock, after sitting in rush-hour traffic for half an hour, all the children are tired and fractious. And yet Jane remains calm – almost serene – throughout. Lucy is full of admiration. Could she cope with three children and a job? she wonders. Plenty of women do. Potential family size is not an issue she has ever had to consider, because there was no possibility of having even one baby. But now, the realisation that this could perhaps be in her future sends a little frisson of excitement through her. *Not three*, she decides. *There's not enough time left for three. But one would be nice. Maybe.*

While Jane bathes Barney and oversees homework, Lucy assembles the beef patties and the hand-cut chips and makes a salad dressing. Barney is fed straight away and put to bed, while the older children join Jane, Robin and Lucy for dinner. There has been no opportunity for Jane and Robin to talk, except perhaps for a hurried word while Lucy is out of the room making a trip to the bathroom, but he welcomes her presence with warm acceptance and doesn't ask any awkward questions. They drink quite a lot of the wine, and with candles on the table and the soothing hum of the washing machine in the background, the meal is a convivial one. Lucy manages to relax.

After they've eaten, Molly is sent up to bed and Oscar is allowed to watch television for an hour, leaving the adults to talk over coffee and more wine.

Eventually, Robin stands up, stretches and says, 'I'd better get Oz to go up. He'll be glued to the box all night if we let him.' As he heads for the sitting room, the doorbell rings. 'Were you expecting anyone?' he asks, sticking his head round the kitchen door, a frown on his face.

'No, definitely not,' Jane replies firmly, shooting a glance across the table.

There's the sound of a second, more insistent ring, then the front door being opened. A familiar voice says, 'I know she's here.'

Lucy's stomach sinks like a stone.

Marcus follows Robin into the kitchen. He's scowling, and the depth of his five o'clock shadow betrays that he went straight to the operating theatre that morning without bothering to shave.

'Come on,' he says to Lucy, beckoning her like a car parking attendant trying to wave a car towards him. 'You're coming with me.'

'Lucy's staying here tonight,' Robin says, obviating Lucy's need to speak. She shoots him a grateful look. Saliva is pooling at the back of her throat and her heart is racing.

'That's right.' Jane speaks calmly. 'She's not going anywhere. Not with you.'

'What is this?' Marcus sneers. 'Some sort of fucking conspiracy? Well, I'll thank you not to meddle between man and wife.'

He grasps Lucy roughly by the left elbow and tugs her towards him. Her right arm flails, knocking over both her glass of red wine and the bottle. It trickles across the table and pools like blood on the floor.

'Oh no you, don't!' says Robin briskly, pulling Marcus backwards. In response, Marcus's fingers dig into Lucy's arm even harder, making her wince with pain. She can smell alcohol on his breath.

'Let her go, you bully!' Jane hurriedly pushes back her chair and comes around the end of the table to help her husband restrain him.

'Or what, exactly?' Marcus demands. He does release his hold on Lucy but grabs the large glass vase filled with tulips from the table and hurls it against the wall, sending damp flowers and crystalline shards spraying everywhere. This is followed by the cast-iron skillet used to fry the burgers, making an unholy banging noise. The dish drainer filled with cutlery is added for good measure.

A shocked-looking Oscar appears in the doorway, his mouth open, and from the top of the stairs, Molly screams, 'Mummy! What's happening?' The sound of her hysterical sobs cuts through the shocked silence, joined within seconds by Barney's crying.

'Now look what you've done,' Jane hisses, hurrying out of the room to comfort the children. 'Happy now?'

'Okay, enough is enough. I'm going to phone the police.' Robin pulls his mobile from his pocket and swipes to unlock the screen.

'It's all right, there's no need to go over the top.' Marcus turns his back towards Robin and addresses Lucy, 'But if you've got any sense, you'll come straight back home.' He waves at the wreckage of the kitchen, as though it has nothing to do with him. 'Not exactly the ideal house guest, are you?'

'I should go,' Lucy says to Jane later, as they sweep up the glass and flowers and mop the wine from the floor. 'You've been so kind, but I can't expect you to put up with this. It's not fair on you and Robin, and especially not on the children. I'm so sorry.' She pulls a tissue from her jeans and wipes away the tears that are the natural by-product of shock.

Jane pats her arm. 'It's eleven o'clock at night; I'm not going to throw you out on the street. Stay for tonight, and we'll get our heads together in the morning and think about the best course of action. Things will be clearer once we've all had a decent night's sleep.'

'I need you to know that I didn't tell him I was here,' Lucy says, collecting up the knives and forks from the floor. 'But when you phoned that night after Fiona's dinner party, he must have realised that you were concerned about me and keen to help. He'll have put two and two together and worked out I could be here.'

Jane empties the dustpan into the bin and straightens up, rubbing her back. 'Very likely. But listen, I've got a couple of girlfriends who could put you up for a bit; people Marcus wouldn't know about. At least until you can sort out a more permanent arrangement.' She moves around the kitchen, boiling the kettle, filling water glasses and hot-water bottles for them both with a natural motherliness. 'Robin thinks you should see a solicitor as soon as you can. Maybe…' She hesitates, holding out a hot-water bottle in a fluffy rabbit cover, 'Maybe organise a restraining order. I know that sounds drastic, but after tonight's little performance…'

'No, you're right,' says Lucy, blowing her nose. 'I think that's a good idea.'

She has been given Molly's bed for the night, with Molly now in Barney's room and Barney in the lower bunk bed in Oscar's room. The mattress, in its painted white frame stencilled with unicorns, proves surprisingly comfortable, and the heat and weight of the hot-water bottle help lull Lucy into a deep sleep. When she's woken by the door being pushed carefully open, she assumes it's Molly looking for a special soft toy. She glances at the Moana clock on the dresser: 3.14 a.m.

But this isn't Molly. This is a tall, well-built man. Robin, checking that she's all right? No, not Robin. Marcus.

'What the hell are you doing here?' she hisses, groping around for her dressing gown. 'How did you even get in?'

'Child's play. The idiots keep their spare key under that bay tree by the front door.' He closes the bedroom door softly behind him. 'And don't think about calling for Jane or Robin. You don't want another scene like there was earlier this evening.' He says this in a detached way, as though he has no personal responsibility for the 'scene'. 'And I know you certainly don't want a disturbance to wake the children and scare them all half to death. They've been traumatised enough; don't you think?'

Infuriatingly, Lucy knows that Marcus is right. About the Standish children, at least. She has no desire to wake the entire household, and she especially doesn't want Molly and Barney upset again. If she resists Marcus, that is exactly what will happen.

'Best you just come home with me, quietly. No more scenes.' He points at the suitcase in the corner of the room. 'That your stuff?'

Lucy nods silently.

'I'll take it down now. Get dressed and meet me downstairs.'

Still groggy from sleep, but accepting that she has no choice but to comply, Lucy starts tugging on her clothes while Marcus carries her case downstairs, moving as quickly and quietly as a cat burglar. All those hours spent in the operating room, working his way around critical blood vessels which would cause immediate death if they were nicked with a scalpel, has given him supreme control over his movements.

Lucy composes a quick text to Jane's phone, struggling to think of something that won't alarm her too much if she reads it during the night.

Have decided to go home. All fine, don't worry. Will call. Xx

Her phone is still in her hand when she reaches the front step and Marcus immediately snatches it from her.

'You won't be needing that, for a start,' he says, pushing it into the back pocket of his suit trousers. When she tries to protest and reach for it, he adds, 'No scenes, remember, Lucinda? Let's just get you home.'

He pulls the Standishes' front door to behind them, replaces the key under the plant pot, then lifts Lucy's suitcase into the back of the car.

'Hop in.' He sounds almost cheerful now. 'I suppose you're wondering how I knew where you were,' he goes on, conversationally, as he steers his car through the empty streets. 'If you already know a phone's number, it's very easy to track its exact location by installing a GPS tracker on your own phone. I simply had to use the app to look at the coordinates on a map. And there you were: a little icon in the Clapham area.'

'Marcus,' Lucy is surprised at how well she manages to modulate her voice, masking her anger. 'This isn't going to work. Dragging me back home isn't going to solve anything. I know that, and you know that.'

As he twists in the driver's seat to face her, she's shocked by the dark hollows under his eyes. He doesn't look well. 'Listen. Can you just for once stop making this all about yourself? I've been up for nearly twenty-two hours straight, ten of those spent slicing up people's hearts in an attempt to keep them in the land of the living. And I've got to be back in the hospital in four hours' time, with steady hands. You've lost me enough sleep as it is. Let's agree to just leave the mud-slinging and accusations, okay?'

She nods mutely.

When they get back to Barnes, she follows him into the house and upstairs to the master bedroom. Marcus tugs off his shoes and trousers and is asleep on top of the bed within seconds, while Lucy stares, blinking, at the ceiling, forcing herself to accept that, for now, she's not going anywhere. There's no point trying to rock the boat in the short term, and nothing to be achieved by stomping off to the spare room. She's begun to realise that if she's going to get out of this marriage, she needs to play a longer, and much smarter, game.

NINE

JULY 1996

Of course, Felicity Gibson's ban is not the end of the matter.

The appeal of Blackwater Pond is too great. When Adele calls round again two days later, only to be told firmly by Felicity Gibson that they will have to find something else to do with their time, she appears to take it well. However, after mooching round the Redgate shopping precinct for an hour, she changes her tune and starts to wheedle.

'C'mon,' she says, hooking her arm round Lucy's neck. 'Let's go to the Pond. We don't have to swim; we can just hang around. See who's there.'

'See if Gary Emsworth's there, you mean,' Lucy says with a grin. Gary is a big, brutally handsome sixteen-year-old on the receiving end of Adele's most recent infatuation.

'Fuck off,' says Adele hotly. 'Well, Miss Goody-Goody, if you're not going to come, I'll just have to go down there on my own, won't I? I don't bloody care either way.' She retracts her arm so forcefully that Lucy is spun round, then flounces off in the direction of the precinct exit. It's the nearest the two of them have ever come to an argument.

'I think I'll go to the library,' she tells her mother the next morning, as she spoons muesli into her mouth. 'I'll take my bike.'

'Not today,' Felicity shakes her head. 'I've got a dental appointment up in London.'

'So? I can still go.'

'I'm not leaving you alone here all day. Not with…' She changes tack and smiles suddenly. 'I've asked Sally Beckett if you can spend the day with them, and she said that's fine. Joanne would like the company, apparently.'

'But I'm not even friends with Joanne,' Lucy protests.

'She's a nice enough girl, and they're only just down the road. You can cycle over after you've finished your breakfast.'

It's hot and sultry again, only today the sky is obscured by a layer of thin, yellowish-grey cloud and the warmth is oppressive rather than benign as Lucy makes her way reluctantly to the Becketts'.

'Joanne's upstairs,' Sally Beckett says with a smile, as she admits Lucy to the house. 'Go on up, sweetheart.' She's wearing a sleeveless dress in fuchsia pink linen, and a pair of high-heeled sandals, a huge pair of sunglasses like insect eyes push her blonde hair back from her face. 'I'm just popping out for a bit,' she says, reading Lucy's expression and surmising correctly that Felicity Gibson would have thought twice about taking up Sally's offer if she'd known Sally wasn't going to be in residence. 'The new computer system at work has crashed and I've got to pop in and sort things out. But I won't be gone long. Joanne's brother's Jamie is around the place somewhere, and my mum's just down the road if she's needed. And her Auntie Sandra will look in on you later, if I'm not back.'

The Becketts have lived in the Redgate area for generations and make up an extended clan of siblings, cousins and aunties. Their family contrasts starkly with the Gibsons, with their only child and complete lack of relatives within a fifty-mile radius.

Loud music from one of the bedrooms is the only evidence of the older brother Jamie's presence, but Joanne is in her room, as promised. She sits hunched on the edge of her bed, as though waiting for a dental appointment of her own, her skin clammy with sweat and her glasses faintly steamed over. The room itself is stuffy and has a sickly smell of foot odour mingled with cheap perfume.

'Hullo,' she mouths at Lucy, without enthusiasm. When she fails to move, Lucy reaches past her and opens the window.

'It's hot,' she explains. 'Why don't you have your window open.'

Joanne mumbles something through the thudding of the bass woofer from the next bedroom. It sounds like 'Allergies.'

'What shall we do?' Lucy asks.

Joanne shrugs.

Lucy, who has positioned herself near the windowsill to try and capitalise on the feeble breeze, looks outside desperately for some inspiration. A few small children are circling the cul-de-sac on trikes and scooters. Below the window, her own bike lies propped against the raised flower bed where she left it.

'Do you have a bike?' she asks Joanne. 'We could go for a bike ride.'

Joanne nods. 'In the garage.'

It turns out that the bike hasn't been ridden for so long that both tyres are flat. There are two other bikes in the garage, boys' bikes with dropped handlebars.

'Whose are those?' Lucy demands.

'That one's Jamie's. And that one's my cousin's. He's been staying with us for a bit. 'Cause he's fallen out with my auntie and uncle.'

Lucy vaguely remembers a whispered conversation between her parents about Sally having a tearaway nephew who had got himself into trouble with the police, but all she's interested in at this particular moment is securing a mode of transport. 'Can't you borrow one of them?' she wheedles.

Joanne is reluctant, but eventually Lucy persuades her to use Jamie's. It's too big, and Joanne perches awkwardly on the seat like a shapeless marshmallow on a toasting stick.

'Where are we going?' she asks Lucy nervously. 'I'm supposed to tell my auntie or my gran where I am if I go out somewhere.'

'Just around,' says Lucy airily, turning round to smile at Joanne. 'You know, nowhere in particular.'

But she does know exactly where they're going. They're going to Blackwater Pond.

The first person Lucy sees is Gary Emsworth. He's in the midst of a gaggle of older boys, their newly acquired tans and the sheen of reservoir water combining to emphasise the developing muscles on their chest and abdomens.

She knows then that there is a good chance that Adele will be there, and, sure enough, she spots her sitting on the edge of the rocky promontory, smoking a Marlboro as though she's had a twenty-a-day habit for years. Her face lights up when she sees her friend but instantly darkens when she spots Joanne at her side, clinging to the handlebars of her brother's bike as though her life depends on it. As though she's in danger.

'Come on,' Lucy says to her encouragingly, and they both drop their bikes on the grass verge next to the path and walk to the edge of the reservoir.

Adele stubs out her cigarette with a frown and climbs off the rock.

'What's she doing here?' she demands, as though Joanne isn't standing right there in front of her.

Dropping her gaze and shrinking into her body, Joanne goes to the water's edge and pretends to be absorbed in throwing in small stones. Her pale shoulders are already scorching in the sun.

'Why the fuck did you bring her?' Adele asks, her voice dripping with disdain. 'I thought you said you weren't friends with her.'

'I'm not,' says Lucy, folding her arms across her chest as though challenging Adele not to believe her. 'It wasn't my idea. I mean, it was my idea to come down here, because I had to do something with her, but it wasn't my idea to spend the day with her. My mum arranged it. With Sally Beckett.'

Adele shrugs, but Lucy can tell she's mollified. 'Well, let's just leave her here and go and play on the rope swing.'

'I don't know...' Lucy is still afraid of the rope swing, of its jerky, unpredictable arc.

'Don't be a baby, Luce. Come on,' Adele catches her by the wrist and drags her over to the rock, where Gary Emsworth is dangling from the rope, curling his hand into his armpit with his free hand and making chimpanzee noises.

When he has let go of the rope and splashed into the water, Adele grabs at the rope and pushes it into Lucy's hand. 'Go on.'

'Virgin!' shouts one of the boys.

Prompted by the teasing to prove a point, Lucy takes off her glasses and leaves them in a clump of grass. Then she lets the rope take her weight, knotting her ankles around it as if she was in gym class, but before she has had a chance to swing herself, Adele gives her a shove and the rope flies out over the surface of the reservoir. It's not blue and sparkling today, but murky and greenish-grey. As the trajectory of the rope goes into reverse, heading back towards the rock, Adele screams, 'Jump, for Christ's sake!' and Lucy lets go, simultaneously closing her eyes. Her foot catches on something as she descends into the water, but she launches herself back to the surface and starts swimming back to the rock. Despite her slight build she's a strong swimmer: the product of several years of private lessons and foreign holidays with outdoor pools.

'Not a virgin now!' crows one of the larger and more intimidating boys. He wears his hair shaved short and has a tattoo across his tanned shoulder blades.

Lucy ignores him. She's decided she loves the rope swing and goes back time and time again, queuing for her turn with the burly teenage boys. She has no idea how much time has gone past but eventually becomes aware of Joanne hovering near her shoulder. Despite the cloud cover, Joanne's flesh has turned from palest baby pink to cerise.

'We need to go,' she says in an urgent whisper. 'My auntie's coming over this afternoon and she won't know where we are.'

'"My auntie's coming",' Adele mimics Joanne's slight lisp. 'Jesus, what are you, Beckett? Five years old?'

Joanne's face flushes, and when she turns to Lucy in silent appeal, Lucy sees her eyes tear up behind the thick lenses. Their ugliness stirs empathy in Lucy, even though the Gibsons have made a point of buying their daughter stylish spectacle frames and have promised she can wear contact lenses once she's in Year 9.

'We'll go in a minute,' she says, attempting to appease both girls.

'Tell you what Joanne,' Adele grins, thrusting the rope at her. 'One go on the rope swing, then you can leave.'

Joanne shakes her head. 'I don't want to.'

'Go on,' Adele wheedles. 'There's nothing to it. Everyone else has done it.'

Joanne shoots Lucy a desperate look.

'Just one go,' says Lucy encouragingly. They're the only ones on the rocky platform now that the older boys have slunk off under the tree cover to drink cans of beer and smoke. And the truth is she's hungry, and sweaty and a little dehydrated, and just wants to sit indoors with a cold drink. Life will be easier if she just backs up Adele. 'It is easy, honestly. You just hang on till the rope's gone as far as it can, then let go, really quickly. Like this.' She mimes the action.

'Okay.' Joanne positions her feet on the edge of the rock, pushes her glasses up her nose and reaches towards the rope.

As she does so, Lucy's brain leaps forward in time so that she knows exactly what is going to happen even before it takes place. Adele pushes the knot of the rope in Joanne's direction, then, with a fast, whipping motion, snatches the rope away just as her fingers are about to close round it. Joanne's right arm flails in space, reaching for something that's no longer there. The disorientation makes her clumsy, her glasses fly off and her right foot folds over her left. Both heels skid on the wet surface of the rock. Still grabbing wildly for the rope that isn't there, Joanne bounces onto her right hip before plunging off the edge of the stony platform. There's a horrible hollow smacking sound as the side of her skull hits rock. Then silence.

Lucy's first thought, bizarrely, is about the bikes.

Her own bike lies abandoned on the grass. Next to it is Jamie Beckett's bike. How is she going to get both bikes back to the Becketts' house on her own? The anxiety about this detail overwhelms her.

The silence is suddenly punctuated by loud screams from somewhere, and then there are voices shouting, people running, a commotion.

Lucy waits for Joanne to emerge from the surface of the water – surely she's about to do that? – but she doesn't. She keeps looking over desperately at the bikes, as though the very presence of her older brother's bike will somehow make Joanne okay. She's aware of someone running up the path to fetch help, though she doesn't notice who it is, and then a man out walking his dog comes and jumps into the water. He pulls out what looks like a bundle of wet washing to the sound of his dog's frantic barking. Then an ambulance pulls up in the lane, and two paramedics scurry towards the rock with a stretcher. They bend over the heap of washing, and between their feet Lucy glimpses a thin, watery trail of blood.

'She'll be all right,' Lucy says out loud, to no one in particular. She looks around wildly for Adele, calls her name, but Adele is no longer there.

Lucy's memory of what happened next remained hazy in the years that followed.

Someone – she still has no idea who – must have phoned her father's office, because he appears in the doorway of the second ambulance, where she's sitting with a cotton blanket draped round her shoulders. He embraces her silently, then leads her to where his car is parked.

'Come on; let's get you home.'

'What about the bikes?'

'Don't worry about the bloody bikes.' Jeffrey seems stressed, but he does not reprimand his daughter for being at the reservoir after she has been told not to go. This in itself is concerning.

Felicity has not yet returned from London, so when they get back to the house it's her father who attempts to make her something to eat; her father who never cooks. He burns the toast and the scrambled egg is full of gristly white lumps. Lucy takes one look at it and runs to the bathroom to be sick.

Felicity appears in her bedroom as she's getting ready for bed. 'Lucy, sit down.' She pats the bed and sits herself. Her face is distorted by a strange rictus, almost as if she's trying to suppress a smile. But of course she's not. 'Darling. Joanne…' She closes her eyes briefly, and when she opens them again, Lucy sees with alarm that there are tears there. 'Joanne didn't survive. She hit her head on a rock and her lungs filled up with water because she was unconscious.'

'She's dead?' asks Lucy, trying out the unfamiliar word. A word that doesn't fit with someone of her age.

'Yes,' Felicity nods, and brushes the tears away. 'I'm afraid she is. She drowned. Her poor, poor family… The police need to speak to you, but they've agreed it can wait until tomorrow. Until you're less shocked.'

'But it was an accident,' Lucy says, a jolt of panic making her insides tingle, her pulse quicken.

'I know, darling, but they still need a statement from you. That's how these things work.'

Felicity fetches a mug of hot chocolate; which Lucy doesn't want but drinks anyway so that her mother will leave her alone.

She lies on her bed in the half-dark, staring at the ceiling, unable to banish the image of Joanne's body from her mind. Where is she now, she wonders? In one of those metal freezer drawers like they have on *Prime Suspect*?

There's a sharp tapping noise, as something bounces off the windowpane. Lucy climbs off the bed and finds a piece of gravel on the carpet. Outside, Adele is just visible in the pale glow of the street light, her hand resting on the handlebar of her bike.

'Luce, come down,' she hisses. 'I need to talk to you.'

Lucy holds up a finger to her lips, then creeps out onto the landing. Her parents are watching television in the sitting room and don't notice her coming down the stairs, but Kibble does, skittering across the hall floor to greet her. She picks him up and holds him hard against her chest so that he won't bark while she opens the front door. Sensing an unscheduled outing, he wriggles with delight and follows Lucy down the drive with a dancing motion.

'What did you tell them?' Adele says, without preamble. Her face, half in shadow, is a chalky grey, and she hunches her shoulders.

'Tell who?'

'The police. Who else?'

'I haven't spoken to them yet. Tomorrow, I think.'

'So what are you going to tell them?'

It feels all wrong that she doesn't mention Joanne by name. That she doesn't even acknowledge that she's dead.

'That it was an accident. That… that she slipped.' Lucy reaches down and grabs Kibble's collar before he can disappear into their neighbour's garden.

Adele purses her lips, seemingly satisfied with this. 'Make sure you do,' she says ominously. 'Promise.' She holds out her hand, palm up, and indicates with a jut of her chin that Lucy should lay her own hand flat on top of it in a facsimile of a Freemason's handshake. Lucy obeys the unspoken request. Adele then pulls her hand away and turns her bike around to wheel it in the opposite direction. Before she swings her leg over the saddle, she pauses and looks back at Lucy. 'Best friends don't betray each other: remember that.'

TEN

For the next few days, Lucy plays the perfect wife.

She attends lectures and works on her academic assignments as usual while Marcus is at work, stocking the fridge and preparing food that she knows he likes. That is the outer Lucy. The inner Lucy is in turmoil. She knows with utter certainty that she has reached the point of no return and is simultaneously furious with herself that it took five years for her to get here. Marcus's maturity had been so seductive, extending as it did the nurturing she had always enjoyed from her parents. It felt like manna from heaven to a shy, uncertain twenty-something. But that protection was only one side of a coin. And on the other side was the need to control. Of course, she had come to realise this intellectually some time ago, starting with the trip to Paris. But it has taken this long to accept the emotional truth of her situation: she is an abused wife. And having fully accepted it, there is to be no turning back.

Marcus is exhausted when he returns home from work every day and lacks the energy to argue. Lucy capitalises on this by being blandly agreeable and sticking to neutral topics of conversation. Sensing that their marital crisis has passed, on Wednesday evening, he even makes suggestions about a summer holiday. An hour later, there is another surprise.

'Here,' he comes into the kitchen as she stacks plates into the dishwasher and holds out her mobile. 'You can have your phone back.' He says it as though conferring privileges on a well-behaved teenager.

Lucy feels her insides curdle with anger, but forces a smile. 'Thanks,' she says, putting it down in full view on the counter, to prove she has nothing to hide. 'I don't have lectures or seminars tomorrow, so I think I'll go and see Dad. I'll probably stay the night.'

Which you will know full well, since you'll be tracking me, she thinks privately. She's not sure whether she will actually stay at her father's or not, but she intends to pre-empt her husband checking up on her plan.

'Good idea. Give him my best and tell him to get Malcolm Denehay to phone me if he has any concerns.' He comes over and hugs Lucy, thus declaring an end to their fight. 'I'm going to go up now: I'm shattered.'

Once Marcus is in the bathroom, Lucy goes to her desk in the bay window of the dining room and roots through the drawers. At the back of the bottom one, her fingers brush against something leathery and she pulls out what she was looking for. A small, bound passbook for the savings account her parents set up for her when she was ten. They added money regularly on birthdays and at Christmas, and, with the interest earned, the balance now stands at several thousand pounds. All her other accounts are shared with Marcus, and he checks the statements routinely, so that if she withdraws an unusual amount of cash, he will notice. But she has never mentioned this old account to him. She stuffs the passbook into the zipped pocket of her handbag, and once there is no further sound coming from upstairs, follows her husband up to bed.

In the dark, he stirs and reaches for her, but when she lies still and unresponsive, he gives up and sinks back into deep sleep.

Rhea Gibson is three years older than Lucy: a stringy, energetic woman who has always enjoyed having the upper hand over her younger, more attractive cousin. Having completed her nursing registration, she joined a pharmaceutical company, working her way up through sales to management. She proudly and anachronistically describes herself as 'a career woman', and this – according to Rhea – is why she is single and childless. Nothing whatsoever to do with the fact that she is bossy, inflexible and occasionally aggressive.

'Come in, come in,' she says as she opens the door of Jeffrey's bungalow to Lucy, dressed in sports gear with an apron on top. 'Only, make sure you wipe your feet. I've just hoovered.' She gives her cousin a stiff embrace. 'Uncle Jeffrey's in the lounge: I'll pop the kettle on and make us some coffee.'

Lucy bends over her father's armchair and greets him with a kiss. He seems lethargic, but the deathly pallor has left his face and he smiles warmly at his daughter.

'All okay with you?' he asks, adding pointedly, 'And Marcus?'

'Yes, fine. We're both fine.'

His eyes examine her face, as though searching for clues. 'Are you sure, darling? You look wrung out.'

'Yes, Dad. Just a little tired.'

It occurs to her that her father might think she's pregnant. That he probably hopes she is.

'It's getting to the end of my course, now, and there's a lot to fit in. Once my dissertation's done, I'll get a chance to relax.'

'Let's hope so… I expect that son-in-law of mine is still working ridiculous hours too?' Jeffrey sighs.

Lucy perches on the edge of the armchair, which allows her to avoid further scrutiny of her face, and examines her fingernails. Rhea bustles around, plumping cushions and polishing the occasional table before she puts the coffee tray down on it, all of which seems quite unnecessary to Lucy, as does the ridiculous apron.

After a couple of home-made shortbread biscuits and half an hour of awkward small talk, Lucy is relieved when Rhea heads back to the kitchen to prepare some soup for lunch.

'Don't tire him out, he needs to rest!' she admonishes, as though Jeffrey is her father and not Lucy's.

'Better do as you're told,' Jeffrey says with a conspiratorial wink.

Lucy bends to hug him, then lets herself out, shouting goodbye to Rhea.

The kitchen is at the back of the bungalow and Jeffrey's armchair faces towards the back garden, so there is no one to see her place her phone inside the little wooden mailbox nailed to the wall next to the garage. Jeffrey long ago asked the local postman to put all the post through the letter box, so this mailbox is now redundant. Having thus fixed her GPS coordinates at her father's home, she gets back into the car and drives into the centre of Redgate.

Her first port of call is the building society, where she withdraws five hundred pounds in cash from her childhood savings account. Then she goes to a mobile phone concession, where she tries to explain to the gangly, acne-scarred salesman that, no, she doesn't want or need a contract phone, she just wants the pay-as-you-go handset with optimal web browsing capacity. A frustrating forty minutes later, Lucy emerges from the shop with the new phone unpacked, charged and ready to use.

She walks down the street to The Copper Kettle, an old-fashioned tea shop where her mother used to take her as a child, and orders a pot of tea and a toasted teacake. She's not in the least bit hungry, but her mother always used to order teacakes when they were there, and it feels wrong not to do so now. The place hasn't changed in thirty years: the tables are still covered with red and white checked PVC tablecloths, each sporting a bowl of sugar lumps and a metal serviette dispenser, and the shelves on the walls are still crammed with an assortment of dusty knick-knacks, none of them an actual copper kettle. Lucy feels the years roll away, and she is transported back to the comfortable, untroubled days of her childhood. When she first moved to London after university, this was the last place she wanted to be, and if anyone had told her she would be sitting here fifteen years later, deliberately trying to conjure the ghosts of her past, she would have laughed in their faces.

She signs into Facebook and types 'Adele Watts' into the search box.

There are a lot of Adele Watts out there in the world, far too many to trawl through in one sitting. And that's assuming Lucy's Adele uses social media, which – if her contrarian and non-conformist character has remained unchanged – she may not. Perhaps she could start with someone connected to Adele who might be less difficult to find. Lucy remembers the spelling of her sister's name was unusual; wrong even, in some people's estimation. Chelsee, rather than Chelsea. She tries searching for Chelsee Watts. A lot of Chelsea Watts come up, but only one Chelsee Watts.

Lucy squints at the pictures. She barely remembers the five-year-old Chelsee she first met in 1995, but this could well be her. Her profile settings are open, and her location is listed as 'Surrey, UK'. She clicks through the photos on her account and sees that this is definitely the right Chelsee. She's now a petite pretty young woman in her twenties, fond of heavy pencilled brows and stripes of brown highlighter under her cheekbones. Here she is with a short, dumpy woman who is just about recognisable as Dawn Watts, and with various half-siblings and boyfriends. The boyfriends conform to a distinct type; all dressed like would-be rappers, in branded sportswear, gold chains and designer trucker hats. And here she is, finally, with Adele. They're seated in a pub beer garden, with a cohort of empty glasses in front of them, each brandishing a lit roll-up. The way they are lolling back on their elbows, their poses unfocused, suggests a degree of intoxication.

The caption reads: *Standard weekday night: me and my big sis down at the Dog #secondhome.*

It's dated about six months ago. So Adele and her crowd must still drink at the Dog and Fox. Lucy glances at her watch. It's only half past three, and she does not relish the idea of hanging about in a grotty pub for hours. But her only other option is to send a message to Chelsee and hope she'll pass it on to her sister. If she doesn't check Facebook regularly, that could take days, or even weeks, or not happen at all.

She visits the newsagent across the road and buys a handful of magazines before driving to the Dog and Fox and parking in the far corner of the pub car park. The pub itself is all but empty, so she waits in the car for a while, flicking absently through the magazines but not really taking in what she's reading. The pictures and words just blur.

At six thirty when regular drinkers start to shuffle into the pub in ones and twos, Lucy goes inside and orders a gin and tonic, positioning herself at a table opposite the door. The main bar has cheap wood panelling and swirling floral wallpaper on the walls and torn, sticky carpets. The fittings are cheap, and everything is covered with a faint patina of ancient tobacco smoke. Lucy knows that people are staring at her, a woman with her long hair expensively styled, rather than scraped onto the top of her head in a tight bun. That alone makes her stand out. She orders a second gin and tonic and a packet of crisps and tries to deflect attention by studying her phone.

At eight forty-five, just as she's at the bar ordering a Diet Coke and wondering how much longer she can spin out her solitary drinking session, she catches sight of Adele, standing with a group of people near the pool table.

Taking a deep breath, she walks over and clears her throat.

'Adele?'

Adele turns and looks at her, but her slanting eyes betray no surprise, no emotion at all.

'It's me, Lucy Gibson.'

'Yeah, I know who you are. Not likely to forget, am I?'

There is a hint of the old Adele grin, but it's gone as soon as it's appeared. She's wearing tight jeans with a top that exposes her shoulders, and Lucy realises it was the padded coat that she was wearing in the supermarket car park that had made her appear big. She's still stockily built, and a rim of flesh hangs over the waistband of her jeans, but she's barely overweight. There are creases at the corners of her eyes, which are accentuated with heavy eyeliner.

Silently she takes in Lucy's J Crew blazer and £200 trainers, her Prada bag and chunky gold bracelets.

'I knew you'd come,' she says eventually.

ELEVEN

'You knew?' Lucy repeats, surprised.

'Ever since I saw you.'

Lucy frowns, even though the answer is obvious.

'In the Costcutter's car park. And, also, my mum's friend Janet Leary is friends with the lady who cleans your dad's house, and she told Janet that your dad had been taken poorly. Gone into hospital. So I reckoned you'd probably be coming down here at some point.'

'Can I buy you a drink?' Lucy asks.

Adele has come into the pub with two men and a girl, all in some variation on the theme of sportswear, and they are staring over at her and Lucy with frank curiosity.

'Go on then: I'll have a pina colada. Just kidding. I'll have a double rum and black, since you're buying.'

Lucy goes to the bar and returns to the table where Adele is waiting alone, carrying drinks and two packets of salt and vinegar crisps. Adele always loved salt and vinegar.

'You remembered,' Adele says with another faint grin, ripping the packet so that it opens up and the crisps are spread out, just as she always used to. 'So, how's my bezzie mate?'

She's being sarcastic, of course. It has been a long time since she and Lucy were best friends, and even then it was only for a year. And yet the intensity of that friendship and its terrible ending affected them both deeply. Lucy knows this is true for her, and looking into Adele's oddly slanting eyes, she can tell it's the same for her. Even so, the steadiness of her gaze is unnerving.

'Fine,' Lucy says, because that's what's expected, and because it's a bit too soon to delve into the truth. 'You're right: I've come down to visit Dad. He's out of hospital now.'

'And so you thought you'd just pop into the old Dog and Fox. Bit random, isn't it?'

'I remember seeing you here once, years ago.' She becomes aware that Adele is staring at the huge diamond solitaire on her left hand and buries it in her lap. 'And I fancied a drink after the stress of dealing with Dad, so I thought I'd try here on the off-chance you'd come in.'

Adele reaches out her arms in an expansive gesture. 'Well, here I am. Still hanging around this shithole. Never did get round to moving away from our dump of a home town. Not like you.' She narrows her eyes. 'I hear you got married.'

Lucy nods. 'Yes. My husband's a doctor. In London.'

'Very nice,' says Adele, though her tone implies anything but. 'Got kids?'

'No. Not yet.'

'I've got two,' Adele's face softens slightly. 'Two girls. Paige and Skye.'

'Lovely,' says Lucy. 'Lucky you.'

Adele shrugs. 'Their dad's a useless bastard, but my mum gives me plenty of help.'

'Do you ever see anyone from Redgate High?' The truth is that, apart from Adele, Lucy can barely remember the names and the faces from her brief stint at the school.

Adele shakes her head. 'Not really. Occasionally I bump into Gary Emsworth and Elaine Castle.'

'You liked Gary, I remember that much,' Lucy says, the memory of Adele's high-octane crush prompting a smile. 'Elaine… yes, I think that name rings a bell.'

'They're married now. You see people round and about, you know, in a small place like this.'

Lucy wonders if she will mention Joanne Beckett. If either of them will. Her presence hangs there between them, as awkward in death as she was in life. 'Can I buy you another drink?'

Adele shakes her head. 'I've got to get back to the kids. My neighbour's with them, but she needs to get home. Tell you what, why don't you come back with me, and we can get something to eat. Order a takeaway.'

Adele's flat is a short walk from the Dog and Fox, so Lucy leaves her car parked at the pub and accompanies her on foot. They stop at an off-licence to pick up a bottle of white wine, which Lucy insists on paying for.

'Ooh, posh stuff,' Adele remarks, and Lucy is transported back suddenly to her scrutiny of Lucy's bedroom and her ridiculing the embroidered sampler with her full name. She feels exposed, just as she does when she's introduced to Adele's babysitter, Jackie, and receives a long, suspicious appraisal through narrowed eyes.

'Luce was at Redgate High for a year, same time as us,' Adele tells her.

'Don't remember anyone like you,' Jackie says doubtfully, gathering up her bag and coat but keeping her eyes on Lucy all the way to the door. 'Kids are fast asleep, Dell; you shouldn't hear from them till the morning.'

Adele's flat is on the second floor of a building on the Danemoor estate, where she lived as a child. 'Haven't moved very far, have I?' she laughs, finding a corkscrew and wine glasses. Despite patches of peeling wallpaper and flaking paint, the place is tidy and well-organised, and although the decor and furnishings are cheap, they have been put together with a certain amount of flair, and pride.

Adele pours them both wine, then kicks off her imitation Ugg boots, heaves her bare feet onto the sofa and lights a cigarette.

'Best fag of the day,' she says, adding with a cackle, 'but then I say that about all of them.' She gulps at the wine and pulls a face at its dryness. 'Blimey, bit sour isn't it?' Disappearing into the kitchen, she comes back with a bottle of lemonade and splashes some into the glass. 'Bit more like sangria now.' She proffers the bottle to Lucy, who is about to shake her head, then, not wanting to seem prissy, holds out her glass for some. 'So you've done all right for yourself,' Adele says without bitterness. 'Rich husband, house in London. What do you do for work?'

'I'm just finishing a postgraduate degree.'

Adele shrugs. 'You were always good at exams, and tests, and stuff… Remember when we had the maths tests and we always used to try and sit next to each other so I could copy your answers?'

Lucy nods. 'Yes, I do remember.'

'And that camcorder you had… I remember all those stupid home movies we used to make.'

A pin-sharp mental picture comes to Lucy then, of the two of them laughing so helplessly they used to roll off the bed and onto the floor. When has she ever laughed as hard as that, before or since? Probably never. It was the first proper friendship she'd had, and the most colourful. 'That was such good fun,' she says, smiling. 'Mum used to come and check we were okay, we made so much noise.'

Adele sits up, tapping the powdery column of ash into an empty coffee mug, before taking another deep drag. 'So,' she says, her expression changing abruptly. 'Why are you really here?'

Lucy looks down at her feet. Awkward or not, it's time to come clean. 'It's kind of hard to explain. To know where to start… I saw that you spent some time in prison.'

Adele shrugs. 'What of it?'

'I need to find someone who might have some sort of connections… someone who's brushed up against the wrong side of the law. To help me… with something.'

Adele gives a derisive snort. 'You mean you want to have someone bumped off? A hitman.'

Lucy shakes her head. 'No! God, no. Sorry. I'm not explaining very well.'

'No, you're not.' Adele grinds out her cigarette and lights another one.

'I want to disappear.' Lucy has been holding her breath, and she lets it go now, in a rush. 'Change my identity. I need to find someone who can help me do that.'

Adele tilts her head and puffs smoke at the ceiling. 'Why on earth would you want to do that? You've got the perfect life.'

'No,' Lucy shakes her head. 'It's not. My husband and I… it's not a happy marriage. Quite the opposite.'

'So. Just leave him. Divorce him and take half the wonga.'

'It's not quite as simple as that. Even if I do leave… he's made it clear he's never going to leave me alone. He'll never let me get on with my life. I'll never be able to start over.'

Adele shrugs unsympathetically. 'He can't really stop you though, can he? And if he tries to… well, that's what the police and the courts are for.'

'It's not quite as simple as that… Marcus – my husband – has friends in high places. He's a member of the Freemasons. You know who they are?'

Adele nods. 'I've heard of them, yeah. Old boys' club.'

'Lots of them are in the police, and the legal profession. They've got a particularly strong grip on the Family Court. So yes, he could make a very good job of stopping me.'

'A proper rich girl's problem.' Adele's tone is distinctly unsympathetic.

'So you don't know anyone?'

'No. I don't.' She sets her jaw. 'You obviously think I'm some sort of criminal mastermind, but the fact is all I did was fail to declare some earnings while I was claiming benefits. The judge was way too harsh for a first offence, everyone said so. And I just did a few months in an open prison. It hardly makes me Myra Hindley.'

'I know; I didn't mean to imply that.' Lucy becomes flustered, tries desperately to back-pedal. 'I just thought you might have met people inside who have certain connections, that's all.'

'Well, I don't, okay?' Adele's smile returns briefly. 'Tell you what, though, it makes me fucking glad I never got married.'

'Are you still single now? No man in your life?'

'Yep, still single and planning to stay that way. Well, there is someone, kind of, but…' She stops herself and forces a smile. 'Probably a good thing you never had any kids. In the circumstances.'

Lucy nods. She's not about to go into the history of her childlessness. Not now. 'How old are your two?'

'Paige is nine and Skye's six.' Adele picks up her phone and pulls up a photo. 'Here.'

Two pretty little girls with curly blonde hair and wide smiles fill the screen. 'They're lovely.' Lucy's about to hand the phone back when she spots something. She swipes her fingers across the screen to zoom in on the image. There, on Skye's chubby wrist is a familiar silver bracelet. The same one Adele took from her childhood jewellery box. Her response is automatic, and she has no idea how much she will come to regret it. 'Oh my goodness!'

'What?' Adele reaches for her phone.

'She's wearing my bracelet.'

'What do you mean?'

'That's my silver christening bracelet. The one you took from my house.'

Adele sticks out her chin, that stubborn gesture of old. 'No I didn't. What are you talking about?'

'You did. I saw you take it, and I never said anything.'

'What the fuck?'

'But it's okay, it's fine,' Lucy says hurriedly. 'I didn't mind about it; I was given loads of stuff for my christening. I never wore any of it.'

Adele snatches the phone from her, jolting Lucy's glass and splashing the wine over her shoes. She feels a tightening in her ribs, and she's suddenly that same timid, bespectacled eleven-year-old girl who first met Adele.

'Oh, so I'm a thief as well as master criminal now, am I?' Adele says with a curl of her lip. She grinds out her cigarette and stands up. 'You know what, I think you should go. It was a dumb idea inviting you back here. Stupid.'

'Adele, I'm sorry. I wasn't implying—'

'Go on – just go. Fuck off.'

TWELVE

It's far too late for Lucy to return to her father's house, and her blood alcohol level means that driving back to London is also out of the question.

At least her mobile is still at the bungalow, she consoles herself, and therefore Marcus won't call her whereabouts into question. She trudges back to the Dog and Fox and folds down the rear seats of her car, wrapping a picnic blanket around herself once she's curled herself up inside. There isn't quite enough space to lie down comfortably and her feet are sticky from the wine and lemonade that spilled over her shoes. She shifts miserably like a dog in a cage while a cold, spring rain drums at the windows. After a couple of hours, she is prepared to throw in the towel and check into a hotel but is held back by the fact that the charge will appear on her joint credit card statement and Marcus will start asking questions. She has what's left of the five hundred pounds in cash but doesn't want to waste around a fifth of it on a hotel room. It will be needed soon enough.

Eventually she sleeps for a while, waking at dawn with an aching back and stiff legs. Hunger gnaws at her stomach: she and Adele never got round to the promised takeaway, and all she's eaten in the last day is one of Rhea's shortbread biscuits and a handful of salt and vinegar crisps. Her original mobile phone will have to be retrieved from the mailbox, so after picking up a takeaway coffee and two croissants from a 24-hour petrol-station shop, she drives to the bungalow. The dashboard clock tells her that it's 6.51, and dawn is just breaking. Parking a few metres from the bungalow, she walks up the drive and gropes inside the mailbox for her phone. To her relief the battery has a modest amount of charge, which means it will still be discernible by a tracker. Less welcome are the two missed call notifications from Marcus's mobile.

As she turns to go, the front door opens and Rhea stands there in a lilac velour dressing gown and fluffy slippers. 'Lucy,' she says, confused. 'Is everything all right? Only, when—'

'Absolutely fine,' beams Lucy, with manufactured brightness. 'I stayed down here at a friend's last night, and I just thought I'd pop in and say goodbye to Dad before I head home.'

The expression on Rhea's face is hard to interpret, but it makes Lucy uncomfortable. 'Jeffrey's still asleep.'

'Never mind then; tell him I said goodbye and I'll see him soon.'

Before her cousin can speak, she hurries down the drive and gets back into her car, pulling away with such haste that the engine almost stalls.

'So where were you?'

Marcus stalks into the kitchen at 8 p.m. as Lucy is preparing a fish pie, his suit jacket slung over one shoulder. He has shaved today but still has purplish shadows under his eyes and his hair looks as though it could use a wash.

Lucy pauses, potato in one hand, paring knife in the other. 'Where was I? I told you, I went to Dad's.'

He shakes his head. 'No. You weren't there. When you weren't answering your phone, I rang your father. Spoke to your cousin actually. She said you'd been and gone. Seemed to be under the impression that you were back here in London with me.'

Lucy concentrates on peeling the skin from the potato.

'So where were you, Lucinda?'

'I bumped into a friend from school and we went to the pub for a few drinks. Time sort of ran away with us, and I ended up staying over. That's all.'

'A male friend, was it?'

'No, of course not.'

Marcus snatches the knife from her hand and pushes the chopping board away. 'Just stop that while I'm trying to talk to you. Is that too much to ask?' He holds the knife aloft for a few seconds before tossing it into the sink. 'Have you got another man? A lover? Is that what all this nonsense is about?'

'No of course not,' Lucy keeps her voice low and calm, even though prickles of anxiety are racing through her body. 'That's a ridiculous suggestion.'

'Is it though? Isn't that what's normally going on, when a wife starts acting up?'

Lucy's instinct is to protest at this turn of phrase, but she knows that if she's to maintain control of her situation she has to turn offence into defence. 'I understand that you're overworked and stressed, and that's making you on edge,' she says in the most conciliatory tone she can muster. 'But I can assure you I'm not having an affair, nor do I want to.' She picks up the knife again, smiles, and resumes her task. 'Why don't you go up and run a bath and I'll bring you a G and T. Then we can talk over supper, once you've decompressed a bit.'

Marcus takes in a long breath, closes his eyes and exhales slowly. 'All right,' he says after a few seconds. 'But only because I don't have the energy for this.' He pauses at the kitchen door. 'But don't think this is done with.'

No it's not, thinks Lucy grimly. *Not by a long way.*

*

The following morning, Lucy retrieves the pay-as-you-go phone from its hiding place at the bottom of her underwear drawer and switches it on. Finding Jane Standish's number in her regular Contacts list, she punches it in on the new handset.

'Hello?' Jane's response is tentative, as she picks up the call from an unfamiliar number.

'Jane, it's Lucy Wheedon.'

'Ah.' A warm note creeps into Jane's voice. 'New number?'

'Alternative number. Look, I've been meaning to get in touch.' She has left a couple of texts from Jane unanswered and feels bad about it. 'Mostly to apologise for the other evening. And for disappearing in the middle of the night. I really wanted to phone you, but…'

'But you couldn't,' Jane says briskly. 'And I think after Marcus's performance we're all pretty clear why.'

'I'm so sorry.'

'Are you all right, Lucy? That's all Robin and I are concerned about. I phoned Fiona and dropped a few hints, but she said as far as she was concerned you and Marcus are still together and you're fine. Is that right?'

'No,' Lucy says heavily. 'No, nothing is fine. I just decided that rather than run away I needed to do some forward planning. And that involves outside help. So…' She takes a deep breath. 'I wondered if you knew any solicitors who were experienced in dealing with this kind of… situation.'

'Let me think…' There's a beat of silence, then she says, 'My friend Vanessa went through a horrendous divorce. Her bastard of a husband was obstructive about absolutely everything, but I remember she said her legal firm were fantastic. Why don't I call her and get their contact details, then phone you back? I take it you want me to use this number from now on?'

'Yes, please. The other one's under surveillance.'

An hour later, Jane sends a text with a phone number for a practice called Russell, Parker and Payne.

Frances Harper is the woman you need, apparently. Good luck and keep in touch. J x

Lucy phones the firm's enquiries number and a very brisk young woman tells her that in order to secure an initial consultation with Ms Harper, she will have to pay a fee up front.

'It's a little difficult,' Lucy tells her. 'With the… current marital issues. I was planning on paying with cash when I saw her.'

The woman disappears to consult a colleague and comes back a minute later. 'We can put a hold on a credit card and you can settle the account with cash when you come in, if you like. But we do still need the card number in order to book an appointment.'

'You won't actually charge the card though?' Lucy asks, shuddering inwardly at the thought of Marcus's reaction if he sees the law firm's name on his statement.

'No, as I said, we'll just hold the funds until you can come in.' The woman speaks slowly, as if dealing with a child or a simpleton. 'I'm sorry, it's been declined,' she says. She may as well have added, 'No surprise there.'

'But it can't have, there's a ten-thousand-pound limit. Hold on…' Lucy rummages in her wallet for an alternative card. That, too, is declined. 'I'll have to phone you back.'

'I can only hold this appointment slot for a few hours: Ms Harper is extremely booked up.'

Leaving her regular phone at home, Lucy drives to Clapham, where she first withdraws money from her old savings account, then tries one of her joint account cards in a cash machine. It's sucked into the card slot with an ominous clicking sound, and '*Please contact your issuing bank*' appears on the screen.

She drives to the Standishes' house and is relieved to see Jane's car parked outside. When she opens the door, Lucy brandishes a handful of twenty-pound notes at her.

'Help for the fiscally compromised, madam? If I give you this, can I stick £375 on your credit card?'

Laughing, Jane invites Lucy in for coffee and makes the call to Russell, Parker and Payne in order to secure Lucy's appointment.

'Weird about your cards not working though,' she says, but then catches sight of Lucy's expression. 'Unless…'

'Marcus,' Lucy says simply. 'I don't have any credit issues, so it has to have something to do with him.'

Once she's back home, she tries phoning her husband, but his mobile goes to voicemail as it always does when he's at work. She's certainly not going to humiliate herself by contacting Beryl and asking for a message to be passed on to her husband. Instead, she tackles him as soon as he gets home from work.

'Yes,' he says coolly. 'You're damn right. I did close those accounts. You've just proved to me that you can't be trusted, and as far as I'm concerned that includes being trusted with my money.'

'It's our money,' Lucy reminds him. 'I'm your wife.'

'Really? Well why not try acting like it?' He starts up the stairs towards his study. 'Now, if you don't mind, I've got a clinical research paper for peer review.'

'What am I supposed to live off?' Lucy shouts up the stairs after him. *Thank God, I've got that solicitor's appointment*, she thinks. It can't come soon enough.

Marcus thunders halfway down the stairs, his wallet in his hand. He opens it and peels off a handful of notes. 'Here you go, darling. From now on you get housekeeping. Or – more fitting for a spoilt child like you – pocket money.'

He tosses the money over the banister and the notes flutter to the ground, landing like confetti around Lucy's feet.

THIRTEEN

Frances Harper is a handsome woman in her early fifties, her ash blonde bob streaked faintly with grey. She wears a white silk shirt with a no-nonsense black trouser suit and a few discreet but expensive pieces of jewellery.

She allows Lucy to talk at length and without interruption, scribbling fluent notes on a yellow legal pad. Eventually she leans back in her chair, pen still in hand.

'Well, Mrs Wheedon, the good news is that you have ample grounds to file for immediate legal separation. Moreover, the new criminal offence of coercive and controlling behaviour has had a knock-on effect on the family courts, and there are new rules in place when it comes to divorce, which undoubtedly apply in your case. Although it's unlikely to affect the financial settlement you're awarded, especially as you don't have children.'

'I don't care about the money.' Lucy is aware that her voice is trembling. 'That's not what this is about. It's about freedom. Getting my life back.'

Harper smiles sympathetically. 'Yes, I can see that. However, that brings me onto the bad news. In order to achieve the physical separation from your husband you so desperately want, and which he seems hell-bent on preventing, you would need to make a police complaint. Given, from what you've just told me, that he's determined to follow you wherever you go. And that he's using financial means to control you. If he ended up on police bail, it would mean that he would be prevented by law from contacting you or even coming near you. But the criminal complaint would take precedence over divorce proceedings, which would almost certainly be delayed until after a court case. And any financial resolution would be delayed too. You would have to be prepared to weather that storm, which wouldn't be easy.'

Lucy nods. 'I see.'

'The other thing it's only fair to warn you about is this. The burden of proof for coercive control is high in a criminal case. And from what you've said about your husband – an eminent and widely respected man – he would no doubt tell a completely different story about your marriage when put on the witness stand. There is clearly an issue of credibility here.' She holds up a hand as Lucy starts to object. 'Which, I must stress, does *not* mean I don't believe you. Far from it: what you've said is very compelling, and sadly all too familiar... You say some of your friends have witnessed the controlling behaviour in action?'

Lucy nods.

'That's a point in your favour. In the short term, you could apply to the court for an exclusion order. That would effectively bar your husband from the marital home. The courts are normally reluctant to grant them unless there's violent or threatening behaviour, which is arguably the case here. Is that something you would consider as a starting point? I imagine he'd be keen to avoid the publicity, so might then go voluntarily. That often happens.'

'Not Marcus.' Lucy gives a short, deprecating laugh. 'If he gives any ground, it will be over his dead body. That's what he tells me, anyway.'

Harper frowns. 'Goodness, let's hope it doesn't come to that!' She straightens her jacket and checks her watch, signalling that Lucy's allotted time is over. 'A lot for you to think about, I know, and I do recommend you give it plenty of thought.'

'And if I want you to go ahead?'

'You would have to pay my retaining fee up front. Fifteen thousand pounds.'

'Fifteen?' Lucy croaks.

'The entire bill is likely to be at least fifty thousand.' She gives a small smile. 'Sixty to seventy would be a more realistic estimate. Though I would, of course, be applying for your costs to be covered by your husband. Anyway, Mrs Wheedon,' she stands up and extends a hand, 'as I said, you need to think about this. Do please get in touch again once you have.'

Back in Barnes, Lucy pulls out her savings passbook from the zipped pocket in her bag.

After withdrawing the cash to refund Jane for her legal consultation, there is £5,800 in the account. She still owns some shares, valued at around three thousand pounds – a purchase that pre-dates her marriage – and has a few good pieces of jewellery. They would be unlikely to raise their true value on the second-hand market, and the entire pot of cash if she sold everything would still fall short of fifteen thousand pounds., let alone the full legal bill if things went that far. And if she hands every penny to Frances Harper, what will she have to live on, now that Marcus intends to keep her on cash handouts and freeze her out of their bank accounts? She could try and get a job, but that would mean missing the final, critical two months of her master's course.

Her father has plenty of savings and might be persuaded to lend her some cash. But he would insist on knowing what the money was for, and once she had told him, could she trust him not to tell Marcus about what she was doing? She doesn't think so. Jeffrey has already proved himself all too vulnerable to her husband's manipulation. And after his stroke, she doesn't want to risk his health by adding anxiety about her welfare.

Using her new burner phone, she logs on to an auction site and starts trying to work out realistic prices for her favourite dress rings and gold bracelets, one of which turns out to be worth at least two thousand pounds. The doorbell rings, forcing her to abandon her task midway through drafting a listing.

Adele stands on the doorstep.

'Adele! What a surprise!' This is all she can manage; her brain desperately struggling to catch up. *How the hell did she find me?*

'Yeah, I bet it is.' Adele gives a broad grin and lopes into the hallway, looking around in wonder. Lucy half expects her to start stroking the wallpaper. 'In case you're wondering, Mum's mate Janet got Gwen – your dad's cleaner – to look in his address book when she was working round his place. She said there was no phone number written down for you, otherwise I'd have phoned you obviously.'

'Obviously,' says Lucy weakly. 'Come on through. Coffee?' If they're quick, Adele can be on her way before there's any risk of Marcus returning.

'Yeah, go on then,' says Adele, staring open-mouthed at the bespoke Tom Howley kitchen units with their carbon grey doors and cream marble counters. 'Wow. This place. How much did this lot set you back?'

'A fair bit,' Lucy admits, switching on the espresso machine.

'So how much does your old man earn, then?'

Lucy just gives a faint smile. She doesn't know the exact figure anyway.

'Quarter of a mill a year?' Adele asks.

'More, I think.' She reaches into one of the cupboards for cups and saucers.

'And you want to give all this up? You must be smoking drugs.'

Lucy sighs. 'There's more involved in a marriage than just the trappings,' she waves a hand round the room, 'the stuff.'

'Nice problem to have,' sniffs Adele. 'Anyway, that's actually why I'm here. Sorry about the other night. It was a bit weird seeing you like that, and it made me a bit, you know… touchy.'

Lucy presses the button on the coffee machine and a hot, fragrant stream hisses into the cup. 'It's okay. I know my turning up like that after all these years… it was a lot to deal with.'

'I lost my shit and I shouldn't have done. Like I said: sorry.' This craven, eager-to-please Adele is unfamiliar to Lucy and is making her feel oddly disorientated, even in her own home.

She sets the cups of coffee on the table and gestures for her to sit down.

Adele takes a sip of the espresso and pulls a face. 'Christ, Luce, that's a bit fucking strong! Give us some more milk, will you, and some sugar.'

Lucy obliges.

'Anyway, that's not the reason I'm here. The other night… we didn't mention the obvious. You know what I mean.'

Lucy feels fear creeping up the back of her neck.

'Joanne Beckett,' supplies Adele.

Lucy pinches her fingers together as though she's trying to warm them up. 'No, we didn't. I guess neither of us could face it.'

'Exactly.' Adele scrunches up her face. 'But the fact is, I know that since I last saw you, you haven't told anyone about my… about what happened when she fell in the water. About my part in that.'

'I promised,' Lucy says simply.

'I know. And you kept the promise, which means a lot. After I'd asked you to leave the other night, I got to thinking about that. About how much I owe you.'

'We were very young,' Lucy reaches out her hand and touches Adele's. 'You weren't to know what could have happened.'

'Yeah, I know. But I was still over the age of criminal respon-sibility. I could have ended up in Young Offenders. For years. So, anyhow, I was thinking about that. And then I thought about what you asked me. About wanting to start a new life.' She stirs two heaped spoons of sugar into her coffee. 'So I decided I should help you. Plus, I get it, I really do. Why you might want to leave. The girls' father… well, he could be a real pig, and there were times I wanted to just grab them and take off. Never come back, you know?'

Lucy nods.

'So I asked around a couple of people I met when I was inside, and I've been given a name. A guy local to me who's done time for insurance fraud and knows about this kind of stuff. He'll be able to help. For a small fee.'

'How small?' Lucy thinks back to the prohibitive cost of hiring a lawyer like Frances Harper.

Adele shrugs, pulling out a cigarette and lighting it, without asking for her host's consent. Lucy fetches an ashtray, but makes no comment. 'I mean; you'd have to sort that with him obviously, but maybe a couple of grand? Something like that?'

'And what would I get for that?'

'Again, you'd have to speak to him, but it would be along the lines of a new passport and ID, somewhere to stay, that kind of thing.'

Lucy is suddenly reminded of the Netflix documentary series about the FBI. There was an episode focusing on their witness protection programmes, and the former agent that they interviewed on camera explained how it takes immense strength and discipline to walk away from your life and never go back. That even the most innocent backtracking can place lives in danger. 'Can he be trusted, this contact?' She puts her cup down and makes eye contact with Adele. Those deep-set, slightly slanting eyes can still unnerve her. 'I'd have to be certain that he wasn't going to tell anyone where I was. I mean, not just Marcus – my husband. That bit's obvious. He'd have to make sure he didn't give away my new information to anyone.'

'Not even me?' Adele twirls her cigarette between her fingertips thoughtfully. 'Best friends forever, and all that.'

Lucy hesitates, remembering how happy that friendship once made her. Then she shakes her head. 'Not even you. Nobody. That's the only way these things work.'

Adele wrinkles her nose. 'Fair enough. Let me take your number, and I'll ask him to contact you.' She pulls out her phone and swipes away the screensaver of her daughters, 'Shoot.'

'0734…' Lucy starts to recite her contract phone number then checks herself. Of course, she'll have to supply the number of the new handset bought in Redgate. 'Hold on a second.' She goes upstairs and fetches it, still unable to remember the digits off by heart. 'You'd better take this one.'

'Ooh,' Adele grins. 'A secret phone. Good thinking, Batman.'

'It's pretty much essential given my situation, I'm afraid.' Lucy reads out the number.

'Okay, noted. Wait for my contact to get in touch, yeah? His name's Denny Renard.'

Denny Renard. Lucy types the two words into her Contacts list, as yet blissfully unaware what this name will come to mean to her.

FOURTEEN

The day after Adele's visit, Lucy switches on her 'secret' mobile and finds a text.

hi this is denny r here adele gave me yr number, need to arrange a meet

Her heart sinks. Denny's communication style is a lot less literate than she was expecting. This man is supposed to have committed insurance fraud, which must involve a degree of intelligence, but this missive suggests an amateur. How can she entrust her future to someone like this? She thinks about telling him she's changed her mind, but decides that since Adele went out of her way to find him, she should at least hear what he has to say. Then, to keep her options open, she'll look into finding a cheaper solicitor. There must be someone out there who won't require such a huge payment up front. She vaguely recalls Helen saying that her brother was a lawyer: she could ask him.

She texts back.

When and where did you have in mind?

Her phone pings with a reply almost immediately.

how bout the dog?

Lucy types back.

*Not Dog & Fox. Don't want to meet in Redgate, I know too
many people there. Needs to be a distance away.*

ok how about red rooster diner tonight 6pm

He names a fast-food place on the dual carriageway that links
Redgate with the A3, next to a truck stop and a petrol station.
Lucy calculates that she can drive there and back for 6 p.m. and
still be home again before Marcus gets back from the hospital.

She buys herself some time with advance preparation of a
casserole for their supper, then scribbles a note on the pad in the
kitchen, telling Marcus that she and Helen are planning to go out
for a drink after their last lecture of the day.

Dressing for an assignation with a hired criminal is not
something she's ever had to consider before. The last thing she
wants is to look conspicuous. She'd like to blend in, which isn't
straightforward at 5'10" with long, luminously blonde hair. In the
end she dresses in yoga leggings and a hooded sweat top, tying
up her hair and stuffing it under a baseball cap, which she keeps
pulled down low over her face as she walks into the Red Rooster.

Denny's texts were not what she had expected, and nor is he
in person. He's taller than average and heavily muscled in the
artificial way of someone who is naturally slight but spends all
their time bodybuilding with weights. His thighs are so thick
that they knock up against each other awkwardly when he walks
and bulge through his skinny jeans. Under his T-shirt (featuring
the slogan 'Muscle Monkey'), his overdeveloped pectorals bunch
forward, folding over on themselves, and his tanned biceps are
like two huge hams. He has two full sleeves of tattoos, and one
that extends up from his chest and over most of his neck: a red
and blue swirl of Japanese-style fishes and flowers. His trendy fade

haircut is deceptive: when she looks more closely at the lines on his face, she realises that he must be around forty.

'All right?' he says, thumping his body down in the chair opposite Lucy. 'Adele told me you were a looker.' His smile reveals long incisors which give him a vulpine appearance.

Lucy hands him a menu and spends a long time deciding what she wants to eat, because she has no idea how to start the conversation, or negotiation, or whatever this is going to be. She orders a toasted cheese sandwich and a coffee, and Denny asks for a double hamburger ('Well done') and a beer.

'So,' he says easily, extending his thick thighs so that they're taking up all the space under the table and she has to tuck hers under her chair. 'You've got yourself every little girl's dream and married a rich, successful geezer, but you want to jack it in. Why's that: not getting enough action in the bedroom?'

Lucy stares at him: shocked at both his casual sexism and the personal nature of the enquiry.

'Aw, come on,' he says, tapping his menu rhythmically on the edge of the Formica table, then straightening the cuffs of his shirt sleeves. He seems unable to keep still, full of pent-up, animal energy. Lucy wonders if he uses steroids. He looks the type. 'It's just banter.'

'Let's not go into my reasons: it's really not necessary,' she tells him, avoiding contact with his unsettling pale green eyes. 'I just need to know what you can do to help, and how much it will cost.'

'Righto then, Blondie, have it your way.' The waitress brings their food, and he starts ripping the beef patties into shreds with his knife and fork. 'I can get you a passport and a driving licence in a new name. The idea is that you can then use those to get whatever other ID or accounts you might need. And I can fix somewhere for you to stay for a bit when you first leave home; somewhere secure, where you won't be found.'

Lucy sips her coffee, thinking about this. 'And the price?'

'Five bags.'

She frowns at him.

'Bags of sand. Thousand. Five thousand.'

Lucy's shaking her head. 'No. I can't pay that much. For that much I could employ a solicitor to take my husband to court and get a restraining order.'

Denny shrugs, unperturbed, and thrusts a huge piece of meat into his mouth. 'Would that stop him though? Your old man? From what I heard via your mate, he's not going to give up that easily.'

He has a point, Lucy thinks. Any legal action she took would be interpreted by Marcus as designed to humiliate. It would rile him up rather than put him off. And there was a risk he would charm his way out of it, blind any judge with his stellar reputation and royal connections.

'Three thousand,' she says, taking a bite of her sandwich. 'That's all I can afford.'

'No can do, sweetheart,' Denny says sadly, tipping back his head and letting the beer run down his throat. 'It costs more than that. The accommodation ain't going to be cheap for starters. If you don't want a fleapit.'

'Four thousand would really be all that I can manage.'

He pretends to think about this. 'Go on then. Only 'cause I'm a sucker for a pretty face, mind.'

Suppressing a shudder, Lucy ignores this. 'How long would it take?'

'Passport's going to be about five days, minimum. I'd need the cash first, obviously. And you'll need to send me a passport-size photo of you that's high enough res to reproduce my end.'

'Okay. I'll still need to think about it.' Pushing her plate away, Lucy reaches into her bag to pull out her wallet, but her hand touches something smooth and hard. *Christ*, she thinks, *I forgot*. Her phone is in her bag: the one that Marcus tracks via his app. She meant to leave it on the kitchen table, as though she had forgotten it.

'Don't think for ever, darling.' Denny pushes out his lower lip and taps his empty beer bottle against the edge of the table. 'My services are available for a limited time only.'

'I'll bear that in mind.' Lucy returns the baseball cap to her head and hurries out into the car park.

'Shit!' she swears under her breath as she drives back into London. 'Shit, shit, shit!' *Please let this be one of those times when Marcus is tied up with patients all day. That I get home first, so he never discovers I've left town.* But when she gets back to Barnes, his car is parked on the driveway and the lights are on downstairs.

She walks into the kitchen, but there's no one there. The house is deadly quiet.

'Marcus?'

He's sitting in the drawing room in semi-darkness, the room illuminated only by the light from the hallway. She catches the glitter of his eyes, the jut of his cheekbones, which has become more pronounced in recent days as he's lost weight.

'Have a nice day, darling?' His voice is cold, quiet.

He knows.

He holds up the note that she left for him. 'Good lecture was it?'

She shrugs. *Maybe he hasn't actually checked on her phone. Bluff it out.* 'Okay, I guess.'

'I checked your lecture schedule online. You didn't have any today. So where have you been? Only, the location of your phone would suggest it's somewhere on the A427.' His voice is getting louder.

'I went—'

'And *don't…*' this word is almost a shout, '… don't say you went to see your father, because I've already phoned him and he hasn't seen you.' He stands up, his full height menacing, then strides to the drinks cabinet and takes out a bottle of vodka, pouring himself a glass and swallowing it down neat. 'So, where were you?'

The pounding of Lucy's heart makes her chest tighten and her ears ring.

'What's the point in me telling you, when you already know?'

'Ah, but I don't know who you were with…' Marcus swallows the remains of the vodka and pours himself another glass. His voice thickens, becomes indistinct. 'Lover boy, was it?'

Lucy turns and heads back towards the staircase, but Marcus blocks her path.

'Oh no you don't, Lucinda. Not until you've answered the question.'

She pushes past him and runs up the stairs. There's a crashing sound as something explodes within earshot and, turning round, she sees that Marcus has thrown the vodka bottle after her, narrowly missing the backs of her legs. It shatters against the wood trim of the stair treads, a glittering firework of clear glass and colourless liquid, followed by Marcus's heavy footsteps. With a little whimper, she sprints up to the landing.

'Don't be ridiculous, I'm not trying to hurt you, you stupid girl!' he shouts. 'I just want to know what's going on. After all I do for you, is that too much to ask?'

Lucy runs into the spare bedroom and drags the heavy chest of drawers against the door. Marcus hammers against it with his fists, then thumps it so hard with his shoulder that the hinges threaten to splinter away from the door frame. Eventually, realising that he can't get in, he changes tack.

'Actions have consequences! Have you thought about that? Eh? If I can't trust you with the car, can't trust who you're going to meet in it, then you can't have it.'

'What do you mean?' Lucy asks, her voice shaking. Although she already knows.

'I pay for the bloody thing. It's my name on the lease agreement. So tomorrow I'll tell them we don't need it any more. Get them to take it away. Let's see how you get on making assignations with lover boy using public transport.'

'Marcus,' Lucy keeps her tone reasonable. 'We can't go on like this. Surely you can see that? This is not how marriage is supposed to work.'

'Oh, so you think instead you'll just piss off with someone else and take half my hard-earned money with you, do you? Let me tell you, Lucinda,' he spits the last word, 'that is not going to happen. I'll kill you before I let that happen.'

Sinking down onto the spare bed, Lucy drops her head into her hands. She can still hear her heart, its wild pounding filling her skull. The fact is, part of her believes Marcus is serious. She has no idea how long she sits there, but eventually becomes aware of Marcus's footsteps stumbling away, and the master bedroom door slamming. She waits, and waits, shivering even though the heating is on. When she hears the muffled sound of the clock in the dining room striking two, she drags the chest of drawers back into position and opens the spare room door. Silence.

She heads towards the master bedroom. Marcus is asleep on his side of the bed, breathing heavily. Lucy creeps towards him and stands there looking down at his face. There are hollows under his eyes, and even though he's asleep, the impression he gives is not one of peaceful rest but something more comatose. As her eyes grow accustomed to the gloom, she notices a prescription bottle on his nightstand; not one she's ever seen before. She leans over her husband's upper body and picks it up. It's too dark to read the label, so she carries it onto the landing where the light is still on.

Temazepam 20 mg. Take one tablet daily, as required. MAY CAUSE DROWSINESS. Do not drink alcohol or operate heavy machinery.

The dispenser is St Mary's Hospital pharmacy, and there's no patient name on the label. He must have prescribed the drugs for himself. She removes the lid of the bottle and, without knowing exactly why, removes a few of the tablets, hiding them in one of the drawers of the spare-room dresser. Then she tiptoes back into the bedroom and replaces the bottle on Marcus's nightstand. The digital display on his alarm clock reads 2.17.

Confident that he's not going to wake, she goes downstairs to the kitchen and presses the 'on' switch on the kettle. While she waits for it to boil, she pulls her second phone from its hiding place at the back of the drawer, where she keeps spare napkins and tea towels, and turns it on. It vibrates immediately with a text. Denny.

don't keep me hanging ok gorgeous

She exhales hard, a breath it feels as though she has been holding for hours.

Please go ahead and get the stuff I need. I'll organise the money.

FIFTEEN

Disorientation overwhelms Lucy when she wakes the next morning. Why is she lying on the spare bed, partially clothed? And then, with a hollow, sinking sensation, she remembers.

'Marcus?'

She steps out onto the landing, but the house is eerily still. In the master bedroom, the plastic pill bottle is gone from the bedside table and the empty bed is unmade. Pulling back the bedclothes, she undresses, showers and changes into clean clothes. As she's coming downstairs to make coffee, rubbing a towel through her damp hair, the doorbell rings. A large, balding man is standing there with a clipboard clutched against his chest like a shield.

'Mrs Wheedon?'

'Yes?' She blinks at him, the wet towel hanging limply in her hand.

'I'm here to take the car.' He frowns down at the clipboard and haltingly reads out the registration plate. 'I understand it isn't needed any more.'

'Your understanding is quite wrong,' Lucy says hotly. 'It's very much needed. My husband's just doing this out of spite.'

The man reddens slightly. 'Nevertheless, I am legally authorised to take it. You can give me the key, or I can come back with a tow truck. Up to you.'

Sighing, Lucy goes into the kitchen and pulls the electronic fob from the ring with the house keys, placing it on the man's outstretched hand. There's no point arguing, and no real point in keeping the car, which, like a giant tracking device, would allow her to be found. It just would have been useful to have it for a few days longer.

Once the man has left, she takes out her laptop and boots it up, realising that she will have to leave this behind too. After all, a PC can be hacked, and its flow of information monitored. It's too much of a risk. She copies her half-finished thesis project and course notes onto a USB stick, still intending to finish her degree even though she has let her studies slip in recent weeks. After this, she has some financial housekeeping to do. She creates a Google Pay account on her new phone and sets it up to receive funds from eBay, before listing three pieces of jewellery on the auction site. Then she phones her broker and sells her shares, transferring those funds to Google Pay too. That will be her backup money; her subsistence. The balance that remains in her old savings account will have to be withdrawn in cash to pay Denny.

It's strange but exhilarating to have to think about budgeting and being careful with her expenditure. For the past eight years, she has been cushioned from financial worry, all her bills covered, a shiny credit card always on hand, linked to an endless supply of credit. She has been able to buy exactly what she wants, whenever she has felt like it. To live in this large, stylish house without a thought to how much it costs to furnish and to run. And yet that no longer gives her pleasure. Quite the opposite; it's a desolate feeling. The house is a cage – one worthy of a spread in *House & Garden*, but a cage all the same. And yet she can't help but be aware that to cut herself off from Marcus will be to cut herself off from the financial safety net forever. If she arranges to disappear, there will be no coming back at a later date to take half the house and a share of his earnings. This is it.

The turnaround time for her new documents is unavoidable, but she's not going to wait it out here, in the house. Not after last night. She needs to stay a step ahead and somehow throw Marcus off the scent. And once she has left, she can never come back to fetch anything. Anything she leaves behind is lost forever. What was it that the former FBI agent said in that documentary about witness protection? '*Even your memories become a liability.*' These words echo in her head as she packs her suitcase. She takes photos of her mother, the remainder of her jewellery and as many of her favourite clothes and shoes as she can fit in the case, making sure to leave behind a few key pieces, like her treasured Burberry raincoat, so as not to fuel Marcus's suspicions. Then she texts Marcus.

Going to Vicky's place in Bath for a few days. You and I both need time to think.

'Good God, Luce, this is a surprise! A very lovely one though.'

Vicky Leland is her best friend from her undergraduate days at UEA, now living in a pretty golden-stone cottage in Bath and working as a probation officer. Lucy texted her once she was on the train from Paddington, simply saying that she would be in Bath and in need of a bed for the night. She mooched around the city's coffee shops and boutiques, dragging her suitcase, until five thirty when Vicky would be returning from work.

'Come in, come in!' Vicky hugs her, then straightens up and eyes her suitcase. She's a slight, wiry girl with spiky red hair and an excess of nervous energy. Fun for short bursts of time, a little exhausting after that. 'That's a bloody big case… anything I should know?'

Lucy gives her an edited version of the state of her marriage, leaving out both Marcus's worst transgressions and the fact that she never intends to go back.

'I dare say a couple of days apart from one another will do you good. Give you some perspective. As will wine, of course.'

Vicky ushers Lucy into her small, brightly coloured sitting room. 'Glass of rosé?'

They drink several glasses, then go through to the kitchen and continue to talk as the perennially single Vicky throws together a chilli con carne and regales Lucy with tales of dating disasters. They drink more wine in front of the log-burning stove and eventually climb, a little tipsily, up to the small but cheerful bedrooms.

'I've got to head out at eight for work, for my sins, but take your time in the morning,' Vicky says, fetching towels and a glass of water and giving her friend a warm hug. 'Let yourself out when you're ready. Paracetamol in the bathroom cabinet, coffee in the cupboard to the right of the fridge.'

Lucy hugs her back, harder than she would normally, painfully aware that it might be a very long time before she sees her friend again, if ever.

In the morning, she fully charges her regular phone, then leaves it under Lucy's guest bed, pushed back out of sight. Of course, she had the option to leave the phone somewhere much nearer to home, or to destroy it altogether, but she and Vicky were very close as students, and she wanted the chance to say a proper goodbye. And now – at least for the next twenty-four hours or so while the battery has charge – if Marcus tries to locate his wife, he will think she's still here in Bath.

She catches the train back to London, checks into a cheap hotel in Earls Court and begins the wait for her new life to start.

SIXTEEN

For three days Lucy drifts around West London like a ghost.

She thinks about catching the tube to Russell Square and going to the Social Sciences building to mingle with her fellow students. But now that the taught component of her coursework is over, few of them will be around and the risk of Marcus looking for her there, while not high, does not seem worth the risk. Instead, she sells a gold charm bracelet and a string of pearls online and uses the proceeds to buy the cheapest laptop she can find, filling the empty, angst-ridden hours with working on her thesis. It occurs to her that once she's no longer Lucy Wheedon, she won't be able to use the qualification and this thought nags at her. But complete the thing she must: it's in her nature. At school she was never late with homework, always finished every assignment.

'*Teacher's pet.*' Adele's childhood jibe comes back to her. With her link to Denny, Adele is the only friend who will potentially be able to track her down: to find who she is, and where she is. Part of her really hopes that Adele will defy her embargo and do it. The thought of having one remaining link to her past comforts her.

After three days, a text arrives from Denny, as she is sitting on her single hotel bed with her laptop on her knees.

got yr stuff now, where shall we meet

Her heart thumping, she types back.

I don't have a car any longer, so will have to be London. Can you make it this evening?

She can't bear the thought of further delay.

busy tonight will have to be tomorrow where?

Lucy ponders this for a few minutes. She considers asking him to come to the hotel – after all there is privacy in her room – but something holds her back. The thought of being near a bed with Denny makes her uncomfortable. A public space would be better. If they meet in a crowded café or bar, there's a chance that they'll be overheard, or seen handing over forged documents. They need to be somewhere where they can be inconspicuous, not under scrutiny.

Meet me at Tate Britain. At the foot of circular staircase. Midday.

'What is this bleeding place?' Denny bunches his huge shoulders and gestures upwards with his chin, in the direction of the beautiful rococo ceiling above the rotunda.

'It's an art gallery,' Lucy says, displaying patience she certainly doesn't feel. 'Free to the public.'

'Personally, I don't see the fucking point,' Denny grumbles. 'They'd do better putting that money into housing or a sports stadium.' He's wearing a zipped tracksuit top, baggy branded sweatpants with logos down the side and trainers so blindingly blue-white that sunglasses are required to look straight at them.

The gallery is quiet on this weekday morning, despite it being the school holidays. A few teenagers amble aimlessly around, taking photos with their phones, while older visitors take their time in front on the artwork, standing back to admire what they see and reading from their guidebooks. Lucy leads Denny into a deserted room full of Old Masters and sits on the leather bench at its centre, gesturing for Denny to sit down too. He does so reluctantly, then starts tweaking the laces on his incongruous footwear. They've clearly never been worn before: the soles pristine, unscuffed.

A middle-aged couple in anoraks and sensible shoes wander into the room and embark on an earnest discussion of one of the paintings, the man pointing and gesturing with his hands while the woman nods enthusiastically.

'Just look at those fucking twats,' Denny says, baring his feral front teeth. 'Tossers.'

Lucy feels a frisson of distaste. But she doesn't have to like this man, she tells herself, she just has to trust him to do what he's promised to do. He's just here to provide a service, and in doing so to free her from an untenable situation.

I'll kill you myself first…

'Show me what you've got,' she says in a low voice as the art-loving couple move on.

'Cash first.'

Lucy reaches into her coat pocket for the manila envelope of cash that's been hidden under her hotel mattress for the past three days. The scene would be like something from a spy thriller, if it weren't for Denny's ludicrous shoes.

He glances around them, then thumbs through the notes quickly, counting them.

'It's all there,' Lucy says, because that's what they always seem to say in films.

Denny reaches inside his pocket, pulls out a white A5 envelope and hands it to her. Inside is a UK passport with the headshot she sent to Denny on the photo page.

And her new name. Joanne Louise Chandler.

'Joanne?' She queries.

'Yeah,' he says defensively. 'What's wrong with it?'

She can't explain her discomfort to Denny; of course she can't. 'I just wondered why they chose that.'

'Listen, it's done with some sort of random generator, using popular names from the year you were born. A sixteen-year-old bird called Gladys is going to attract attention, right?' He warms to his theme. 'And a ninety-year-old granny called Kylie would be even worse.'

Lucy looks at the passport again, trying to absorb this shifting picture of her own identity. She consoles herself that at least she's not likely to forget this name. Recalling that witnesses in the FBI protection programme had to practise saying and writing their name in order to retrain their brain not to react if someone called their real name. She tries saying it aloud. 'Joanne Louise Chandler.'

There's a driving licence in the envelope too, registered in Penrith, Cumbria. 25 Asher Road.

'Is this a real address?' she asks, pointing to it.

'Nah. Made up,' Denny says, with pride.

'And Penrith?'

'The idea of it being that far away is that down South fewer people will know if it's real or not.'

She nods, unable to fault this logic. The only other things in the envelope are a print-out of a reservation for a home-sharing site – eight days in a one-bedroom flat with a sea view in Brighton – and a forged council tax bill for that address, in the name of J. L. Chandler.

'Brighton?' she queries. 'But I don't know the place.' She doesn't like it much either, from the few times she's visited, but doesn't say so.

'That's exactly the bleedin' point. It's got to be somewhere you wouldn't normally go. Too easy to guess otherwise.'

'And after the eight days are up? It's not long.'

'You'll have to sort out somewhere else. That's all the money would run to.' Denny fiddles with his shoelaces. 'I've got to make a profit, you know.'

'Does Adele know where I'll be? Will you tell her?'

Denny shakes his head firmly. 'You don't get it, Blondie. Nobody's got to know. Not your parents, your best mates, nobody. That's the only way it works.'

He's right, Lucy has known this all along, but now feels herself wavering. She couldn't confide in her father anyway, that much is clear. He would almost certainly tell Marcus. But someone like Jane Standish? Someone who could be trusted. Perhaps, eventually, that will be possible.

'One other thing… what about academic qualifications?'

Denny stares at her.

'Has Joanne Chandler got any A levels, or a degree? Only, I'll have to apply for jobs, and I might have to produce evidence of my qualifications.'

'Fuck's sake,' Denny sneers. 'Are you serious? Your old man's such a dangerous lunatic that you have to run away, and you're worrying about your fucking exams?'

Lucy feels the heat of anger rising in her but manages to quell it. 'I'll need to make a living, that's all I'm saying.'

'Make up whatever exams you need, then. That's the whole point, Joanne Chandler isn't a real person.' Denny stands up and bends to brush an imaginary mark from his trainer. 'And if you need any more forged documents down the line, you know where to come, don't you?' He winks at her and lopes off. 'See ya, darling.'

I hope I don't, Lucy thinks as she watches him go.

SEVENTEEN

The flat in Brighton calls itself a one-bedroom but is really no more than a studio, with a bed-sized alcove off the living room. The furniture is cheap and functional, the curtains grimy and ill-fitting and the windows so smeared with salt water that they let in little light. The sea view turns out to be a glimpse of a drab grey stretch of horizon.

Reminding herself that this is only for a week, Lucy vows to spend as much time as she can in the fresh air. But wandering streets full of uncleared rubbish, dodging beggars and drunks, does nothing to raise her spirits. Every spare patch of wall is covered in graffiti, every shop doorway a bedroom for the homeless. Walking on the beach is no better. Sinking into pebbles is far from enjoyable, and made worse by the need to dodge dirty nappies, discarded tampons and broken glass. She sticks to strolling around Old Steine Gardens and Queen's Park when the weather is sunny, and when it's not, sits hunched over her laptop working on finishing her master's thesis, often with tears rolling down her cheeks.

The sense of isolation is overwhelming; far worse than she'd anticipated. *I can't do this*, she says frequently, to the empty room. *It's not going to work.* Even something as simple as ordering a takeout coffee seems fraught. She gives her name on the order as 'Lucy', then, blushing and flustered, switches it to 'Jo', earning a quizzical look from the barista.

Even submitting the final draft of her thesis to her tutor is bittersweet. She's proud of her achievement and pleased with the end result, but it's Lucy Wheedon who will be an MSc in Social Anthropology. Not Joanne Chandler.

I can't do this...

But then she considers the alternative, and resolves instead to think of ways to make her life as Joanne a little more bearable. Having decided that staying in Brighton is not an option for her, Lucy needs to look for accommodation elsewhere. No longer having a car is a huge obstacle and makes it difficult to spread her search wide. She'd like to find somewhere in London, but without employment, it's simply too expensive. And even if she picks a distant suburb there will always be a risk of seeing Marcus, or someone he knows. As soon as she has an address, she can start applying for jobs, so accommodation is the first priority.

She narrows the search to either Lewes or Eastbourne but quickly realises the flaw in her plan. To apply for rental properties, she'll need references and a credit history. So the next practicality she tackles is to open a bank account as Joanne Chandler, which proves easy enough using her passport and the utility bill. Lucy tells the clerk that she has just moved to the area from London, which prompts a request for her previous address. She writes down the first flat she lived in when she moved to London as a new graduate, crossing her fingers that they won't actually check, and asks to collect her new card in person from the branch rather than have it mailed to a flat she'll only be using for another three days.

'It's a big block of flats, and all the mail gets dumped in the communal hall,' she tells the bank clerk, impressed with her own ability to think on her feet. 'So really it's a security issue.'

Lucy also falls into the habit of leaving the television on in the flat, simply to fill the unbearable emptiness with voices. She's keeping the new phone switched off unless she needs it; out of habit rather than as a precaution. When she switches it on during her penultimate evening in the depressing studio, there's a text from Jane.

Haven't heard from you in ages… dropped round at the house to check but no one in. Is everything okay? J xx

The temptation to reply is strong. But it would undermine everything she has had to sacrifice to get to this point. Instead she deletes the text and reluctantly blocks Jane's number. This only serves to emphasise her sense of isolation, and she convinces herself that if she could only make contact with Adele, that would provide some sort of human lifeline. They wouldn't need to meet up, but they could at least talk. She sends Denny a message asking for Adele's number. An hour later there's no reply, so she switches the phone off and starts getting ready for bed. As she's brushing her teeth, the intercom handset near the front door makes a squawking noise. Having never used it before, she assumes this is some sort of an electrical malfunction and ignores it. It chirrups again.

Lucy has removed her contact lenses so has to squint at the flickering image on the video screen. The system is cheap and of poor quality, like everything else in the flat, leaving the image of the visitor cropped from the neck down. She can only make out that there's a familiar figure standing there; a tall man.

The sound is distorted too, but down the handset she can just about make out: 'Hello, darling.'

Denny? Why is he here now? Her hand hesitates over the door release button.

'Let me up.'

She presses 'Enter', and it's only as she hears feet thundering up the stairs that it strikes her that this man is not wearing trainers, but shoes. Proper shoes with rigid soles. And the long coat that struck her as familiar is identical to the cashmere overcoat she bought her husband for their fifth-wedding anniversary.

Marcus.

She doesn't have time to work out how he could possibly have found her, because he is already banging his fist on the door of the flat. Even though she's at risk of disturbing the whole building, she stands frozen at the centre of the room, her heart hammering in her chest.

'Open up!' he barks.

Lucy doesn't move. And then there's a splintering sound as his shoulder is hurled against the door, breaking loose the flimsy lock. Slamming the door back against the wall, he strolls into the room with a fixed smile on his face.

'Not up to much, is it, this place?' He looks around at the drab furnishings and Lucy's suitcase, open on the floor and still half unpacked. 'Was it really worth giving up a lovely detached house near the river in Barnes for this dump?' It's a rhetorical question, because before she can open her mouth he extends a hand to her. 'Come on, Lucinda, you need to come with me.'

Lucy pulls her dressing gown around her tightly, shaking her head. 'No. I'm not coming with you. And if you try to make me, I'm going to call the police. I'm not coming back, Marcus.'

He sighs, and his expression softens. 'Darling, it's your father.'

She feels the blood drain from her face and her legs start to shake. 'He's not…?'

'He's had a second stroke. A much bigger one this time. He's in a bad way, Lucinda, so if you ever want to see him again, we'd better go.'

How could I have walked away from my own father, knowing this could happen at any moment? A wave of shock and guilt washes over Lucy. With tears welling up, she heads into the bedroom alcove and gets dressed in the clothes she's just removed, putting her laptop into her bag with shaking hands. When she emerges, Marcus is shoving items of clothing into her suitcase. 'And if you're wondering how the hell I found you, can I just point out that you're not as clever as you think. A second phone. Pretty obvious, wasn't it?' He looks around the room, then takes her bag from her, pulling out the offending phone handset. 'You won't be needing this any more anyway.' He tosses it onto the far corner of the countertop in the tiny kitchenette. To reach it, she will have to squeeze past him.

Lucy wants to argue that she does need the phone, but that will delay them, and all she can think of is that they need to get to her father before it's too late. Before he's gone for ever. So she lets the cheap phone go, little knowing how dearly this decision will cost her.

Marcus shoulders her case and prods open the broken door with his foot. 'Come on; no time to waste. We need to go.'

They drive in silence along the darkened motorway, headlights coming and going and Lucy's head crowded with so many fragments of thought that she feels as though she's hallucinating. But uppermost in them is fear of losing her father, interspersed with flashbacks of the final drive to the hospital to see her mother for the very last time. She closes her eyes and tips her head back, making the tears run down her jawline and drip onto her neck. Marcus turns to look at her every few minutes but remains silent.

When they reach the intersection with the M25, instead of taking the westbound slip road and heading for the Redgate turning, Marcus carries straight on into central London.

'I thought we were going to see Dad,' Lucy says, feeling an acid wash of fear rise up her from her stomach.

'We are,' Marcus says calmly. 'He needed specialist care at a hyper-acute stroke unit, so he's been transferred to Charing Cross Hospital.'

They weave through south-west London and are suddenly on the familiar, tree-lined streets of Barnes, a couple of miles from the hospital. Marcus turns the car into their own driveway.

'Why aren't we going straight to Hammersmith?' she demands.

Marcus gets out of the car, takes her suitcase from the boot and then leans in through the open door to speak to her. Now that the car's interior light is on, she notices how gaunt he looks. He has lost more weight, even in the week since she last saw him.

'It's midnight: we're not going to be allowed onto the HASU now. You can head over there first thing.'

'No,' says Lucy stubbornly. Fuelled by a combustible mixture of anger and alarm, she jumps out of the car and stands under the porch light to check that she has some cash in her wallet. 'If he's really that critical, then I'm not going to risk leaving it until tomorrow. I'll get a cab over there and plead with the staff to let me see him.'

Whip-fast, Marcus lunges at her, yanking her bag from her with one hand and grabbing her upper arm with the other. She stumbles, and he takes advantage of her temporary loss of balance to drag her through the front door, slamming it behind them. Before she can even draw breath, he has double-locked the mortice and pocketed the key. Her heart rate quickening, she darts to the French doors in the kitchen, but they're locked and the keys are nowhere in sight. She tries the windows, but they're locked too and the metal security screens are drawn shut.

The same is true in the drawing room, and the dining room. Burglaries are common in the detached houses in their street – set back from the pavement and untouched by street lighting – so when they bought the place they had lockable security grilles fitted on every ground-floor window.

Marcus stands in the hallway, still in his cashmere coat and holding her bag, watching her dart from room to room like a caged animal. Eventually he intercepts her and holds her arms down hard by her sides. His fingers dig into her flesh, making her gasp with pain.

'You're hurting me!'

'Can you blame me, after what you've put me through?' he snarls. He shakes her hard, then releases his hands abruptly, as though dropping a piece of refuse, causing her to stagger backwards as though she's drunk. She regains her balance and goes to grab the landline in the kitchen, but there's nothing connected to the phone jack in the wall.

Returning to the hall, she pounces on her bag and snatches it from him, rummaging desperately for her new mobile before remembering with a sinking feeling that it's still in the flat in Brighton, lying on the counter of the kitchenette where Marcus flung it. He watches her, his arms folded across his chest.

'You may as well stop trying, Lucinda. You're never going to get out.'

She drops her bag as a terrible thought occurs to her. 'Is my father even ill? Is he really at the Charing Cross?'

Marcus gives a bleak smile. 'As far as I know, he's tucked up safely in his bungalow.' He pulls out his own mobile and offers it to her. 'You can phone and check if you like?'

Lucy stares at him aghast, a nagging, nameless fear curdling her insides.

Marcus shrugs off his coat and tosses it over the newel post. 'I've got two valve repairs and an angioplasty on my list tomorrow; I'd better get my head down.' He starts up the stairs. 'And you may as well do the same, darling.'

She stands motionless in the hall, looking down at her forearms. Purple patches of bruising are starting to appear where Marcus's gripped her.

He keeps walking, not looking back at her.

'Suit yourself. Either way, you're staying here this time.'

EIGHTEEN

MARCH 1997

The doorbell rings again. And, once again, Lucy pretends not to be in.

But she does creep to the window of her room and look out. And, sure enough, there is Adele Watts, with her bike.

The two of them are no longer classmates. Lucy was so traumatised by Joanne's death that her parents removed her from Redgate High before the September term even started and she's now a Year 8 pupil at St Theresa's, a private convent school in nearby Brockington. The breaking up of Lucy's friendship with Adele was almost certainly a big part of the Gibsons' motivation for moving her to a new school. But Adele seemed reluctant to accept the status quo. On several occasions over the past few months, she has cycled up to Haverleigh Park and rung the doorbell of the Gibsons' house. Lucy always pretends not to be in. Adele then hangs around for a while before giving up and cycling off.

Lucy watches her former friend now from behind the curtain. She executes a series of slow, mournful wheelies on the driveway, then stops and balances on the seat of her bike. Pulling a carton of cigarettes from her jeans pocket, she lights one, smoking it as she looks up in the direction of Lucy's bedroom window.

Has she seen me? Lucy wonders, her heart thumping with a sort of excitement. Part of her wants to run downstairs and go outside to join Adele. But she doesn't. She stays watching from behind the edge of the curtain. Eventually Adele stubs out the butt with the toe of her trainer, gives one last look up at the window before shaking her head and pedalling away. And as she does so, Lucy knows with utter certainty and a twinge of regret, that this is the last time.

Adele won't come back again.

NINETEEN

Lucy wakes up on the sofa, where she eventually succumbed to sleep in the small hours after her adrenaline levels subsided.

The sealed house is airless, leaving her with a pounding in her temples and her tongue stuck to the roof of her mouth. The first thought as her addled brain clears is that when Marcus opens the door to leave for work – as he must, because he has an operating list – she will be able to attract the attention of passers-by or a neighbour. But a quick glance through the barred drawing-room window tells her that his car is already gone, and sure enough when she checks it, the front door is double-locked. She bangs on it helplessly until her fists are swollen and sore, but nothing happens.

Then she remembers her old laptop. She can raise the alarm by emailing one of her friends. But when she boots it up and tries to open her web browser, she sees an exclamation mark over the Wi-Fi icon on the toolbar. No connection. Hurrying up to Marcus's study, she looks for the Wi-Fi router, usually plugged in behind the desk. He's removed it, along with the phone handsets. She tries joining her neighbours' networks, but unsurprisingly they're all password-protected.

As she goes into the kitchen to make tea, Lucy's thoughts turn from her confinement to the spectacular failure of Denny's scheme. The fact that it has fallen through so rapidly after she paid thousands to get away leaves a bitter taste. Marcus claims to have tracked her second phone, but she had it switched off almost all the time, so how was that possible? The only period she can remember having it on for any length of time was the previous day when she tried to get hold of Adele. But for Marcus to have turned this house into a fortress and then driven to Brighton, all in the space of a few hours? It was possible, but was it likely?

She realises with a dragging heaviness that, however Marcus tracked her down, it makes little difference now. What matters is that she's a prisoner in her own home. Nobody knows, or even thinks there's anything wrong, with the possible exception of Jane Standish. Will Jane come looking for her if she gets no reply to her text and can no longer make contact? At this moment in time, it seems like her best hope. Probably her only hope.

Lucy carries her mug of tea upstairs and searches both the study and the bedroom for the landline handsets, even though she's pretty sure that Marcus will have taken them with him. The bottle of temazepam is still there on his nightstand, almost empty now, but there's no sign of the phones in any of the drawers or cupboards. Her eye is caught by the roof of the kitchen extension, some six feet below the sill of the bedroom window. If she could get the window open, then she could climb through it and drop down onto the extension roof. Of course, the window is locked. The drop from the first-storey windows at the front of the house is nearly twenty feet, but she could manage this jump onto the flat roof.

Running downstairs, she pulls a hammer from the toolbox in the understairs cupboard and starts smashing at the window. But it doesn't break. Its surface crazes with lines and gives way slightly under the hammer head, but somehow remains intact. Of course, she remembers, with a sinking sensation, after an attempted break-in a couple of years earlier, Marcus had arranged for the windows at the rear of the house to be covered on both sides with a special protective film. 'Used in the Pentagon to prevent the windows blowing out in a terrorist attack,' he had told her proudly at the time. So now she's a princess in an unbreakable glass tower. Sinking on to the bed, she closes her eyes and gives in to tears.

Spending time with neither online connection nor contact with the outside world challenges her sanity. Lucy feels more isolated during that day even than she did in Brighton, a feeling compounded by heart-pounding desperation so extreme that it borders on panic. To try and calm herself, she digs out her old yoga mat from the back of the wardrobe and tries to remember the routines she learned when she was doing classes. *Focus on the breathing*, she instructs herself. *Get out of your thinking mind.* But although the incoming panic attack recedes a little, she still feels breathless with anxiety. Deciding that food will help she goes into the kitchen and makes toast, switching on Radio 4 for company. But the toast sticks in her throat and she ends up throwing most of it in the bin. She decides she can't wait until she is allowed to leave. She has to find a way out.

On the top floor, in Lydia's room, she manages to force open a window that wasn't locked properly. It's too small to climb through and the drop from the second storey is too high to contemplate anyway. But as she breathes in the welcome gust of fresh air, she spots a patch of red and realises with a swell of hope that it's the postman's van.

Getting her face as close as she can to the window, she screams at the top of her voice. 'Help! Over here!'

Footsteps crunch on the gravel. The postman is bringing mail to the house. Hurling herself down four flights of stairs, she positions herself next to the letter box, grabbing it when the sprung hinge is pushed open. Three official-looking letters tumble onto the mat.

'Help!' Lucy wiggles the tips of her fingers through the letter box. 'I'm locked in!'

The gravel crunches again and the footsteps start to recede.

'For God's sake!' Lucy shrieks, and then as the postman reaches the gates, she sees the wires coming from his ears, catches a distant, tinny beat. He's wearing headphones.

Slumping against the wall, she sobs noisily for a few minutes. Then she splashes her face with water, fetches a jigsaw that she spotted in Lydia's room and starts putting it together on the dining room table. The mindfulness of the activity soothes her a little, and eventually she becomes calm enough to think clearly. If she's not going to break out of the house, then she has to find some other way to end this. Her only remaining option is to appeal to Marcus's rational side and sense of fair play. To make him see what's right. Perhaps if she can ensure he gets proper rest and can wean him off the sedatives, he will be more rational. The children are due to visit in a few days' anyway, and Marcus can hardly keep the house in lockdown then. Something will have to change.

She finishes the jigsaw and watches daytime television with only part of her attention on the screen. By the time the sky outside the windows is darkening, she is so oppressed by the house and her own company that she's almost looking forward to her husband's return. But eight o'clock comes and he still isn't back from work.

Eventually there's a loud banging on the front door. Lucy hurries into the hall. Has he forgotten his key? But no, that's not possible: he locked her in, and he knows she's not able to answer the door to him anyway. Perhaps it's Jane, come to check on her in person? Her pulse quickens.

The letter box flap is thrust open. 'Oi, Blondie, you there?' Denny.

Quelling a shiver of disappointment, she squats down on the hall floor so that he can see her face.

'What the fuck's going on?' he demands. 'Only, I've been trying to contact you and your phone's out of service. The caretaker of the building said your stuff was gone from the flat. Get tired of being Joanne, did you? Didn't suit you?' There's an acid note in his voice.

'No!' Lucy feels tears pricking at the back of her nose. 'No, I did not. Marcus tricked me into coming back here by telling me my dad was about to die, then he locked me in.'

Denny makes a hissing sound. 'I'm not gonna lie, I did think it was a little bit weird that the lights were on, but all the security grilles are closed. Fuck. What an arsehole.'

'D'you think you can help me get down from one of the first-floor windows? Can you borrow a ladder or something? Only you'll have to hurry: Marcus will be back any minute.'

Denny grins, and the sliver of him she can see through the letter box is all wolfish teeth. 'Oh. I'm going to do something better than that, darling. I'm going to get this door open.' His face disappears for a few seconds, then he rattles something metallic in front of her three-inch field of vision.

'What's that?'

'Set of pick wires.'

Lucy is about to ask him whether he's always equipped for burglary or just on this occasion, but she realises she can't afford to annoy him. The depressing truth is that Denny is all she has.

He lets the letter box flap swing shut, and there is a lot of tweaking and scraping, first in the mortice lock and then the Yale cylinder lock.

The letter box is pushed open again. 'Okay, try the door now.'

She twists the catch on the Yale lock and the door creaks open. Denny stands in front of her grinning. His hair is waxed to a crest, and he's dressed in ripped, skintight jeans, a polo shirt buttoned at the neck and a Harrington jacket.

'Oh God. Thank you. Thank you, Denny.' She lunges forward and gives him an awkward half hug, filling her lungs with the clear, cold night air. 'Let me just grab some stuff, and then we can go. Did you come here in your car?'

But Denny holds up a hand. 'Whoa, whoa, whoa. You're going nowhere, Blondie.'

She frowns. 'What d'you mean? I've been held here against my will. I'm going to go to the police.'

Denny is shaking his head, using one of his huge arms to propel her backwards into the building she's just escaped.

'No!' she struggles against him, but it's quite useless. He follows her into the hallway and shuts the door.

'Look, don't lose your shit, all right?' He grins, revealing the big teeth. 'I'm going to help you. But first let's just have a little chat about what we need to do.'

Lucy stares at him.

'You're looking at this problem totally arse about face. You've got it the wrong way round. You've tried running away from your old man, but it hasn't worked. The geezer outwitted you. So. You need to switch things.' He flips a meaty hand to his face, palm up. 'And that way you don't lose all this, either.' He gestures around the spacious hall, at the antique oak settle dotted with bright contemporary cushions and the tasteful framed lithographs.

'What d'you mean?'

'What I mean is that instead of you getting away from him, you need to get *him* away from *you*. Permanently.'

Lucy's eyes widen, as he makes a slitting gesture across his throat.

'And, guess what: Uncle Denny here's going to help you.'

TWENTY

Denny's pale green eyes glitter under the hall light.

'You mean?'

'We're going to kill him.'

'We're going to kill him,' Lucy repeats stupidly, feeling as though she has been teleported to an episode of *EastEnders*. 'You and me?'

'That's it. Keep up.'

'How?'

'Have you got something that will knock him out. Sedative or something?'

'Yes…'

Denny nods, pleased. 'What, exactly?'

She thinks of the tablets she took from the bottle by Marcus's bed. 'He has temazepam. I've taken some of the tablets out of the bottle. But—'

'All you need to do is make sure he takes them, get him well out of it. Then I come over, we shove him in his car, pipe the exhaust in, leave the engine running and job's a good'un. He's an NHS doctor, so he overworks, right?'

'Yes. Of course.' And lately to an insane extent, she thinks.

'And his marriage is in trouble. That must be common knowledge by now. So no one would be that surprised if he topped himself. Meanwhile, if you're still locked in here, then no one can point the finger at you.'

Lucy hesitates, but only for a second. 'No, look… this is crazy. However much I might want my marriage to be over, I'm not doing *that*. I don't want Marcus dead.'

Denny advances slightly nearer, grinning. 'You sure about that?'

'Okay, there have been moments when it's a case of "God, I wish he was dead." But thinking it and doing it are two completely different things.'

He shrugs. 'Suit yourself, sweetheart. But at least take some time to think about what I've said. The door's open now, right? So if you want, you can go and tell the police. And…' He reaches in his pocket and pulls out an unfamiliar mobile handset. 'Only one number programmed into this: mine. So if you change your mind, at least you've got some way of letting me know.' He places the phone in her palm and gives her shoulder a lingering squeeze, before lumbering back through the front door. 'Speak soon, yeah?'

If she's to go to the police station, she'll have to leave the door on the latch, Lucy thinks, pulling on her jacket and applying some lipstick to counteract her deathly pallor.

But then, one hand on the front door, she hesitates. What exactly will she tell the police. That she's a prisoner in her own home? Appearing in person at the police station will give the lie to this: she will clearly have left the house under her own steam. No longer locked in. Free to come and go. How could the police take her claim seriously, or do anything but dismiss the incident as a marital spat: a domestic? Taking temporary refuge at the Standishes is a much better idea, and in the morning she will visit her father and plead with him to give her the money for her legal bill.

Lucy looks down in distaste at the phone Denny has left for her, then – because, with no other option, she can't contemplate leaving it behind – thrusts it to the bottom of her bag. She runs up to the bedroom and grabs clean underwear and a few other essentials, then leaves the house, slamming the front door behind her with an overwhelming sense of relief.

Car headlights temporarily blind her and she stands on the spot, motionless as a hunted animal. The crunch of gravel under tyres sends a shiver of despair through her.

Marcus cuts the engine and jumps out of his car. 'How the hell did you get out?'

'You can't do this!' Lucy shouts in his face, her saliva landing on his cheek. Her bag clutched to her chest, she swerves round him. Marcus tries to rugby-tackle her, but the element of surprise and her fight-or-flight reflex work in her favour and she dodges him, slipping out onto the pavement and starting to half walk, half run away.

'Lucinda, please.' He flaps his arms by his aide in a gesture of helplessness. 'I'm sorry. Can we please just talk?'

Now several metres away from him, she turns round and shakes her head firmly. 'Oh no. I'm not going to fall for your tricks again, Marcus. There's no way I'm going to get locked in again. Never.'

'Okay, look…' He selects a key from the bunch on his keyring and unlocks the metal window grilles at the front of the house. Then he tosses the whole bunch in her direction. They land at her feet, gleaming under the street lamp. 'Have the keys. You can keep hold of them while we talk. And once we've talked, if you still want to leave, then go. I won't try and stop you.'

Lucy narrows her eyes, trying to read his facial expression, but he's too far away and it's too dark. She simply doesn't know if she can trust him any longer. She should just keep going. But she aches with emotional exhaustion and the excess adrenaline is making her legs wobbly. She bends down and picks up the keys. The keyring is shaped like a silver Eiffel Tower, bearing the legend '*I love Paris*', only with a red enamel heart in place of the word 'love'. She bought it for Marcus in a touristy shop in the Latin Quarter on that fateful weekend trip to the city. It was several years ago; years that now stretch like decades.

'Please, Lucy.'

He almost never calls her Lucy, even though he knows she prefers it. She steps a few paces closer and she sees for the first time how terrible he looks. His hair is dirty and unkempt, and the cuffs of his shirt look grimy.

'All right then,' she says quietly. 'But I keep hold of the keys.'

He nods, and they walk into the house together. She has the mobile from Denny in her bag, she tells herself, and even with outgoing calls blocked, it will still make an emergency call.

'We'll feel better if we eat something,' she says, once they're inside. Marcus's house keys are pushed deep into her trouser pocket, but she keeps her fingertips on them as a talisman of safety. 'I could get something out of the freezer. Or we could order in.'

But Marcus ignores her, striding into the kitchen and opening a bottle of Barolo. He drinks deeply from his glass as though he's a marathon runner at a water stop.

'Is it really so bad being married to me?' he asks Lucy. His gaze, over the rim of his wine glass, is steady, curious. 'I mean, look,' he gestures around him at the beautifully finished kitchen, the double doors out into the pretty garden, 'you're well provided for. I let you go to college and mess about getting a degree you didn't really need. Paid the fees without complaint. I take you—'

'You "let" me,' says Lucy as calmly as she can muster, though her heart is still racing. She fingers the keys again. 'That's the problem, Marcus. That word. It's not in your gift to allow me to do things. I'm a grown woman.'

'It is if I'm paying for it.' Marcus empties a third of the bottle into his emptied glass and slumps down onto one of the kitchen chairs.

'When you're married, your money is shared: that's a given. It still doesn't give you the right to track my movements. To monitor who I speak to and who I see.' Heat rises in Lucy's chest, as she experiences a rush of anger so intense it makes her shake. 'Can't you see? I'd rather not have your money – any money – and be able to live my life without your constant control. You're an intelligent man: surely you understand that?'

Marcus ignores this. 'You know, Lucinda, people told me I shouldn't marry you. Nobody was in favour of it. They thought you were just a silly bit of a girl. A pretty airhead.' He's slurring his words slightly now, taking frequent mouthfuls of the red wine. 'Okay, Amber could be a bit of a nightmare, and things weren't perfect on that front, I grant you. But at least she was a grown woman. A woman of substance.' He glances up at Lucy, but she stands stock-still, her hands clenched. She parts her lips to speak, then decides against it. 'You were just an overprotected child. No substance at all. So. Whole thing: a mistake.'

'If it was a mistake, then shouldn't we just bring it to an end? Can't we find a way to do it amicably? I'm happy to sign anything you like saying I won't take half your money from you—'

'Amber's already had most of it anyway,' Marcus snorts, draining the remains of the bottle into his glass.

'And I would still like to see Tom and Lydia occasionally.' She was fond of her stepchildren, enough to want to maintain some sort of contact.

Marcus's face darkens. Lucy notices for the first time that his hands are shaking. Mr Marcus Wheedon, FRCS, the steadiest hand in the business, is shaking like a long-time alcoholic. 'Leave my children out of it,' he mumbles.

Lucy sighs, taking the empty wine bottle and carrying it over to the recycling bin. As she does so, she takes in the face of the vintage kitchen clock. It's after 10 p.m. After only a few snatched hours on the sofa the night before, she is dizzy with fatigue. It's not just physical tiredness but a profound emotional torment that makes rational thought painful and constructive argument impossible. Now that her agitation has receded, she's simply too

drained to think of leaving. 'Look, Marcus, we're both worn out…
we're not going to get anywhere like this. Why don't we just go to
bed and talk some more tomorrow? I'll sleep in the spare room.'

'But you'll just leave,' Marcus says, wiping his hand back and
forth across his chin as though he's surprised to find stubble there.
'You'll wait until I'm asleep and you'll just piss off again.'

Lucy shrugs, taking two glasses from the cupboard and filling
them both with water. 'I won't. But for once, you're just going to
have to take a chance and trust me on that.'

He sighs, and pulls himself up unsteadily from his chair. 'Fair
enough. You win.' He stumbles to the stairs and mounts them
slowly, using the banister to haul his weight.

Lucy follows him with a glass of water in her hand. 'Here –
you'll need this.'

He takes it from her and, placing it on his nightstand, unscrews
the cap on the temazepam bottle. Lucy hurries into the bedroom
after him, but before she can stop him, he has tipped three of the
pills into his mouth and washed them down with the water. She
opens her mouth to query whether this is a good idea, then thinks
better of it and retreats to the spare room. After placing the keys
under the pillow, she tugs off her trousers and shirt and sinks onto
the bed, giving way within seconds to a bone-deep exhaustion.

When Lucy wakes, the room is still in darkness and a phone is
ringing somewhere.

She glances at the clock, and realises with a sinking sensation
that far from being pre-dawn, it's only five to midnight. Behind
the closed door, cracks of light appear and she hears Marcus's voice
speaking in a low, urgent tone.

'Marcus?' She opens the door and looks out onto the landing.
Through the open bedroom door, she can see that he's out of bed
and getting dressed. 'What's going on?'

'I'm on call,' he mutters, bending over and fumbling under the bed for his shoes. 'Need you to drive me to the hospital.'

'But you can't go in now! It's out of the question.'

He raises an eyebrow at her, swaying slightly with one shoe in his hand.

'Marcus, you've drunk a whole bottle of wine and taken several temazepam. Which you're not supposed to have with alcohol. Even if I were to drive you, you're not in a fit state to operate.'

'Try telling that to the patient who needs corra— coronary revascularisation.' He stumbles over the words. 'I'm the only surgeon this side of Birmingham who can do it.'

He straightens up, and Lucy sees that he has buttoned his shirt all wrong. For the first time, she sees that middle age has well and truly caught up with him. He always seemed Peter Pan-like, with his vital energy and full head of glossy hair. Now he looks all of his forty-eight years and more.

'Keys. I'll need my keys back.' He holds out a hand, wiggling his fingers impatiently.

'I'm not giving them to you,' Lucy says firmly, crossing her arms and blocking the bedroom doorway. 'No way. You're not in a fit state.'

'Suit yourself.' He pushes past her roughly, stumbling against the door frame. 'I've got a spare car key.'

He stamps into his study and comes back holding the key aloft, a smile of triumph on his face that would have been ridiculous if it weren't so alarming.

'Marcus, you can't!'

Lucy tries once more to block his path to the stairs, but he thrusts both hands at her shoulders, knocking her against the wall. She loses her footing on the top step and tumbles down the stairs, winding herself and cracking her head against the wall. Marcus runs down after her, but rather than checking that she is unharmed, he steps over her and heads for the front door, swinging it wide open.

A rush of cold, night air hits Lucy's face. Disorientated, she struggles to her feet, as the Range Rover engine roars to life. She runs out onto the drive, temporarily blinded by the headlights. As her eyes adjust, she catches a glimpse of Marcus's face, skin pale, eyes opaque and unfocused.

'For God's sake, stop!'

Ignoring her, appearing not even to see her, he throws the car into reverse and shoots out of the driveway, clipping the wheel arch against the stone gatepost. He needs to be stopped, Lucy thinks. She should phone the hospital. But the landline phones are still unplugged and put God knows where, and she no longer has a mobile; only the pre-programmed one that Denny gave her.

Fumbling in her bag, she grabs it and runs out onto the street after Marcus's car. It's going too fast, weaving precariously back and forth across the central white line. Waving her left arm to try and catch the attention of one of the few passing motorists, she switches on the phone with her other hand and presses the 'Emergency' button.

'999: what's your emergency?'

The car revs with a horrible loud, grinding sound and picks up speed. Lucy sprints down the road after it, phone still in hand.

'Hello? What's your emergency, please?'

It's as though the accelerator has got stuck somehow, because the car's trajectory is unstoppable, heading across the opposite lane and into the path of an oncoming car.

'Police, fire or ambulance?'

The other vehicle, a small white hatchback, swerves just in time, but Marcus's car continues its deadly path, right across the road and up onto the pavement. Lucy holds her hands up to her mouth, the operator still faintly audible on her handset, as the Range Rover hits a tree trunk at seventy miles an hour. The bonnet crumples and Marcus's car turns into a single, roaring ball of flame.

PART TWO

TWENTY-ONE

The outside of the place is familiar: she has seen it so many times before.

But despite Lucy's numerous visits to the home of her husband's first wife – to drop off or collect her two stepchildren – she has never been inside it until now.

Amber holds open the door of the pretty terraced house off Westbourne Grove and allows Lucy to cross the threshold, but there are no words of welcome. At Marcus's funeral, which she attended with the children, Amber's face was impassive under her hat's black veiling. She gave Lucy a stiff embrace and an air kiss, but Lucy knew that it was purely for show, because the two women were being scrutinised by two hundred mourners.

'Have you got the stuff with you?' Amber demands. She's a handsome woman in her mid-forties, always immaculately made up and with glossy sable curls that look as if they've had the benefit of hot rollers. Today she's wearing a grey cashmere roll-neck sweater and well-cut black trousers.

'It's in the back of the car,' Lucy says, gesturing outside to the cardboard boxes of the children's possessions that Amber has demanded she return. 'But listen… are you sure you need them? I wouldn't want Tom and Lydia to feel the door was closed to them. As far as I'm concerned, they still have their rooms in the house.'

'No,' says Amber coldly. 'That wouldn't be appropriate.'

'Appropriate?'

'Under the circumstances, I don't want the children returning to… where it happened. It's too much for them.'

Lucy sighs. 'Okay, if you're sure that's what they want.' She turns back to the front door, then pauses a beat. 'The coroner's inquest is next Tuesday: I don't know if you've been told?'

'Surely *you're* not going to attend?' Amber folds her arms across her chest, her expression stony, and Lucy realises with a chilling rush of shock that Amber blames her for Marcus's death. Of course, she hasn't said as much, but she doesn't need to. It's spelled out in her body language.

'Of course I'm going to attend.' Lucy struggles to keep her voice level. 'Why on earth would I not?'

Amber narrows her eyes. 'According to Beryl, Marcus crashed the car because of extreme stress. Stress caused by you walking out on him.'

According to Beryl. No surprise there. Any chance for the old bag to stick the knife in.

Lucy knows she shouldn't argue, that she should let the facts do the talking at the inquest, but she can't help herself.

'Marcus crashed the car because he had combined a whole bottle of wine with 60mg of temazepam. I was the one who tried to stop him driving.'

Amber shrugs. 'Sitting pretty now though, aren't you?'

Lucy turns back, her hand still on the front-door catch. 'Meaning?'

'Well, the house is paid off, there's a huge life insurance premium and a considerable death-in-service payout. Four times his salary, if I remember rightly. That alone must be getting on for a million. I see you've already treated yourself to a brand new car.'

Lucy decides against explaining that Marcus got rid of her old car as a way of trying to keep her prisoner in her own home. Instead, she runs down the steps and hefts the cardboard boxes from the boot of her car, dumping them on the driveway. Then, without another word, she drives away.

Sitting pretty.

Amber's words come back to her over and over again once she is back in the house in Barnes. Is that really how she is seen now? The shock, the trauma and the outright ugliness of her widowhood have felt anything other than pretty. Given her desire to end her marriage, her extreme pain at Marcus's death has taken her by surprise. Gillian, her bereavement counsellor, has explained to her that the loss of a troubled relationship can be far more difficult to deal with than the ending of a harmonious one. It involves regret, relief, shame and guilt. Guilt most of all. Lucy knows rationally that the hours Marcus was working, the drinking, the abusing sedatives – none of these were her fault. And yet still she feels guilty.

'Maybe I should have agreed to drive him to the hospital after all,' she said to Gillian at their last session. 'And kept him alive.'

'And maybe he would have ended up killing his patient,' Gillian pointed out. She has taught Lucy to explore her feelings during therapy but to try and distance herself from them the rest of the time, as a self-protective mechanism. So Lucy closes the doors of the children's now-empty rooms with a sigh and goes back to her desk to continue with the process of job applications. She doesn't need to work for financial reasons; as Amber bitchily pointed out, she's now very comfortable financially. But she wants to. She wants to be busy, and to push herself. To achieve something in her own right.

As she is registering on a couple of graduate recruitment sites, the doorbell rings. She jumps up to answer it.

'Hello?' The figure on the doorstep has their back turned, taking in their surroundings, and at first Lucy doesn't recognise her.

'All right?'

It's Adele. She's changed her hair colour again, to pastel violet, and there's a new piercing on her nostril.

'Gonna let me in?'

'Of course.' Lucy opens the door wide. 'Come in.'

Adele walks through to the kitchen without being asked.

'Coffee?'

She pulls a face. 'Nah, didn't like that strong stuff you made last time. Tea'll do.'

Lucy sets the kettle to boil and turns to smile at her friend. 'It's good to see you... To what do I owe the pleasure?'

'I heard about your husband,' Adele says simply. 'Read about it in the papers. I didn't get any reply when I tried to text you, so I thought I'd better come around in person and check on you.'

'Sorry, I don't have that phone any more,' Lucy says, swirling a teabag round the mug, adding milk and handing it to Adele, 'I would have replied otherwise.'

'So,' Adele takes a noisy slurp. 'To be honest I'm not quite sure what I'm meant to be doing.'

'What d'you mean?'

'I mean, am I meant to be giving condolences or congratulations?'

Lucy flushes slightly, busying herself with searching for biscuits. Adele does have a point. She was approached with a request for help, help in escaping a marriage that was intolerable. And now Lucy has well and truly escaped: through her husband's untimely death.

'Obviously, you know better than most that things were not great between Marcus and I.'

'But you'd gone back to him.' The sharpness of Adele's tone takes her aback.

'No, not exactly...' Lucy continues to rummage in the cupboard, reluctant to turn round and face the full force of Adele's cross-examination. 'Things were... The night he died we were in the process of trying to work something out. Something that would involve us separating though.' She pulls out a tin of oatmeal biscuits and slides them across the table to Adele. 'I wasn't going to stay with him.'

'Dead convenient, in that case.' Adele's slanted eyes glitter with something bordering on malice. She waits for Lucy to respond, and when she stays silent continues: 'That he's out the way and you end up with all this.' She waves her hand around the large, beautifully appointed kitchen.

'It might look that way, but, trust me, this wasn't what I wanted.' Lucy's voice cracks. 'The last two weeks have been an utter nightmare.'

Adele turns down her lower lip to show that she doubts this. 'You gonna keep this place?' she asks. 'Or will you sell it? Bit big just for one person, isn't it?'

Lucy thinks of the two rooms on the top floor, now stripped of their books, games and clothes. 'Yes, it's definitely too big. So I'll probably put it on the market. Not yet, but maybe in the summer.'

'How much is it worth then, a gaff like this?' Adele asks, as gauche and tactless as she was when they were children.

'About three million.'

Adele's eyes widen. 'Bleedin' 'ell, Luce. You're a millionaire. You get the old man's life insurance payout too?'

'The payment has been delayed until after the inquest, but yes, I will.'

'And how much is that?'

Lucy feels suddenly queasy at this questioning. Especially from Adele, who was once convicted of taking a few extra thousand pounds in benefits to try and keep her family afloat.

'I don't know,' she lies. 'I'll need to speak to my solicitor about it in due course.' She clears away Adele's empty mug to indicate that their chat is over.

'Nice though, eh?' Adele looks straight into Lucy's eyes with an unreadable expression; one that hints at secrecy. 'Nice problems to have.'

'How *are* you?'

Helen adopts that special tone people use when speaking to the recently bereaved, one Lucy knows only too well.

'Fine,' she answers, then regrets the glib choice of word. 'You know: getting there.'

'Hope you don't mind me phoning your landline, only I couldn't get through on your mobile.'

'Yes, sorry about that.'

In fact, Lucy is not sorry. Having a brand new mobile phone with no numbers yet stored on it has been a convenient way of keeping well-meaning enquiries away. Though some people – like Jane Standish – have called round in person bearing casseroles.

'Anyway, the reason I'm phoning is to ask you over for supper with me and Pete. Nothing fancy; just the luxury of a meal you haven't had to cook.'

'That's sweet of you, Helen, but I'm not sure. I'm not very good company.'

'Nonsense,' Helen's voice is warm but brisk. 'It'll do you good to get out of that house. Tomorrow evening, and I'm not taking no for an answer.'

Lucy assumes it will just be the three of them for supper: herself, Helen and Pete. But when she arrives at Helen's flat in Crouch End, there's a fourth person, introduced as Pete's friend Noah Kenyon. He's a bear of a man, with shaggy hair and a slightly scruffy beard, but his hazel eyes have a roguish twinkle and there's a warmth about him that Lucy can't help but respond to. To her relief, he deals matter-of-factly with her newly widowed status, telling her that he's sorry but without gushing, probing or – most importantly – doing the sympathetic head tilt when he asks her about it. He's quick to move onto other topics of conversation and soon they're talking about the perils of cycling in London, the joys of getting to the end of a master's degree course and the mysteries of Article 50. Helen has made a hearty chicken and lentil casserole, Noah has brought several bottles of wine and Pete supplies a 90s soundtrack from his collection of vinyl. To Lucy's surprise, the evening turns into a robustly cheerful affair: so much so that she is sorry when it comes to an end.

Minutes after the taxi has dropped her at home in Barnes, the doorbell rings. Lucy determines to ignore it, but it rings a second time. *Surely not Adele again*, she thinks, her good spirits evaporating. *Here for another round of contrary needling.*

But the figure outlined in the fanlight is far too tall. Tentatively, she slots the chain into place and opens the door.

'Hi again.'

It's Noah Kenyon, in bike leathers and holding a crash helmet under one arm. He extends the other arm sheepishly, and she sees he's holding the leopard print scarf she had been wearing earlier that evening.

'Sorry to disturb, but you left this at Helen's flat, and since I only live just across the bridge, I offered to drop it off for you.'

Lucy releases the chain and opens the door wide, revealing a huge blue Kawasaki parked across the driveway.

'That's very kind of you: thanks.' She hesitates a second, then remembers her manners. 'Want to come in for a nightcap?' Nightcap sounds wrong. It has a suggestive ring, like an invitation to look at her etchings. 'I was just about to have a herbal tea,' she goes on quickly. 'Before bed.' This sounds even worse, and she blushes like a schoolgirl.

Unfazed, Noah grins. 'I could use a camomile. Or a pepper-mint,' he adds quickly. 'Whatever you've got.'

They settle on spearmint and lime leaf. Noah sprawls on the kitchen sofa, apparently completely relaxed. He gives a brief, appreciative glance at his surroundings but doesn't fawn about the decor or query the economic wisdom of one person living in such a house alone. His lack of self-consciousness is infectious, and for only the second time in months, Lucy is able to relax. It feels wonderful.

'Thanks for this evening,' she says as she hands him the tea, feeling she should acknowledge this. 'It was good just to forget everything for a while. I'm grateful.'

Noah gives her his easy grin. His hazel eyes are fringed with surprisingly long and lustrous black lashes. Noticing this, Lucy feels both a jolt of dismay and the pull of attraction. She has an unsettling impulse to reach out and touch him.

'No problem,' he tells her. 'You've had a shitty time, but that's in the past. Things can only get better from here.'

'I hope you're right.' She gives him a careful smile.

'I am: you'll see.' He pushes his unruly dark hair back from his forehead and stands up, leaving his tea half drunk. 'I'd better be off. You're probably very tired. I should think sleep's been in short supply.'

Lucy nods. 'Right again.'

'Tell you what, how about we go for a drink some time, and you can let me know how things are going? I'd love to hear first-hand if I was right. About things getting easier from here on in, I mean.'

'That's a lovely idea.' She hesitates. She likes this man. She even – to her utter surprise – feels something more than mere liking. And yet. 'Thank you. But I'm sorry; it's a little too soon.' Suddenly her mind is full of Marcus again, and the imminent inquest. It's as though she's been punched in the solar plexus. 'I'm just not ready.'

TWENTY-TWO

'It's really a family thing, but it's quite fun, and I thought it might be nice for you to get out of the house. Enjoy this lovely weather.'

On a Saturday morning in late May, Jane Standish phones to invite Lucy to a spring fair on Clapham Common.

'It would be nice to go out…' With the phone pinned against her shoulder, Lucy unfolds the written copy of the coroner's verdict that she has just received in the post: *Marcus James McAdam Wheedon, D.O.B 16.08.69. Death by accident (road traffic collision).* '… As long as you're sure I wouldn't be in the way?'

'Nonsense, the more the merrier. It will be good to see you.'

Lucy decides to put on a floaty grey summer dress that always lifts her mood when she wears it and ties up her hair in a high ponytail. And it is indeed a lovely day, with high clouds scudding across a picture-perfect blue sky, the trees vibrant green and the air carrying birdsong and a faint scent of blossom. Even south London is pretty in this weather, Lucy thinks, as she strolls towards the common from the bus stop.

'You look so well,' Jane says, as soon as she spots Lucy at their meeting place near Long Pond. She embraces her warmly. 'Doesn't she, Robin?'

'Yes,' he says kissing her on both cheeks. 'I'm pleased to see it.'

Jane's tone has a faintly accusatory edge. Does she look *too* well? Lucy wonders. If she seems okay, will people assume that she doesn't care about Marcus's life being over?

'Sleep,' she says simply. 'I've finally started sleeping again.'

Ever astute, Jane gives her a lingering look and says, 'It must be a very confusing time for you. Lots of competing emotions, I should imagine. Including relief.'

'Yes,' Lucy agrees but does not elaborate.

Jane links arms with her. 'Come on, let's find somewhere that's serving coffee. I don't know about you, but I'm desperate for caffeine.'

The fair turns out to be little more than an extended farmers' market with entertainments for children thrown in: an oversubscribed bouncy castle, a ball pit and a fire engine to clamber over. A few weary-looking Shetland ponies have been press-ganged into giving rides to the under-eights. Robin takes the children to buy candyfloss while Jane and Lucy sit at a picnic table with their coffee.

'Mostly I feel shell-shocked,' Lucy admits. 'As though this is all a bit unreal. You know: like it's happening to someone else.'

'It'll get easier. Bit by bit,' Jane says, squeezing her hand. She narrows her eyes slightly. 'Do you miss him?'

'I don't know,' Lucy replies carefully, looking across the expanse of grass to where the ponies are ambling back and forth. 'I miss the Marcus from the early days of our marriage. But maybe not the recent Marcus.'

'And are you still planning on moving away from London?'

Lucy shrugs. 'That job I was interested in – the one in Bristol – will be long gone. But maybe if I find something else as appealing, I would consider it. If I end up staying in London, I think I'll certainly sell the house and move somewhere smaller.'

Robin comes back with the children. Barney – every available bit of skin covered in sticky pink sugar – needs the loo and Oscar wants to go and investigate a stall selling computer games.

'Daddy will go with you,' Jane tells her oldest son, 'And I'd better take Barney. Lucy, would you mind keeping an eye on Molly for a few minutes. Meet you back here in ten?'

Molly slips her hand through Lucy's, and at her request, they walk over to pet the ponies.

'Didn't have you down as the 'orsey type.'

The low voice comes from somewhere behind her, but Lucy recognises it straight away. Denny Renard.

He's wearing indigo-wash jeans, aviator shades and a short-sleeved cotton shirt, the sleeves so tight round his straining biceps that they almost cut off the circulation. 'You look very pretty, Blondie, I must say. Widowhood's obviously suiting you.'

Molly clutches her hand more tightly, gazing up in confusion at this threatening stranger.

Lucy drops to her haunches and plucks a handful of long grass. 'Why don't you take this and give it to that brown pony over there?' She points to a rotund caramel-coloured one with a blonde mane. 'Make sure you hold your hand flat, like I showed you.' Molly nods solemnly and runs over to the pony.

'What are you doing here,' Lucy hisses at Denny once the little girl is out of earshot. 'How did you even know I was here?'

He taps the side of his nose. 'Ways and means. I like to keep tabs on my friends.'

He must have followed her here from Barnes, or how else could he possibly know? Had he been on the same bus?

'We're not friends,' she says crisply, still watching Molly out of the corner of her eye.

'Aw, come now, that's not very nice,' Denny wheedles.

'I'm sorry, I'm here with friends, I can't talk to you.' She turns her back, indicating that the conversation is over.

'You still got that mobile I gave you?' The tone of his voice changes. It's hard-edged, and not the slightest bit friendly.

'I don't know,' Lucy says truthfully. She used it to call the police on the night that Marcus died but can't even remember what happened to it from that point. What followed is a blur of sirens, cups of tea from well-meaning neighbours and witness statements.

'Well,' Denny says in the same menacing tone, 'I suggest you find it. And you'd better hope you do.'

Before Lucy can react, he's turned on his heel and disappeared into the crowd.

She eventually finds the mobile when she gets home, after searching for twenty minutes. It has slipped down behind the settle in the hall, where she must have flung or dropped it on the night of the accident. The battery is flat, but one of the children once had the same brand of phone and there's a spare charger in the kitchen drawer.

Once it comes to life, it bleeps with a text. There's no written message, just an audio file. Lucy clicks on the link to play it out loud.

Her own voice comes into the room, startling her. There's no doubt that it's a recording of her, but there's also no doubt that the things she said have been rearranged to completely alter their context and, by implication, their meaning.

'I wish he was dead... he has Temazepam. I've taken some of the tablets out of the bottle... of course... we're going to kill him.'

TWENTY-THREE

A few days go by without Lucy hearing any more from Denny, but she already knows better than to breathe easy. He won't leave matters there.

Sure enough, three days later, another message arrives on the cheap and nasty mobile handset. She has come to loathe the thing, as though it's a plastic and lithium avatar of Denny himself.

what did u think of my bit of damming evidence then

She has replayed the audio message several times. Of course, she knows that the phrases on it are out of sequence, but they have been seamlessly spliced together and, to a less attuned ear, it does indeed sound as though that's what she said when she and Denny were talking on the evening Marcus died. It must have been digitally altered by an expert; presumably one of Denny's convict pals.

She doesn't reply, but as though he's somehow watching her, another text arrives.

interesting wasn't it. what a jury will call proof of intention. we need to meet

Furious, she snatches up the phone and types back.

There's no way I'm going to meet with you. Forget it.

Ten seconds later there's another bleep.

oh yes you are if you know what's good for you. dog and fox tomorrow 6pm

Lucy switches the phone off and shoves it to the back of a kitchen drawer, hidden behind spare light bulbs and balls of string, as though that will neutralise its threat. Then she snatches her denim jacket, shoves her feet into flip-flops and heads off for a walk to clear her head.

She ends up walking past the huge detached houses on Castlenau and over Hammersmith Bridge. When she reaches the main shopping thoroughfare, her eye is caught by a stylish new delicatessen selling mainly Japanese and Korean foodstuffs. She picks up a basket and browses the aisles, picking out some kimchi and some rice vinegar, for the simple reason that she's attracted by their colourful labels. Then she spots a familiar figure, procrastinating over which brand of rice to choose.

'Hello,' she says to Noah Kenyon. 'Didn't expect to see you in a hipster heaven like this.'

His mouth forms an 'o' of surprise, which morphs rapidly into a delighted grin. 'Not really my natural habitat,' He holds up his basket. 'But I work from home – just round the corner – and I've run out of rice. Any excuse to get away from staring at a computer screen…'

Lucy wracks her brains to recall what Noah does for a living. Something to do with design? Computer graphics?

'Anyway, how about you? Not exactly your neck of the woods, is it?'

I was trying to escape my criminal tormentor and this is where I ended up.

'I fancied a walk, and before I knew it I was in the fleshpots of Hammersmith.' She smiles. 'I'm only really window-shopping. If you can window-shop for food.'

'How d'you feel about getting a coffee?'

Lucy readily abandons her impulse purchases, Noah pays for his rice and they walk a few metres down the road to a small Italian bakery that also has an espresso machine.

'I'm glad I bumped into you,' he says after they've made small talk for a few minutes. He fixes her with his incongruously beautiful eyes.

'I think it was the other way round; I bumped into you.'

'However it was, I'm really glad. I've been trying to pluck up the courage to ask Helen for your number. And now I don't need to: I can go straight to the source.' Lucy's smile is hesitant, and he says quickly, 'I know you said you weren't ready for… involvement, or a date even, I get that. I'd simply like to offer to be a friend, should you need one. That's all. I promise.'

She can't resist Noah's warmth and his disarming lack of game. He proffers his phone and she types in her number, noting the return of his delighted smile as she hands it back to him. She wishes she could tell him about the loathsome Denny and his campaign of harassment, but she can't.

'I'd better get going,' she says, sliding down off her stool and kissing him swiftly on his cheek. 'See you around.'

The Dog and Fox is quiet at six o'clock on a Wednesday evening, with no workers splurging their Friday pay packets, or Saturday clubbers preloading before moving on elsewhere.

A few of the regulars were in the pub the night Lucy went there to find Adele, what feels like half a lifetime ago, and they nudge one another and give her curious stares. She half hopes Adele herself will appear and provide some much-needed moral support. At least she's not obliged to make a duty visit to her father, who is visiting his widowed sister – Lucy's Aunt Dorothy – in Torquay. The stroke, so closely followed by the shock of Marcus's death, has left him frail and anxious, and she's glad that he's enjoying a few days of home cooking and sea air.

At six fifteen, Denny lopes in wearing the sort of shiny nylon tracksuit that professional athletes wore in the 1970s and another pair of box-fresh trainers, neon yellow this time.

'Get you a drink, darling?'

Lucy shakes her head, her teeth gritted. 'Let's just get this over with.'

'Suit yourself.' He shrugs and heads to the bar, coming back with a double whisky. 'Now, let's just have a nice little chat... You enjoy that tape I made of you discussing killing your old man, did you?' He leans back in his chair and leers, making his neck tattoos bulge.

'That's not what I really said to you, and you know it.' Lucy keeps her arms pressed tightly by her sides, her hands in her lap. She avoids looking at Denny.

'I know that, and you know that: sure. But anyone else listening to it, they're going to hear your voice. And those words.' He smiles, pleased with this summary, and takes a mouthful of Scotch, swilling it round like mouthwash. 'Soliciting to commit murder, I think they call it.'

'Come off it, Denny,' Lucy says, with more conviction than she feels. 'What are you planning to do with it? Go to the police? And risk implicating yourself? And, anyway, expert analysis would be able to prove that audio has been messed around with.'

'Ah, but are you willing to risk that though?' Denny asks cheerfully, exposing his long incisors. 'Some jurors might have reasonable doubt about that. Especially if there's other evidence.'

'What other evidence?' Lucy snaps. Her raised voice attracts the attention of the other drinkers, who turn their heads in her direction. 'You know perfectly well there isn't any.'

Denny merely taps the side of his nose.

To give herself a few seconds to calm down, rather than because she's thirsty, Lucy fishes her wallet from her bag, which hangs over the back of her chair, and walks over to the bar to buy a glass of mineral water.

Don't let him see he's rattled you, she tells herself, as she returns to the table. *Stay in control.*

'Look,' Lucy sits down again and glances around her before leaning in a little closer. 'I'm assuming this is about money. You want me to pay you to keep this fiction to yourself.'

'Give the girl a gold star.' Denny licks his fingertip and holds it up in the air.

'If I give you some… some cash… call it a bonus for the services you provided… will that be the end of it?'

'Well now, that all depends.'

Lucy clenches her fists in her lap. 'I can give you five thousand.'

Denny gives a short bark of laughter. 'Five K? You're kidding me, right?'

'All right then. Ten.'

He leans in closer. 'Come on now, Blondie, you're sitting on a pile, we both know that. That house. The dead doctor's cash. It must all add up to millions. You can do a lot better than a few poxy grand.'

Lucy stands up abruptly, her knee knocking the table and spilling Denny's drink. It drips onto his massive, shiny thigh. 'I'm not going to be blackmailed by you,' she says in a low voice, her fists clenched at her sides. 'You get that? You can fuck off.'

But as she strides out of the pub, she knows only too well that her counterpunch will make no difference. She knows that Denny will be back.

The next morning Lucy receives an email inviting her to an interview. The Pink Square Agency is a small digital company serving charities, and the job itself is administrative and poorly paid, but nevertheless she is delighted to have been shortlisted without any directly relevant experience other than her recently completed degree. She emails back her intention to attend, and goes downstairs to the kitchen to make coffee.

Despite herself, Lucy's eye is drawn to the drawer where she has hidden Denny's phone. She turns her back to fill the water chamber on the coffee machine, but still the wretched phone draws her back. She can't ignore it. She pulls it from the drawer and switches it on, holding it at arm's length like a grenade. There is a text waiting for her. Of course.

It takes her a while to work out what she's looking at. It's an image, slightly blurred, but when she walks over to the French windows and holds it nearer the light, she eventually discerns that it's a screen grab of a text message.

I need you to find someone who will help me kill my husband

Frowning, she reads it again, then a third time. This is not a text she has written; she's quite sure of it.

Then a second message arrives; another photo. This one has zoomed out slightly, and it shows the text on the screen of a phone identical to the one she bought in Redgate when she was about to embark on her life as Joanne Chandler. The 'secret phone'.

Ignore it, the rational part of her brain insists, but in a surge of fury she's already typing.

This is ridiculous. I didn't type this, and that's not my phone.

Five minutes later, the handset vibrates with a reply:

oh yes it is, you left yr phone in flat in brighton

And then she remembers: Marcus snatching the phone from her and hurling it across the kitchen and she – in her panic about her father's imminent demise – only too willing to leave it behind. And what was it Denny said when he picked the lock on the front door: '*the caretaker said your stuff was gone from the flat*'? He must have gone to Brighton himself, looking for Lucy, and found her phone in the empty flat.

She forces herself to take deep breaths to slow her racing pulse, and as she calms down, her thoughts clear. This is ludicrous. There's no way Denny will be able to prove she sent that text: he can't even prove that the pay-as-you-go phone in question belonged to her. And if she's supposed to have sent it to him, how can he avoid calling his own involvement into question? He's got a criminal record; it would not be a stretch to conclude that murdering Marcus was his idea.

She's about to switch the phone off without replying when another message arrives. Another photo.

This one is taken from black and white CCTV footage. The quality is questionable, but it's clear enough to show the back view of her blonde hair as she hands over cash to the spotty youth serving in the phone store in Redgate. A second text arrives almost immediately.

they have record of handset serial number in the shop and here u r buying it

The phone buzzes again.

& if ur wondering how I got picture, shop manager is friend of friend

A chill runs through Lucy's blood. Denny's resourcefulness is unexpected, and unnerving. She bought the phone for cash some time before she first met with Denny. How long had he been planning his blackmail attempt? Against her better judgement, she replies this time.

If that text is supposed to be to you, then you can't implicate me without implicating yourself. Think again.

She tries to power down the phone before he can respond, but he's far too quick for her.

who said anything about it being sent 2 me? it's you who needs 2 think again

TWENTY-FOUR

The Pink Square Agency is on the fourth floor of a building just off the Old Street roundabout.

'Hi, I'm Ellen,' says the girl who meets Lucy in reception. She has a cloud of ginger hair around a broad, smiling face.

'Nice to meet you,' Lucy says. She has worn a linen suit and is now regretting it because all the agency employees seem to be in a uniform of dungarees, slogan T-shirts and Converse sneakers. She feels like a headmistress making a surprise visit to a sixth-form common room.

The interview is conducted by Ellen and two others, Megan and Ari, and the tone is relaxed and informal; so much so that after ten minutes Lucy is chatting away, forgetting that she's at an interview at all. The agency's roster of clients is interesting, and she asks as many questions about them as she is asked about herself.

'Sorry,' she says eventually, flushing slightly. 'Rabbiting on a bit.'

'It's fine,' says Megan, who's one of the directors. She wears her dark hair in a severe pixie cut and teams the obligatory Converse with a Breton top and chunky necklace. 'It's great that you're so passionate about working with charities. The thing is, although the role involves a bit of client liaison, there'd also be quite a bit of basic admin work. Spreadsheets and so on. Would you be okay with that?'

'Fine,' says Lucy, meaning it. She would just be happy to have a job and be able to leave the house every day like a normal adult.

'The other thing is…' says Ari, a slight, handsome man with greying temples. '… we've pitched the salary at the level of a recent graduate, but you're obviously a little older, and you have a master's degree.' His gaze fixes on Lucy's tailored suit and Russell and Bromley loafers. 'I'm not sure if that would be in line with your expectations. Only, since we work with charities, we have to keep our payroll spend to a minimum.'

'It's not a problem,' Lucy says quickly. She glances along the line of faces on the other side of the desk. 'Cards on the table – I may as well be completely honest – I don't need the money. My husband died recently, and he's left me extremely well-provided for. But he also left me with an empty house and a surfeit of my own company. That's one reason I'd really like this role.'

You shouldn't have said that, she chastises herself as she walks back to the tube station. *This isn't the* X Factor*: they don't want a sob story, or to give a sympathy job.*

It's a warm, sunny afternoon, so she gets off the tube at Hammersmith and walks the rest of the way home. As she's reaching the parade of shops in Barnes, she gets a text.

Hi, this is Noah. Fancy meeting for a cup of tea? x

She smiles to herself and types back.

Too nice to be inside. How about a walk instead? x

Twenty minutes later, they meet at Rocks Lane and walk along Beverley Brook towards the bank of the Thames. She tells Noah about the interview she's just come from.

'Well done,' he says, adding kindly, 'They'd be silly not to snap you up.'

Lucy pulls a face. 'Not sure I'm exactly what they're looking for, but it was good experience. A step in the right direction.'

They walk and walk, talking about all sorts of stuff: their childhoods, their idiosyncratic culinary likes and dislikes, the point of watching sport, where they would live if they didn't live in central London. Noah – who has the faintest northern burr – says he would return to Cumbria, where he spent his childhood. Lucy tells him about her short-lived plan to move to Bristol and how she would probably choose that or Bath, where Vicky lives. They're still walking when it starts to go dark.

'I should be getting back,' she sighs, though, in reality, she has no reason or desire to be back in her empty house.

'I'm starving,' Noah says disingenuously. 'There's a nice tapas place just on the other side of the bridge: why don't we grab a bite and a glass of wine. Celebrate your return to the world of employment.'

'It's a bit early for that, but... why not?'

Lucy isn't especially hungry, but she's happy to pick at some pickled anchovies and *patatas bravas* over a glass of chilled Albariño, and happier still that the conversation continues to flow organically. Losing track of time in this way feels at once unfamiliar and a luxury.

'That was fun,' she says, as they part company halfway across Hammersmith Bridge; Noah has insisted that it's gentlemanly to at least walk her to the midpoint.

He smiles at her, then cups her chin and kisses her very gently on the lips. Lucy's first instinct is to pull away, but she successfully fights it, and obeys her second instinct, which is to lean in and enjoy it. It turns into something much longer and more passionate, something that makes other pedestrians turn their heads as they pass.

'Thank you,' she says simply, before walking away.

*

Surfacing from a deep sleep a few hours later, Lucy becomes aware of an unfamiliar noise. A creaking noise.

She tells herself that it's just the contracting of floorboards and door frames as the house cools and settles into itself. But it's early June, she remembers. The night air is mild and the central heating hasn't been in use for weeks. She pushes herself up on her elbows and listens.

There's something deliberate and rhythmic about the creaking, and as sleep recedes she realises that she can hear footsteps. The heavy footsteps of someone large. And then there's a thud that can only be a door closing.

Lucy's body is fuelled by a surge of terror, and without meaning to, she has jumped out of the bed. If it's a burglar, she needs to call the police, but even the thought of using her voice seems impossible. What if the burglar hears her and comes upstairs to attack her?

Worse still: what if it's not a burglar.

She stands stock-still for a few seconds, listening. The footsteps recede, there's another thud, then silence. Tiptoeing across the carpet, she edges open the bedroom door and steps out onto the landing. She can hear nothing, except for the ticking of the antique clock in the dining room.

'Hello?' she calls, feeling ridiculous as she does so.

Nothing.

For the first time, she truly understands the expression 'can't think straight' as her mind veers in all directions. The thud could have been the front door closing, she tells herself, but maybe whoever it was opened and closed it so that she *thinks* they've gone. Maybe there's more than one of them. She creeps along the landing and peers down the stairs to the hall. There's no sign of life, and the house is still quiet, but she is quite certain there *was* someone in the house. And that means they could come back.

Retreating into the bedroom, she throws on a pair of leggings and some flip-flops and then runs down into the hall, grabbing her bag with one hand as she flings open the front door with the other. The moonlit driveway is void of life, apart from a large dog fox. It pauses and regards her curiously with glittering eyes until the squawk of her car unlocking makes it hurry on.

Lucy throws herself into the driver's seat and locks the doors internally before pulling her mobile from her bag and phoning Noah.

'Hello?' He answers after five rings, his voice thick with sleep.

'Can I come over?' she asks without preamble.

'Sure…' Even half-asleep he sounds pleased. 'Is there a problem, or can you just not live a moment longer without me?'

'I'll tell you when I get there. What's your postcode?'

It's hard to discern much about Noah's flat with the benefit of only a small lamp in the sitting room, apart from it being clean but somewhat untidy. In the semi-darkness, Lucy can make out a lot of framed posters on the walls, some houseplants, piles of books on every surface and clothes drying over an airer.

'If I'd known you were coming, I'd have tidied up,' Noah says, ruffling the hair on the back of his head and yawning. 'Might even have changed the sheets in your honour.' He realises what he's just suggested and backtracks quickly, 'Not that you're obliged to get into my bed, obviously.'

While he makes them both tea, Lucy explains why she's visiting him at 2.15 a.m.

'And you have no idea who the intruder might be? Can't think of anyone who'd want to scare you?'

'No,' Lucy lies.

'The sensible thing would have been to call the police anyway and get them to check the place over,' Noah reproves her, handing her a mug with the teabag still in it. 'But I'm sort of glad you didn't opt for the sensible thing, or you wouldn't be here now.'

Since she has disturbed his sleep, it seems only fair to Lucy that they take their mugs through into the bedroom and lie down on either side of his bed.

'Are you sure you're all right with this?' he asks her. 'I can kip on the sofa and you can be in here: it's no problem.'

'No,' says Lucy simply. 'I'd rather not be alone.'

They finish their tea in a comfortable silence, then, as if it's the most natural thing in the world, Noah switches off the light and with the same lack of self-consciousness they roll into one another's arms. He strokes her back gently, then kisses her, and as naturally as if they've discussed it beforehand, they start to have sex. Not sleepy, 'couple' sex, but the passionate, abandoned coitus that Lucy had all but forgotten about. She allows herself a few hours of thrilling sensuality before, as the midsummer morning dawns, her mind returns inevitably to Marcus.

Noah senses the shift in her mood and, without saying anything, goes to the bathroom and showers, before coming back with a tray of orange juice and coffee.

'I've got croissants too, but you don't strike me as the sort of woman who's ever hungry before nine in the morning.'

Lucy grins. 'And the crumbs in the sheets are a nightmare.'

Noah eases himself down onto the bed beside her, looking straight ahead as he sips his coffee. 'Do you feel guilty?' he asks, as though reading her mind.

She shakes her head. What she feels, she decides once she is in her car and heading back to Barnes through rush-hour traffic, is plain old shock. Shock that she was capable of acting so sponta-neously, and enjoying it. She refused Noah's offer to come with her as a bodyguard, and in the golden light of a June morning, the house looks as benign as it ever has. She unlocks the door cautiously, having first checked it for signs of damage or forcing. There's nothing, or at least nothing that she can discern. A check of the other rooms, and all their windows, reveals nothing either.

Her jewellery is untouched on the dresser, her laptop is on her desk, and next to it her iPad. All fine. But still, something doesn't feel right.

Lucy glances at the way the iPad is positioned on her desk. Is it her imagination or has it been moved slightly? Just a centimetre or two. She opens the cover and presses the home button and it comes to life, seemingly untampered with. The truth is dawning on her, and it forces her to sit down heavily, as though winded. If there was someone in the house – and she's certain there was – then there was no breaking in. Whoever it was used a key. And if they didn't steal anything, that means they must have had a more sinister purpose.

Her mind races back to the night at the Dog and Fox. She went to the bar to get a drink of water, leaving her bag hanging over the back of the chair. Someone could have taken out her front door key and made an impression of it to use for a copy. Someone who knew just how to do such a thing.

Someone like Denny Renard.

TWENTY-FIVE

As she continues to stare warily at her iPad, the mail app bleeps with an incoming email. It's from Pink Square.

> *Hi Lucy*
>
> *We all enjoyed meeting you yesterday afternoon, and I'm delighted to tell you that we were so impressed, we'd like to offer you the position of Client Accounts Coordinator. This offer is subject to a check of your references, but I'm sure that won't be a problem. I'd be grateful if you could get back to me and let me know if you'd like to accept before the end of tomorrow. Best wishes, Ellen.*

A little shiver of pleasure and surprise runs through her, and she hugs her arms across her chest as she re-reads the email three times. Then, as if fearing it might vaporise, she hits 'reply' and types a hasty acceptance. Once it has sent, she enters a name into the search bar: *Denny Renard.*

Immediately, the search engine spits back at her: *Do you mean Denny Reynolds?*

She tries ignoring this and looking at the results for Denny Renard, but there is nothing linking those two words. She clicks on the results for Denny Reynolds instead and finds a site engineer on an oil drilling platform in Texas and a woman called Denny Reynolds in Inverness. But nobody resembling 'her' Denny emerges. Denny could be short for Dennis, so she tries Dennis Renard next, but this yields nothing of relevance. Nor does *Denny Renard Redgate.*

After making herself more coffee and some toast, Lucy sits down at her desk again. then logs onto Facebook and revisits Chelsee Watts' page. She presses 'Add friend.'

While she's waiting for a response, she fires off a text to Noah, telling him she's got the job. *And thank you for your hospitality*, she adds, with a winking emoji.

> *I knew you'd do it! And thanks for your visit ;) How are things back at the house? All okay? xx*

> *All fine. I was probably just imagining I heard someone. xx*

> *Call the police anyway, and get them to check xx*

I will, Lucy replies, though she has no intention of doing so. Because if she does, she will be forced to explain her connection to ex-convict Denny Renard and why she engaged him to illegally change her identity.

When she logs onto Facebook again twenty minutes later, Chelsee has accepted her friend request. Lucy fires off a direct message.

> Hi Chelsee, don't know if you remember me from back in the day… I've been in touch with Adele again recently, but since she gave me her number I've switched phones so I don't have a way of getting in touch with her. Can you ask her to contact me? Thanks, Lucy (Gibson).

She adds the number for her new phone at the end of the message and presses 'Send'.

There's no response to the message, but that evening, as she's going through her wardrobe and trying to assess what would constitute suitable workwear at the Pink Square Agency, her mobile rings.

'Hey. It's Adele.'

Instantly, she can picture Adele appearing at the front door of the house in Haverleigh Park, balancing the weight of her bike with her toes, her backside still on the seat. That same blend of eagerness and bullishness is discernible in her voice.

'Hi Adele, thanks for calling.'

'Why did you message me?' Her tone is distinctly wary.

'I wanted to talk to you about Denny Renard.'

There's a beat of silence. 'Why?' Adele asks coolly. 'I mean, I thought that was all over and done with now.'

'How much do you know about him?'

'Nothing, okay?' A defensive note creeps into her voice. 'Like I said, I heard of him through someone I met inside.'

'Who exactly, though?'

'She's called Pauline. Pauline something.'

'Can I talk to her?'

Adele is scornful. 'Not unless you get a visiting order from HMP Bronzefield, no: she's still inside. Anyway, why does it matter?' A distinct belligerence has crept into her manner.

'I'd rather not go into that now.' Lucy sticks to her decision not to tell Adele what Denny is up to, fearing it will only complicate matters. 'I just want any background information you can give me. Like, where does he live? And who with?'

There's another silence, longer this time. 'Sorry, but I don't know any of that stuff.'

'But can you try and find out for me? Please?'

'I'll ask around, okay? But I'm not promising anything.'

And with that, she rings off.

*

Noah is insistent that the two of them go out to celebrate her new job.

'I don't know,' Lucy prevaricates when he phones her. 'I'm not sure I want a big fuss made. Apart from anything else, I might be hopeless at it. The job, I mean.'

'Nonsense,' Noah tells her briskly. 'And I wasn't lobbying for a big fuss. Not my style. Maybe just a drink in a bar. Or two drinks, if we really decide to go wild.'

They agree to meet the following evening, at a newly opened cocktail bar in Ravenscourt Park. Despite not wanting a fuss, Lucy takes great care over her appearance, wearing a clingy top with a pleated silk skirt and high-heeled sandals. She has her hair blow-dried and spends more time than usual over her make-up. It's not a date, she tells her reflection, feeling more than a little foolish. It's too soon to be dating. But if getting all dressed up and heading to a bar to meet a man she fancies isn't a date, then what is it?

This question is still unresolved when she reaches the venue, but the expression on Noah's face when he sees her pushes it to the back of her mind.

'Wow, don't you scrub up well!' he teases. He's wearing a clean shirt but the same chinos he was wearing when she last saw him.

They sit on high stools at the bar because it somehow feels more grown-up and decadent and, as ever, the conversation flows easily.

'So, is this a date?' Noah asks eventually, as though reading her mind. His hand has strayed to the top of her thigh and rested lightly there.

'No,' says Lucy firmly, though she's smiling. 'It's not.'

'Why not? I put on a clean shirt: doesn't that qualify?'

'Because I can't do dating, not right now.' Lucy's tone becomes more serious. 'My husband only died a couple of months ago. It wouldn't be—'

'Seemly? Isn't that all a bit Jane Austen?'

'Maybe.' She shifts her leg subtly so that Noah's hand slides off. 'But it just happens to be where my head's at. For now, at least, I have to think about how this might look to people.'

He frowns, puzzled, then musters a smile and raises his Long Island iced tea. 'Well, here's to you anyway, and to your new career.'

'Thank you.' Lucy raises her mojito in return. 'And look, Noah, I'm not saying we can't see each other. But let's just keep it very low-key. Just for a bit. I'm used to being an old married woman, and this is all very unexpected and a little bit weird.'

Noah responds with a mock salute and they go back to talking about her new daily commute to work.

At the end of the evening, as they walk out into a pink summer twilight, he kisses her lightly. 'I won't ask to come back with you. On account of the not dating thing.'

At home alone, Lucy instantly regrets her puritanical approach. The house is in complete darkness, and as she approaches the front door, it looks bleak and somehow ominous. Her phone starts ringing the instant she switches on the lights in the hall. As she answers it, she's already decided that if it's Noah, she'll backtrack completely and plead with him to come over.

'Hello, sweetheart.'

'Hello?'

Lucy pulls her phone away from her ear so she can squint at the screen. 'No ID' appears where the caller's name would be.

'Don't tell me you don't recognise my voice, Blondie.'

Denny.

She feels the hairs on her bare arms stand up and her breathing quickens. 'How the hell did you get this number?' It emerges as a croak.

'Ways and means, ways and means. Because you and I, we still have a bit of business to attend to.'

'No, we do not.' Lucy tries to inject some steel into her voice, even though she feels far from steely. 'I've already made it clear:

if you want to take your so-called evidence to the police, then go ahead. In fact, if you ever call me on this number again, I'll go to them myself.'

'Aw, come on now, don't be like that. Don't spoil things.'

'What things?'

'Well, you've had such a lovely night out. And you look so pretty.'

Lucy's blood chills and her legs go soft underneath her. She clutches the back of the settle.

'I like the way that silky skirt shows off your legs. Very tasty.'

He was watching her. Following her. She pulls aside the curtain at the hall window and peers out into the street. It's almost dark, with the leaves of the plane trees casting shadows in the orange glow of the street light. Something moves into her peripheral vision, but it's just a neighbour walking her dog. Narrowing her eyes, she thinks she can make out the blurred outline of someone on the opposite pavement, but a supermarket delivery van pulls up, obscuring her view.

'Going to go upstairs to undress now, are you?' Denny asks in a low, leering voice. 'Make sure you draw the curtains; you never know when someone might be looking in.'

Lucy steps back from the window as though she's been scalded. 'Was it you?' she demands.

'Was what me?'

'Were you in my house? The other night.'

'I don't know what on earth you're talking about.' He sounds as though he's suppressing laughter. 'How can you accuse me of that? That would be a crime, wouldn't it?'

'I'm changing the locks, anyway, if you've got hold of a key somehow,' Lucy tells him defiantly.

'You want to be careful though… any lock can be picked; new or old. You were glad of my skills in that department once, remember? You wanted me to come in to your lovely house.'

'And now I want you to just leave me alone!' Lucy feels angry tears burn the back of her eyes. 'I can give you more money, if you'll just stop this. I can give you fifty thousand, but it will have to be on condition that you don't contact me again.'

For a few seconds all she can hear is his breathing. Then he gives an exaggerated sigh. 'We've been over this, Mrs Wheedon. You're going to have to do a lot better than that. I'm looking at seven figures, not five.'

'I'm sorry, but that's not possible. Be reasonable.'

'It's you that's not being reasonable. Why shouldn't you share some of your old man's wealth around. Especially as you're not on your own any longer.'

Lucy was about to cut the call, but this makes her stop in her tracks. 'What do you mean?'

'*What do you mean?*' He mimics her voice, making it high and girlish. 'I mean, you've got yourself a lovely new boyfriend. Or is he new? Maybe you had him all along, which is why you wanted rid of the crazy doctor.'

Noah. He knows about Noah.

'So, I'll give you forty-eight hours to better your offer. If you want to keep lover boy out of this.'

TWENTY-SIX

Forty-eight hours come and go, and Lucy ignores Denny's ultimatum. But then so does he. She hears nothing further from him.

Maybe he's come to his senses and realises that, legally, he's playing with fire, Lucy reflects. That he stands to get into far worse trouble with the authorities than she does. Even so, her uneasiness persists for a while, and although she has changed the locks and installed pick-proof and bump-proof German steel deadbolts, she still checks the house frequently during the night, glances over her shoulder when she heads out on foot and is wary when she unlocks the front door and comes in from the inside.

Her non-dates with Noah continue, though Lucy tries to space them several days apart and keep overnight stays to a minimum. Although they are growing closer and she trusts him, she still tells him nothing about Denny's campaign of intimidation or his blackmail attempt. Of course, she's confident that Noah would be supportive – protective even – but to pull on that particular thread would mean delving back into the dysfunction and the ugliness of her marriage to Marcus. It would reveal a side of herself she's not proud of. One she wants to leave behind. In order to do this, she resolves to put the Barnes house on the market at the end of the summer, once the schools are back. The target demographic of buyers for a property like hers are all about to depart to Salcombe, or Rock, or the Dordogne for the summer.

She desperately wishes there was someone she could confide in about all the events of the past two months, but there is no one. Jane knows some of it, but Lucy baulks at telling her about Denny's stalking. If there were someone she could talk to, they could speculate jointly about whether he is gone for good, or whether he's just biding his time. In the wakeful small hours, she even wonders if Denny has pushed some other victim too far, and ended up meeting a fitting end.

Eventually she phones Adele again.

'I was wondering if you found anything out,' she says.

'What? What do you mean?' There are muffled voices in the background and Adele sounds distracted.

'Denny Renard. Did you find out anything?'

'Oh. That.' Her voice is flat. 'No, not really,' she goes on vaguely. 'Look, sorry, but Paige has been poorly. She's been in the Royal Surrey with her asthma, so…'

'Oh. Okay. Never mind then. Hope she's better now.'

There's a taut silence, then Adele says, 'If you really want my advice, Luce, you'll forget it. Just leave well alone, eh?'

On the first of July, Lucy starts her job at Pink Square.

She struggles, at first, to get used to the physical and mental tiredness of a cross-London commute on top of an eight-hour day in an office, returning to Barnes exhausted for the first couple of weeks. She struggles, too, to master the in-house communications systems: the intranet and the diary management software and the billing. But gradually she adapts and starts to relax a little. She gets to know her colleagues, who are universally warm and friendly to her, and joins them for Friday night drinks at a pub in Clerkenwell; an outing she starts to look forward to. And her wardrobe adapts well enough to the Pink Square ethos. It's an advantage, being able to wear jeans and trainers every day rather than skirts and heels.

She cuts her hair shorter and copies the bold red lipstick the girls in the office favour, contrasting with their fresh faces. Most of them are a decade younger than she is.

'Goodness,' Jane exclaims, when they finally get round to meeting for coffee one Saturday morning. 'Aren't you quite the working girl? You look great though.'

'Thanks.' Lucy touches her bobbed hair self-consciously.

'You're moving on,' Jane is approving. 'Putting the whole Marcus… debacle behind you. Which is exactly what you need to be doing.'

Buoyed up by this positive encounter, Lucy goes to the farmers' market to buy cheeses and a big bunch of flowers, before she returns home to complete traditional weekend tasks. It's a warm sunny day, and the garden is inviting. Changing into T-shirt and shorts, she decides to tackle the weeding, taking the radio outside with her. She's singing along to 90s hits and feeling lighter of heart than she has done in months, when she gets a text.

U didn't think I'd forgotten did you

Her palms grow clammy as she stares at it. The trowel slips from her fingers and clatters onto the path at her feet. *Ignore it*, she tells herself. *That's proven to be the best way to deal with Denny Renard. Call his bluff.*

There's nothing more from him, but that evening Lucy notices a missed call from Noah. Half an hour later, she sees with dismay that it's not one missed call, but seven. At first she wonders if she's forgotten about an arrangement to meet. As far as she's aware, they are not due to see one another again until the following Thursday.

As she's about to call him back, the doorbell rings. She slots the chain into place before opening the door a crack. But it's not Denny, it's Noah.

'Can I come in? I think we need to talk.' His easy smile has vanished.

Lucy's hand instinctively goes to her mouth. She has never seen him like this before.

'What is it?' she asks, alarmed, as she removes the chain.

Noah steps inside and closes the front door behind him. 'Let's go through to the kitchen.'

He sits down at the kitchen table, but Lucy hovers. 'Can I get you anything?' she asks weakly.

He shakes his head and indicates the chair opposite him. She sinks in to it, heat thumping.

'I had a visit from a friend of yours.'

'Who?' Lucy asks, although she knows.

'He didn't give his name,' Noah says, looking down at his fingernails. 'Big guy: bit of a muscle Mary. Tatts everywhere.'

'He's not a friend of mine,' Lucy says quickly. 'I can assure you of that.'

'Associate then.' There's distaste in his voice, and the way he's now looking at Lucy makes her heart pound even harder.

She runs a quick visual scan of Noah's body, but can't see any cuts or bruises. 'He didn't hurt you?'

Noah shakes his head. 'No. But he did have some very interesting things to say.'

Lucy breathes out hard. 'Go on.'

'This thug… does he have a name?'

'Denny.'

'Denny told me that while your husband was still alive, he'd helped you out with changing your identity. New name, new life.'

There's no point in denying this, so Lucy simply nods. Behind her, the kitchen tap is dripping like a metronome. It's the only sound in the room.

'So who are you exactly? Only, I'm confused.' Noah can't keep the bitterness out of his voice. 'Are you Lucy Wheedon, or are you "Joanne"?'

Drip-drip, drip-drip.

She jumps to her feet, marches over to the tap and wrenches it closed. 'Of course I'm Lucy.' She has to consciously prevent her voice from rising hysterically. 'Marcus was controlling, abusive. I ran away from him, and yes – I paid Denny to help me.'

'How would you even know how to find someone like him?'

'I've got this childhood friend… a school friend… She was in prison for a while. She put me on to him.'

Noah is staring at Lucy as though she's a stranger, his expression bleak.

She grabs a bottle of water from the door of the fridge and gulps some down, slaking her thirst. The afternoon has become baking hot and the sun is beating in through the west-facing windows. With the water still in her hand, she comes back to the table and sits down again. 'I went away, but only for a very short time. Marcus found me. So I ended up coming back.'

Noah looks up at the ceiling, rubbing his hands over his bearded chin, then down at the floor. Anywhere but at her face. When he does look up, his hazel eyes are as hard as pebbles.

'So you came back and changed your plan. You decided that instead of divorcing your husband, like any normal person would, you'd kill him.'

'No!' Lucy slams her palms on the table, knocking over the water bottle. The contents drain out, leaving a dark stain on the wooden table top, and trickle onto the floor. There's a fraught silence as they stare at one another. 'That's not what happened. Is that what Denny told you?'

Stupid question. Of course he did.

'He told me you'd drugged your husband deliberately on a night when you knew he was planning to drive. So that he'd crash his car. Which he did.' Noah's face is stony. 'I checked the news reports.'

'Noah, for Christ's sake!' Lucy can't help but raise her voice. 'That never happened. Are you going to believe him over me? Seriously?'

'Your jailbird buddy – one of several you have, it seems – played me a recording of you saying that's what you were going to do. And he showed me texts where you plead for help in killing Marcus.'

'Denny faked those,' Lucy is aware how weak this sounds. 'Marcus's death was ruled an accident by the coroner. It was investigated properly.' Lucy feels heat burning in her neck and face, as though she's been caught in a shameful deception. 'Yes, he took sleeping tablets and alcohol, but of his own free will.'

Noah presses his fingers against his closed eyes for a second. 'So you weren't questioned by the police?' he says, when he opens his eyes again.

'Well, yes, I was, but that was a routine part of their enquiry. They talked to several of his colleagues too, and their account of his last days corroborated what happened. That Marcus was suffering from stress and behaving erratically. That his focus had gone and a couple of times he seemed drunk.'

'So you didn't take some of his temazepam tablets from the bottle and hide them then?' Noah asks, almost hopeful.

Lucy's cheeks burn. 'Okay… yes, I did. Three of them. But I didn't really know why I was doing it. And I never used them, I swear. Wait…'

She runs upstairs and comes down again with the pills, which were at the back of the spare room dresser drawer where she'd left them.

'Look,' she says, holding them out on her palm. 'I've still got them.'

Noah nods, letting out his breath as though he's been holding it.

'Trust me, Denny Renard is a real operator. An opportunist. He knows I've been left comfortably off.' She despises herself for the middle-class euphemism. 'And he's trying to extort money from me. It never occurred to me he would go to these lengths, but it's all part of his plan to wear me down. He's been stalking me, following me. And I'm so sorry you got involved. I really am.'

Noah stares back at her, clearly thinking this through. 'So was it him that was in your house that night?'

'I don't know. Probably, yes.'

'Why on earth didn't you tell me? You've never so much as mentioned any of this. Lucy, can't you see how odd it looks?'

She lets her head drop forward. 'I'd only just met you, and it was so soon after… it was only a couple of weeks after the funeral. It just seemed wrong, somehow.'

'Surely it's never wrong to share something as serious as this.' Noah lets out a long sigh. The hard glint has left his eyes now. He just looks sad.

'You can't honestly think I'm a murderer?' Lucy makes a feeble attempt at a smile. 'Me? I even put spiders out into the garden alive.'

He doesn't return her smile. 'Right now I really don't know what to think. This is a proper headfuck.'

'Are you breaking up with me?'

Noah runs his fingers through his hair, avoiding her eyes. 'Lucy. I think you're great, you know I do. But you've got to understand, this isn't the sort of thing you expect to hear about someone you're seeing.' He reaches out and covers her hand with his fingers briefly. 'I think perhaps for the moment we should cool things. Take a bit of a breather.'

She looks at him mutely, tears welling in her eyes as he repeats back to her the words she used to him on the night they met.

'I just need some time.'

TWENTY-SEVEN

AUGUST 2000

Lucy checks the screen on her brand new phone, even though she knows that this is a pointless exercise. She is one of the first girls in Year 11 to get a mobile phone of her own, but most of the others don't own one, including Holly Paterson, who she is meeting this evening. Supposed to be meeting this evening.

She's outside The Back Room, a rock music venue on the outskirts of Redgate, waiting to go and see Hot Box. The band has been hailed in the press as the UK's answer to Green Day, and are only appearing at such an unstarry venue because their pin-up of a lead singer, Travis Heyter, grew up in the area. Lucy, like thousands of girls her age, has posters of Travis Heyter on her bedroom wall. Tickets for the Redgate concert sold out within a couple of hours, but Jeffrey Gibson has managed to secure a couple through a corporate hospitality contact at work. Lucy could have found at least a dozen classmates keen to take the second ticket off her hands, but she gave first refusal to Holly, who is the nearest thing she currently has to a best friend.

It took several terms, but she eventually settled in at St Theresa's and started to thrive academically. As her confidence grew and contact lenses replaced her glasses, she began to take part in drama and sport and debating society. She has become one of the popular girls, and the Gibsons are congratulating themselves on having made the right decision over her schooling.

The gig is supposed to start at seven thirty, and at seven twenty-five there is still no sign of Holly, despite them having agreed to meet outside at seven fifteen. Lucy considers going to check the other side of the building, but what if she does so and Holly then arrives and assumes Lucy is not there? She would go into the venue and wait in her seat, except that she has Holly's ticket. The truth is, Lucy has no idea what to do. She has never been to a live music event before. Her parents would no doubt know and their numbers are programmed into her mobile phone, but they were a little reluctant to let her and Holly go out unchaperoned, so Lucy is not going to prove herself too immature by calling home for advice.

The street outside the Back Room is thronged with people; ticket holders queuing to go in, touts selling tickets, people trying to buy tickets and others – like Lucy – waiting to meet up with friends.

'Hey, sexy!'

A thickset man of about twenty spots Lucy, who is dressed in her trendiest outfit of crop top, low-slung combat trousers and wedge-heeled sandals, her pale blonde hair twisted up into a high ponytail. He's holding a bottle of lager, and is already so drunk that the contents are dribbling onto the pavement without him even noticing.

'All right, gorgeous?' says one of his friends. 'All on yer own, are you?' He nudges the first man, who stumbles towards Lucy, splashing lager onto her trouser legs. He grabs at her ponytail, and she has to step quickly backwards to avoid him pulling it.

'Give us a kiss,' says another. There are five or six in the group in total. Lucy tries to move away to another area of the pavement, but they follow her.

'Please,' she says, in a low voice. 'Just leave me alone.'

'Shouldn't go all tarted up like that if you don't want the attention,' one of them complains.

'Begging for it, if you ask me,' says another, sticking a stubby finger into her exposed navel.

Lucy pulls her mobile phone from her bag, although she is not at all sure what she is going to do with it.

'Ooh, look at her with her own phone,' one of the men says mockingly. 'Proper little princess.'

Her original tormentor tosses his lager bottle in the direction of a bin. It misses and shatters into pieces, but he ignores this and grabs Lucy round her waist. The feel of his hot, sticky hands on her skin makes her queasy and fills her with terror. Tears spring to her eyes.

'Get off,' she says in a low voice. 'Please!'

'OI!' A voice shouts from somewhere to her left. 'GET YOUR FILTHY FUCKING HANDS OFF HER!'

The voice is vaguely familiar and so is the person it belongs to, despite the heavily kohled eyes and sandy hair knotted into cornrows. It's Adele Watts.

The men swivel their heads and look at Adele with disdain, but she lunges forward and slaps the one pawing Lucy hard with the flat of her hand, before grabbing the belt loop of his jeans and dragging him away. Inebriated and unsteady, he loses his footing and crashes to the ground. One of his friends reaches for her, but she digs long, neon-painted talons into the flesh of his cheek.

'Little bitch!'

'Well, if you don't like it, piss off out of here!' Adele snarls. 'My uncle's one of the bouncers; want to talk to him about it, do you?'

Grumbling, the men shamble away.

'All right, Luce?' says Adele with her customary nonchalance. 'Long time no see.'

When you smoked a cigarette outside my house and left the butt on the driveway, Lucy thinks. 'Thanks,' she mutters to Adele, not quite able to make eye contact. 'I'm supposed to be going to the gig, but my friend isn't here yet.'

'Well, they'd better hurry up; it's about to start. I just came down on the off-chance there'd be a spare ticket. I'd fucking kill to see Hot Box.' She realises what she has said and flushes slightly.

'I'm sure she'll be here any second,' Lucy says, looking around desperately.

'This one of your mates from your posh new school?' Adele asks.

'Yes. Holly. Holly Paterson.' She's not quite sure why she's giving the full name, except that it lends credence to her waiting there on her own.

The crowd is thinning now; touts have sold their last remaining tickets and nearly everyone has headed into the venue. It's seven fifty.

'I'll wait with you if you like,' Adele says, pushing her fists into the pockets of her denim jacket. She's wearing a tiny fake-leather miniskirt and Timberland boots.

'There's no need, really: I'm sure she's on her way.' Of course, Lucy isn't sure of this at all. In fact, she's now convinced that, for whatever reason, Holly isn't coming.

'Tell you what, why don't you go in, and I'll wait here with her ticket. What does she look like?'

'Um, she's about an inch shorter than me, dark hair cut in a bob. With a fringe. Wearing white jeans.'

Still unsure of the merits of this plan, Lucy heads inside on her own and finds her way to her seat. The house lights are down, and there is an expectant tension in the air. Pink and purple strobes flicker across the darkness of the stage, making the audience gasp. Then the first few bars of 'Bandage My Heart', Hot Box's biggest hit, are sounded out on a bass guitar, and there are a few muted screams. People in front of Lucy stand up, and she is forced to stand too, so that she can still see the stage.

As the lead guitar strikes up, the audience response becomes deafening, and Lucy is only vaguely aware of someone saying something in her ear. She turns to see Adele.

'I don't think your friend's coming,' she mouths above the din. 'Sorry.'

Lucy shrugs, but there's no time to reflect on Holly's absence or debate whether Adele should have waited longer, because a spotlight flashes on, revealing Travis Heyter in all his glory. His shirt is open to the navel, revealing tanned abdominal muscles, his shoulder-length hair sun-bleached like a surfer's.

'My God,' Adele groans, 'will you bloody look at him!'

'I know,' Lucy breathes. 'He's a total god.'

When he starts to sing, the rapture in the audience reaches fever pitch, and Lucy is so electrified with excitement, she feels faint and has to clutch at Adele. The two of them link arms and jump up and down, squealing in unison as 'Bandage My Heart' reaches its crescendo, then segues into dance number 'Teflon Girl'. Adele stumbles into the aisle and drags Lucy after her.

'Is this allowed?' Lucy mouths, but Adele ignores her protest and soon others have joined them, dancing until they're pouring sweat. Lucy has never known a feeling like it, the dopamine hit that courses through her body in a chemical expression of joy, making her more wired, more alive, than she's ever felt. She grins at Adele and Adele grins back, and their dancing gets so wild that they start to laugh and don't stop for the next forty minutes. Holly, who Lucy will later discover had to go to hospital with a dental abscess, is completely forgotten.

'That was completely brilliant,' Adele sighs, as they're carried outside by the surging crowd, arms linked.

'Best night of my life,' sighs Lucy.

'You know…' Adele pauses on the pavement, suddenly serious, '… what happened?'

She means Joanne's death. Lucy nods.

'You didn't tell anyone?'

'Of course not. I promised, didn't I?'

Adele seems satisfied with this. She pops a piece of chewing gum into her mouth before giving a casual wave and turning away. 'Laters then. Thanks for the ticket.'

Lucy thinks about that night, and how much fun it was for a long time. It seems Adele has been thinking about it too, because a few nights later, as the Gibsons are sitting down for supper, the front doorbell rings. Felicity Gibson goes to answer it and has a brief exchange with someone; someone female.

'Anything important?' Jeffrey enquires mildly as Felicity returns to the table and slides her linen napkin back onto her lap.

'It was the Watts girl,' Felicity says tersely. 'Let's just say I wasn't going to encourage her.'

'Mum!' Lucy puts down her fork. 'You should have told me. I would have liked to speak to her at least.'

'No, darling,' Felicity shakes her head firmly, 'that would not have been a good idea. Trust me: this is for the best.'

TWENTY-EIGHT

In the two weeks that follow, Lucy is deeply grateful that she has a job.

It allows her to fill her days and slump at home exhausted in the evenings, leaving little time to dwell on the rapid demise of her relationship with Noah. After he left her house, she texted him to apologise for Denny's harassment, which was the only thing she could think of to do. After twenty-four hours, she received a two-word reply: *Take care x* – the digital equivalent of a door slamming in her face.

She soon falls into a pattern of extending her working day little by little, until she's arriving in the office soon after eight and rarely leaving much before seven. With no partner or children to go home to, this represents displacement activity rather than dedication. Even so, she makes it her business to learn about every client and every project on Pink Square's books, quickly becoming indispensable. Lucy has become the co-worker that others can turn to when they're stuck or under particular pressure.

One morning in August Megan appears at her desk. It's still only 8.45, but Lucy is already onto her second coffee of the day.

'Oh, Lucy, you're here, thank God.'

Lucy gives her the bright, professional smile she has been cultivating, while continuing to update a budget spreadsheet. 'Morning. How can I help?'

'Ari was supposed to go and visit a potential new client, but his little boy fell out of a tree and fractured his collarbone yesterday and he can't come in…' She tilts her head to one side, pleading. 'If I give you a copy of his background brief, do you think you could go and talk to them? It's just a question of getting a feel for what they want in an agency, and the sort of work they need, and then we can get the creative team working on a formal pitch.' Megan shrugs her shoulders and gives a helpless smile. 'I'd go myself obviously, but I've got a funding meeting with St Michael's Hospice and it can't really be moved.'

'Sure,' Lucy says. 'No problem at all.'

And so she finds herself catching a train down to Beckenham to talk to the staff of the Starflower Trust – a homeless charity. It feels good to have a challenge to rise to, and she establishes a good rapport with Nick Dalgliesh, the charity's director. Even the process of writing up her notes for the creative team is enjoyable, and she stays in the office until 9 p.m. For once she falls into bed without wondering whether she should text Noah again or checking three times that the front door is locked securely.

A few days later, Megan seeks her out again.

'Lucy, we've got the Starflower Trust coming in to hear our pitch this afternoon, and since you made the initial contact with them, we thought you should sit in on the meeting. About three o'clock?'

'Of course,' Lucy says briskly, 'I'd be happy to.'

Nick Dalgliesh greets her warmly when she arrives in the meeting room a few hours later, clutching a copy of her notes and some hastily scribbled ideas in case she's asked for contributions to the potential marketing campaign. He introduces her to his creative director Andrea Morris and a junior account executive called Karl, who looks about nineteen. Pink Square's creative team make their presentation and Lucy chips in a few thoughts in the subsequent discussion, although she's self-conscious about doing so and feels her cheeks colouring slightly when the attention of the entire room is focused on her.

'Lucy's our in-house expert when it comes to factors influencing homelessness,' Ari quips. 'She's got a master's degree from UCL to prove it.'

Pippa, the receptionist taps lightly on the glass door. 'Lucy, there's someone here to see you.'

She frowns. 'I'm not expecting anyone… can you tell them I'm in a meeting?'

Pippa lowers her voice slightly. 'I've tried, but he's refusing to go.'

Once again all the eyes in the room are on Lucy, only this time their gaze is curious rather than admiring. The colour in her cheeks intensifies to a deep flush.

'Whoever it is will just have to—' And then she sees the looming figure behind Pippa, bulky and ominous. Denny. He's wearing a baseball cap with the logo 'WARNING: OFFENSIVE' on the brim, and a sleeveless T-shirt that exposes his overworked muscles. He eases Pippa out of the way as if she was a tiny child and reaches for the half-open door. A wolf in wolf's clothing.

Lucy pushes her chair back so fast that the legs make a squeal on the polished floor.

'You'll have to excuse me,' she says quickly, hurrying out of the room and closing the door firmly behind her. 'It's okay, Pippa, I'll deal with this.'

She walks briskly back towards reception, hoping that Denny will follow her. He does so, but only after her colleagues have had the chance to take a good look at him and he's treated them all to one of his signature leers.

'What the fuck are you doing here?' she hisses, keeping her voice as low as she can manage.

Denny waves around the open-plan office space, where heads are peering surreptitiously from behind computer monitors. 'This is your place of work, a place of business. And you and I have business to discuss, don't we, darling? Like the new hairdo, by the way. Very sexy.'

Behind him, Pippa – now back behind the desk – is trying to catch her eye. '*Shall I call security?*' she mouths, picking up the phone handset and waggling it. The commercial block that houses Pink Square is home to various businesses and their lease agreements include the services of an on-site security guard. Most of the time, he loiters in the lobby, checking security passes and directing pedestrian traffic.

Lucy gives Pippa the most discreet of nods but not discreet enough to go unnoticed.

'Getting me chucked out, are you? That's not very nice.' Denny lowers himself into an armchair and blocks most of the reception area with his huge legs.

'I'm sorry, but you can't be here.' Lucy folds her arms across her chest to make herself seem in charge, but her heart is beating wildly, and she's overwhelmed with relief when the lift doors slide open and Lewis, the security guard, steps out. While not as sinewy as Denny, he's at least 6'5" and works part-time as a nightclub bouncer.

'All right, all right, mate!' Denny throws up his hands in mock surrender. 'I'm going.'

He pauses at the lift and looks back at Lucy. 'I'll see *you* later.'

When the meeting's over, the Pink Square staff treat their guests to drinks at a bar round the corner on Leonard Street. Ari orders several bottles of chilled cava, and once glasses are filled and bowls of olives and cheese straws handed round, the atmosphere becomes relaxed and convivial.

'It went well,' Megan whispers to Lucy, giving her a discreet thumbs up. 'I think they like us and they were definitely impressed with the presentation. So thanks for your input.'

'No problem at all,' Lucy smiles. 'I was glad to help. And I rather enjoyed being thrown in at the deep end.'

Megan refills Lucy's glass, and then her own. 'There's not much wiggle room on your salary, but Ari and I were discussing the possibility of revising your role slightly. If this goes the way we want it to.' She holds up her crossed fingers again, glancing across the table. 'Nick certainly appreciates you,' she adds with a smirk.

After three bottles have been emptied, the conversation becomes louder and more animated. Nick Dalgliesh waves over a waiter to order some more. 'Our round this time,' he grins. 'We've got to show we can keep up with you creative folk… Oh. Can I help you?'

Lucy follows Nick's gaze. Instead of a member of the wait staff appearing at his elbow, Denny stands there, feet splayed, hands thrust into the pockets of his tracksuit bottoms.

'Room for a small one?' he says, with a mocking grin. 'Don't mind if I do.' Ignoring the nonplussed expressions of the group, he settles himself down on a spare chair, opposite Lucy, who is too shocked to react. 'Sorry, better introduce myself since Lucy here's not going to. I'm a good friend of hers. Denny Renard. Nice to meet you folks.'

There are puzzled glances, several pairs of eyes moving from Denny's 'WARNING: OFFENSIVE' hat to Lucy's blonde, Home Counties wholesomeness.

Another bottle appears on the table in an ice bucket and, without asking, Denny grabs it by the neck, spraying drips of water everywhere as he pours himself a brimming glass. 'Cheers!'

Both Pink Square and Starflower Trust employees look on in strained silence. Her face burning, Lucy tries to speak, but she's trapped in the role of observer, as though this is happening to someone else.

'Nice to see little Lucy here fitting in so well, I must say.' Denny slurps his cava noisily, then wipes his mouth with his hand. 'You wouldn't think to look at her that she was fingered by the pigs for murdering her old man.'

Lucy's limbs abruptly turn numb. She attempts to shrug her shoulders and make light of this statement but ends up looking as though she's having a seizure. All eyes are on her now and her cheeks blaze scarlet. 'That's ridiculous. I think you should leave.'

Nick's colleague Andrea reaches for her handbag. 'Nick, I think maybe it's time we all—'

'It's true you know. Her husband was loaded, you see, and then he went and died in suspicious circumstances just after Lucy here decided she was leaving him. High levels of sleeping pills in his blood. Pills she admitted to taking from his supply.'

Megan and Ari exchange appalled glances.

Ari reaches over and touches Denny on the shoulder. 'Mate, I think you should go.'

But Denny swats him away, still warming to his theme. 'She's got a whole other identity too; did you know that? Passport, driving licence – all forged. In the name of one Joanne…' he stresses the word heavily, 'Chandler.'

Ellen makes a small, gasping sound.

The colour drains from Lucy's face, and saliva pools in her throat, making her feel as though she's drowning. 'No,' she shakes her head. 'Absolutely not. This is rubbish.'

'You're surely not going to deny it, Lucy? Because that would mean telling all these nice people lies, wouldn't it?'

Ari has stood up and is looking around for a member of the bar's staff.

'It's okay,' Lucy says, getting to her feet too, gripping the arm of her chair because her legs are shaking. 'You guys stay here. I'm going.'

Clearing her throat, she shoulders her bag and hurries towards the front door. She avoids eye contact with Denny but can't help but see his feral grin as she passes him.

Once out on the pavement, she looks back through the window and sees the bar manager and one of the waiters manhandling him away from her colleagues. But it's too late; she knows that. The damage has been done.

TWENTY-NINE

It's no surprise when, as soon as Lucy arrives at work the following morning, Megan calls her into her office for 'a little chat'. In fact, it's something of a relief. She'd rather deal with yesterday's events head-on than be the subject of office Chinese whispers.

'I'm not sure exactly what was going on yesterday,' Megan begins, indicating that Lucy should sit in the chair opposite her desk. She looks embarrassed, fiddling with the chunky green beads round her neck. 'Obviously everyone's entitled to a private life, but when it spills over into a work event, especially one where clients are present, it's a little… unfortunate.'

Does she think Denny is a spurned lover? Lucy wonders with horror.

'I need to explain,' she says quickly. 'He – Denny – he isn't a friend. Barely even an acquaintance. He's… I suppose you could say he's a stalker.'

Megan's face registers alarm. 'Have you contacted the police about this?'

'Well, no, I—'

'Surely you should? Surely that's the first thing anyone would do? I know *I* would.' She holds out her hands and splays her fingers, as if trying to keep such unpleasantness at bay.

'It's… it's a little more complicated than that.'

'So you do know him? This man.'

Lucy nods.

'And what he was saying about your husband's death?' Megan twists hard at her necklace.

'It's not true, obviously,' Lucy says quickly. 'Marcus died in a car crash while over the alcohol limit: that's a matter of public record. I spoke to the police, of course, to help them establish the facts, but that's all.'

'So all that other stuff he said… you don't have a forged passport in another name?'

Lucy could tell a bare-faced lie. She could tell Megan that this piece of information is fabricated too. But the problem is, she's a terrible liar. She has never been able to pass off even the most innocuous fib without blushing or some sort of giveaway facial tic. 'No,' she says. 'I mean, no, that's not made up. I do have a passport in the name of Joanne Chandler… Like I said, it's complicated.'

Megan raises her eyebrows slightly and looks round the room as though expecting someone else to tell her what to do next. She's clearly out of her depth now. 'I see.'

Lucy looks down at her hands. 'I really am sorry. It's embarrassing.'

'So… moving forward, we have to think about the Starflower Trust account. Assuming we're still lucky enough to be considered, after the… after what happened last night. If we are, I'll need to be able to reassure Nick Dalgliesh that we are capable of giving him a thoroughly professional service. So I'll have to tell him you're no longer slated to work on their account. I hope you understand.'

'Yes,' Lucy sighs. She had expected nothing less.

'And just until we can be sure that there are no more incidents like yesterday's, I think it would be best if you work from home for the time being.'

'Is that really necessary?' Lucy asks desperately. Leaving the house every day, chatting with her colleagues, even the hassle of the commute – they have all been part of her survival, her reinvention. She no longer even has Noah's company to distract her from herself. 'It won't ever happen again; I promise.'

But she knows she's in no position to make this guarantee and, what's more, so does Megan.

'I'm sorry, but we believe it is necessary.' Megan hides behind the corporate plural but does at least look genuinely sorry. 'IT will show you how to set up the mail server and the intranet on your own laptop. It won't be much different from being here. And,' She attempts a smile, 'I'm sure the coffee will be better.'

'How long will this be for?' Lucy is aware she sounds desperate. Because working from home will be different. It will be a whole world of different.

'Hopefully not long. Let's see how things go.'

It could have been worse, Lucy tells herself as she catches the tube home. *I could have been sacked.*

And on her first morning of working in her own house, it doesn't feel too bad. It's quite nice to lie in bed with a cup of tea until eight, and then wander down to her desk dressed in her pyjama bottoms. She can throw open the doors onto the lavender-scented garden and almost believe she's on holiday.

But this novelty is short-lived. She receives a few emails, with sundry queries to answer, but as these problems are resolved one by one, the communication starts to dry up. And Lucy is no longer there in the office to pick up new tasks and enquiries to tackle. She's not part of the conversation. Does it really matter if she's emailed to ask her vote for either sandwich lunch or hot buffet for the monthly accounts meeting, if she's not even going to be there? Within a few days she has become redundant, in all senses of the word.

After two weeks of haunting her own house like an underemployed ghost, with nothing to do beyond answering a few emails each day, she smartens herself up and takes the tube to Old Street to visit the office. Heads turn as she walks in, and her co-workers give her awkward little smiles before returning to staring at their screens.

Lucy taps on the open door to Megan's office.

'Lucy… hi!' Megan pauses midway between desk and filing cabinet. 'Do we have a meeting?'

'No, I just thought I'd pop in for a quick chat.'

'Sure.' Megan smiles, but it doesn't quite make it all the way to her eyes.

'I've got to be honest, Megan, I'm finding this working at home thing tough. I just don't have enough to do. So I was wondering if we could set an end date on it. Maybe the end of next week? Or the week after.'

There's a heavy pause. 'We didn't get the Starflower Trust account,' Megan says eventually. 'They assured us it was nothing to do with what happened over drinks, but—'

'So can I come back?'

Megan rubs her forehead. 'Lucy, I'm afraid it's not that simple. We had another visit from him today. From your acquaintance.'

'From Denny?' Lucy repeats stupidly.

'Yes. Now, I'm bound to say, he didn't make any trouble. He asked for you, and once he knew you weren't here, he left peaceably enough. But the visit was unsettling for your colleagues, you have to understand that.'

'Yes.' Lucy feels an acid surge of panic curdling her insides. 'Yes, but—'

'Now that he knows you're working at home, and not here, hopefully that will be the end of it.'

'You told him that?' Lucy's voice rises to a squeak.

It's Megan's turn to look disturbed. 'Sorry, should I not have done that? We didn't give him your address or anything; we'd never give out an employee's personal information. Only we didn't want him making further visits to the office.'

'No,' Lucy says heavily, standing up. 'No it's all right. He already knows where I live anyway.'

The text comes first.

you lost yr boyfriend and now you lost yr job

Strictly speaking this isn't true: Lucy is still on the payroll of The Pink Square Agency. She ignores it, which she knows will prompt a further message. Sure enough, it arrives ten minutes later.

never mind you've still got all that lovely wonga

Her mobile rings with a withheld number, once, twice, a dozen times or more. She turns off the sound, but still the calls keep coming every few seconds, so she switches it off altogether. Tomorrow she will have to go and buy a new mobile phone; her fifth in as many months if she counts the handset Denny gave her. The landline starts ringing next, over and over until she's forced to unplug it. She phones the locksmith who fitted her super-strong German locks and pleads for reassurance: are they absolutely sure that they can't be picked or forced? Could they send someone round to check, and to fit an additional bolt, just in case?

The next day is a bad day. There are far worse to come, but as yet Lucy has no way of knowing this. You believe you've hit the bottom, until you fall still further.

After another frustrating eight hours of sitting watch over an inert email inbox, she decides she needs to do something physically active. Something that will exhaust her and help her to sleep. It's a sultry, humid August evening, but she changes into running shorts and sports bra, sets her phone to flight mode and plugs in her headphones, then heads at a slow jog along Lonsdale Road and

towards the river. Lost in her playlist, and without really think-
ing about an end destination, she ends up crossing the bridge to
Hammersmith. She's pounding along the Thames path past the
Blue Anchor when she sees him.

The pub's terrace is thronged with people, as it is every summer
evening, so at first Lucy's not entirely sure from the brief glimpse of
the side of his head. But when she glances back over her shoulder, she
catches him in profile and then she is sure. It's Noah, and he's with a girl.

She takes in details, like pieces of a jigsaw puzzle. Petite frame,
auburn hair and freckles. Huge sunglasses that don't leave much
face visible, tight jeans, a low-cut top and high cork wedges. The
girl is hanging onto Noah's arm, tilting her face up to his and
laughing. And Lucy knows instinctively from the tension in his
neck that he's seen her too but is pretending that he hasn't. With
her stomach churning queasily, she dips her head and runs on,
making sure to take a different route back to the bridge.

Showered, and with a fishbowl-size glass of chilled Sauvignon
Blanc in her hand, she hears her mother's voice in her head: *'If he
could move on that easily, then he wasn't for you anyway, darling.'*

She knows this is true, and yet it's hard to completely override
the feelings of rejection. Of humiliation. Then it occurs to her
that the unexpected sighting might have prompted Noah to get
in touch. She switches her phone out of flight mode, but there are
no messages from him. Only another twenty-seven missed calls
from Denny Renard, and one text.

you can't keep on avoiding me I know where u live, remember

Once she has drunk most of the bottle of white wine, Lucy
double-bolts the front door and locks the security grilles before
retiring upstairs.

Strange, illogical dreams assail her as soon as she's asleep: dreams of cooking in the kitchen of Noah's flat and him becoming angry with her because she keeps burning the bacon they're supposed to be eating for breakfast. It doesn't matter how many times she tries again with fresh rashers it still manages to burn.

Burning…

Her eyes fly open and the smell bridges dream and reality. The smell of smoke. And a distinctive sound: that of the letter box thumping shut. She rushes to the landing and sees it immediately on the hall floor: an orange ball of flame. A livid scorch mark is lapping the wooden floorboards and the acrid smoke from the varnish hits the smoke alarm sensor, making it screech at an unbearable pitch.

Lucy freezes to the spot. Are you supposed to open doors and windows or close them in a fire? She knows the answer to this question, but her brain is dulled by the screaming alarm and refuses to dredge up the answer. There is a fire extinguisher somewhere in the house, but she can't remember where that is either. She closes her eyes momentarily trying to picture it. First aid kit. It's near the first aid kit. Which is in the utility room cupboard.

Taking the stairs two at a time, she runs to the utility room and finds the extinguisher. Tries to read the instructions but can't without her contacts in. A vague memory of a fire safety drill at St Theresa's comes back to her: Pull the pin, keep the nozzle down, aim at the base of the fire.

The cloud of chemicals smothers the flames with astonishing speed, leaving a fog of unpleasant-smelling vapour hanging in the air. Lucy opens the front door to let in a draught, and a few seconds later, the fire alarm eventually stops its distracting racket.

Setting down the fire extinguisher, she drops to her knees to inspect the damage. The wooden floor is indelibly marked and an area a metre square will need to be replaced. The pile of sodden ash is more or less all that remains of whatever was put through the letter box. Except for one piece of paper that was not quite destroyed and which reveals the fragment of an all-too-familiar image.

Lucy picks it up and examines it. It's a photocopy of her counterfeit passport. There's her own headshot, blonde and blandly smiling, above the name 'Joanne Louise Chandler'. And handwritten underneath it in heavy black marker are three letters: *R.I.P.*

THIRTY

'Hold on… so let me get try and get this straight.'

After waiting for an hour and a half at Roehampton Police Station, Lucy is finally sitting down in front of a young plain-clothes officer: DC Dale Andrewes. He's black, good-looking and has intricate and well-trimmed facial hair.

'This is you?' He points at the photo on the fragment of burned paper. The image, now in a clear plastic evidence bag, is barely discernible,

'Yes.'

'But you're saying you're not Joanne Chandler?' He looks down at the form passed to him by the desk sergeant. 'You're Lucinda Wheedon?'

'Yes.'

'So this is not copied from your actual passport?'

'No.'

'You'll have to forgive me if I'm confused… why is your photo on a counterfeit passport? Were you the one who made this document?'

'No, that was the man who set the copy on fire and shoved it through my letter box. He's called Denny Renard. Well, that's the name he gave. I'm not sure it's his real one.'

DC Andrewes gives her a searching look, taking in her pink Reiss linen dress, her expensive handbag, her manicured nails. 'Mrs

Wheedon, are you aware that this –' he waves at the evidence bag – 'is a copy of what in legal terms is known as a false instrument?'

'I've never actually used it,' Lucy says quickly. 'And I don't intend to: I'll happily bring the original down to the police station and hand it in.'

'Even having it in your possession is an offence under the Forgery and Counterfeiting Act. Carries a penalty of up to two.' When he sees Lucy's bewildered expression, he adds helpfully, 'Years in prison.'

She takes a deep breath. 'I'm aware there are consequences, yes. I can only tell you I bought it because my… because I was desperate. I was experiencing extreme domestic violence.'

'I see.' He looks down at a manila file on the desk in front of him. 'And this was at the hands of your husband? The eminent heart surgeon who wrapped his car round a tree? I've got a copy of the statement you made at the time of that incident.' Aware that he is sounding callous, Andrewes adds, 'You've clearly had a very difficult few months.'

'Yes,' says Lucy. 'And it's not over. Denny – the one who got me the passport – he's been blackmailing me since my husband died. Well, trying to.'

'I hope you've not given him any money?'

She shakes her head firmly. 'No. And I don't intend to.' She thinks about the fifty thousand pounds she offered Denny to leave her alone, but decides not to mention it, or the audiotape he made of her conspiring to murder, but which she currently can't prove exists. 'He's started a campaign of harassment. Phone calls, texts, showing up at my place of work.'

'I don't suppose you happen to know his address?' Andrewes turns to the computer terminal on his desk and enters a login.

'No, I'm afraid not. I think he's based somewhere in the Redgate area – in Surrey – but I'm not one hundred per cent certain.'

'And his date of birth… I don't suppose you know that?'

Lucy shakes her head. 'I'd say he was somewhere between late thirties and early forties. White. Caucasian.'

'We'll test the paper for DNA, but I think that the fire's probably destroyed anything viable…' He starts tapping a series of keys. 'I've got no one under the name of Denny Renard – or Dennis – on the PNC.' He taps some more. 'Or the DVLA database.'

Lucy frowns. 'So what should I do now?'

'I'll make some more enquiries, but in the meantime we can't do anything about the stalking without hard evidence. I need you to log every incident that happens from now on. Keep screenshots of texts and missed-call notifications.'

'I plan to change my mobile number. Again.'

'Good: do that. And keep a record of anything suspicious that comes through your door. And obviously if "Renard",' he makes air quotes, 'turns up in person, at your house or anywhere else, then you must phone us straight away. And by that, I mean phone 999.'

Lucy nods slowly, shouldering her bag and standing up. 'What about the passport? And I also have a driving licence in the same name.'

'Bring them here to me,' DC Andrewes stands up and proffers a hand. 'But I'm afraid I can't rule out the possibility of you being charged.'

Lucy sucks in her breath and holds it there until her sternum begins to hurt. She looks across the desk at Andrewes and her words tumble out with the gush of her exhalation. 'Honest to God, the way I feel right now…'

The past two days unspool in her head like video tape. Her rampant insomnia, her terror every time footsteps behind her on the street get too close, her heart leaping from her chest at every moving shadow. DC Andrewes has never met her before and therefore doesn't know that these pink-rimmed eyes and these patches of scaly eczema all over her arms are not normal. That this dress now hanging loosely used to fit her snugly round the waist.

'…Prison would be the better option. At least I'd be safe there.'

Dale Andrewes manages a smile. 'I doubt very much it would come to that. Even if your case is passed to the CPS, which isn't all that likely… well, pleading guilty, first time offence, combined with you never actually using the documents, and the mitigation of spousal abuse… you'd be looking at a fine, and maybe community service. Suspended sentence at the very worst.'

A thought occurs to Lucy. 'What if I do some digging and try to find more about Renard? Someone recommended him after all: somebody must know something.'

'If you come up with any new information, then please get in touch with me straight away.' Andrewes reaches in a back pocket and hands her one of his business cards. 'But – please – your priority is to remain safe. My advice would be to go and stay with a friend or a relative for a bit. Get away from it all.' He comes round the desk to open the door of the interview room for her, adding as he closes it behind her: 'This man is clearly dangerous.'

Lucy is only too happy to take police advice.

She emails Megan, saying she plans to take a few days off, painfully aware that since her exile, her absence won't make any difference to her colleagues at the agency. Then she phones Jeffrey and tells him she is coming to visit. It occurs to her that she should stay the night at his bungalow, but she is simply too tired. She can't face the probing, the enquiries about the happenings of recent weeks, the need for an update on her new career at Pink Square. So her father's offer of a bed is politely declined and instead she books herself in to the Eastland Manor Hotel, some five miles from Redgate. Any rising guilt over splurging on a large suite for herself is quickly quashed. She's earned a break.

For a couple of hours after she arrives at the hotel, Lucy treats herself to the luxury of doing nothing. She switches off her phone (reminding herself once again that she should arrange to change the number), then runs a foamy bath and soaks in it until the water starts to grow too cool for comfort. The television stays on at low volume, broadcasting inane daytime TV, because silence is still a threatening commodity. Once she has dressed and dried her hair, she calls in at the farm shop adjacent to the hotel and buys a home-made fruit cake, some jam and a selection of cheeses before driving to the bungalow. *This will be perfectly safe*, she reassures herself, since no one knows that she's here. Jeffrey has never been entirely robust since the stroke but is in good spirits and seems genuinely pleased to receive an impromptu visit from his only child. Nevertheless, Lucy can only distract him for so long with gifts of food before the questions start.

'You're not ill?' he asks. He uses the pad of his finger to pick up the remaining crumbs of fruit cake on his plate, licking them off with the lack of self-consciousness of someone who's used to living alone. 'Only, I must say you're looking awfully thin, darling.'

'I'm fine, just tired. Which is why I've taken a day or two off work.'

'So to what do I owe this honour? Is there some other reason you're in the area?'

Lucy shakes her head. 'I've had so little time to myself since I started work… I just thought it was high time I came to see you.'

This is true, of course, but it's not her only reason for returning to Redgate. There's someone else she needs to see; the one person she can turn to for help.

Once she's back in her hotel suite, she switches on her mobile and calls Adele's number.

THIRTY-ONE

'No.' Adele speaks with a lack of interest that borders on rudeness. 'We can't get together today.'

'Tomorrow then,' Lucy says, trying to keep her tone bright, trying not to come across as manipulative. Not that Adele has ever been someone she could manipulate. 'Please. It need only be for ten minutes.'

Adele gives an exaggerated sigh. 'It's the school bleedin' holidays, in case you hadn't noticed. I'm stuck with the kids round my ankles all day.'

'That's fine. We could go somewhere where they can play, and that will leave you and I free to talk.'

'Places like that cost money. Especially this time of year.'

'That's no problem,' Lucy tells her briskly. 'It'll be my treat.'

There's a brief pause while Adele thinks this over. 'The kids do love Hazelwood World of Adventure.' She names a petting zoo and play centre on the far side of the ring road. 'It's pricey though; just warning you.'

So they meet in the car park at Hazelwood at eleven o'clock the following morning. Adele is in a grey velour leisure suit, worn with chunky silver trainers and huge silver hoop earrings; Paige and Skye are in matching pink tracksuits. They take the girls to pet the goats, and feed the guinea pigs and rabbits, then Lucy buys them milkshakes and burgers.

'They'll be wanting sweeties too,' Adele warns her, so Lucy buys them each a bag of acid-bright pick 'n' mix. There was heavy rain overnight and everywhere is still soaked, but she and Adele settle themselves at a picnic table while the children tackle the play equipment, fuelled by their sugar rush and still clutching their packets of candies in their small fists. Lucy has coffee in front of her, Adele a pint of lager and a cigarette.

'I need to talk to you about Denny. I know, I know…' Lucy holds up her hands defensively. 'Again.'

Adele sticks out her chin, tapping a tube of embers into the ashtray. 'I don't know anything else, okay? I asked but, honest, I've not found out anything.'

'The thing is…' Lucy pauses while she wonders how best to describe Denny's campaign. 'Since Marcus died, he's been stalking me. And blackmailing me.'

Adele raises her eyebrows. But she doesn't look shocked, or even surprised.

'He's claiming to have evidence that I plotted to kill my husband. Which is blatantly ridiculous.'

'Is it though?' Adele sucks in a mouthful of nicotine and releases it through the side of her mouth with a little puffing sound. 'I mean, when I read in the papers what had happened – that your old man had died suddenly – that was my first thought.'

'Seriously?' Lucy grins at the absurdity of the suggestion. 'You've known me since I was eleven, and you thought I was capable of murder?'

'You came to me in the first place because you wanted rid of the arsehole, remember?' Adele's tone is smug. 'You wanted rid, and then, hey presto, he's dead. Bit convenient, isn't it?' Her attention moves to the play area, where Skye has just pushed Paige off the monkey bars. 'Oi, Skye! Be careful with your sister: she's been very poorly, remember!'

'Okay, I can see why you might think that,' Lucy admits reluctantly. 'But the fact remains, Marcus's death was an accident.'

'If that's the case you've got nothing to worry about.' Adele drains the last of her lager and lights another cigarette.'

'Denny tried to set fire to my house,' Lucy says, quelling rising impatience. 'So, with all due respect, I would say that I have plenty to worry about. I really need to track him down, so I was going to try and speak to your mutual friend… Pauline was it?'

'That's right.' Adele narrows her eyes as she sucks on the filter of her cigarette.

'And her surname? If I've got that, and the name of the prison, I can apply for a visiting order, and—'

'She won't give you it,' Adele says brusquely.

'Tell me her name, anyway.'

'Jennings or Jenkins. Can't remember which.'

Lucy sighs. 'I don't suppose there's any way of finding out?'

'I could maybe ask Jamil. He might know.'

Adele holds up her empty beer glass to indicate that another pint will help with this process. Sighing, Lucy peels herself off the damp wooden bench and goes back into the cafeteria. When she emerges again with a second glass of lager, Adele has her back turned. She's talking into her mobile in a low, urgent voice.

'No, no, of course I haven't!' she hisses. 'What kind of a fucking moron do you think I am?' Glancing over her shoulder, Adele catches sight of Lucy watching her and lowers her voice so that her end of the conversation becomes inaudible. When she hangs up and walks back towards Lucy, she's frowning.

'Everything okay?' Lucy hands her the lager.

'Yeah. Some people are dickheads, that's all.' She attempts a smile. Lucy suddenly remembers her saying that she was seeing someone on the night that they first met up at the Dog and Fox.

'Boyfriend trouble?'

'Yeah, you could say that.' Adele stands up and waves at her daughters. 'Girls! Come on – we're going now.'

'I was hoping you might be asking your brother. About Pauline, I mean.'

Adele shakes her head. 'Afraid not. That was a different dickhead.' The girls trudge over to the picnic table, their sugar high and overexertion making them suddenly lethargic. 'I really need to get these two back. Okay if you give us a lift?'

'Sure.'

'You two thank your Auntie Lucy for a lovely day, okay?'

'Thank you,' the girls chorus, and Skye adds 'Can you buy me a pet guinea pig?'

'They've had a lovely time,' Adele says as they walk back to the car park. She gives Lucy the familiar grin of old. 'And I will ask about Pauline for you, I promise.'

'I'm glad you've come in: I was about to phone you.'

The following afternoon, Lucy is back at Roehampton Police Station, handing in Joanne Chandler's passport and driving licence to DC Andrewes. He leads her into an interview room and indicates that she should sit down.

'Have you heard from "Renard"?' He makes the air quotes again.

Lucy shakes her head. 'No. I took your advice and went away for a couple of days.'

'No more texts, or calls?'

'I've kept my phone off most of the time, but no, there's been nothing.'

Andrewes nods. 'That's something I suppose. You look better rested.'

Lucy has been reacquainted with sleep for the past two nights, and as a result her hair has regained some of its lustre and the hollows under her eyes have receded. 'Anyway, I thought you'd want to know that I've searched all the centralised information open to us: birth records, National Insurance, electoral rolls, using the estimated age you gave me, and there's no such person as Denny Renard.'

'You're quite sure?'

'Yep.' He slaps his palms against the desk. 'Doesn't exist. So he's not only in the business of handing out false names, he's definitely using one himself. No big surprise there, but I thought you might want it confirmed. And again, anything else that happens, contact me right away.'

Lucy phones Adele while her car is still in the police station car park.

'I thought you ought to know, but Denny Renard is not Denny Renard.'

'What do you mean?' Adele asks sharply.

'He's been using a false identity. Which explains why I've not been able to find out anything under my own steam. Only the detective I spoke to—'

'Hold on,' there's another indefinable shift in Adele's tone. 'You actually went to the police?'

'Yes of course,' Lucy says hotly. 'I'm not going to be persecuted, and I'm certainly not going to let someone use threats to rob me of all my money.'

'Jesus!'

There's a sudden silence on the line.

'Adele?'

'Look, I'm going to have to call you back, okay?'

Before Lucy can speak, Adele has hung up, but she phones back an hour later.

'Listen Luce,' she says. There's been another change in mood: now she sounds conspiratorial, warm even. 'I've found out something too. About Denny. Something you need to know.'

'You know where he is?'

'Sort of. I'll explain later.'

'Can't you just tell me now?'

'No, it needs to be face-to-face. Come over to mine when the kids are in bed, okay?'

Lucy has no idea what time Adele's children go to bed, but she rings the doorbell of her flat at nine. There's loud music coming from somewhere in the block, and a pervasive smell of takeaway curry.

'Come in.'

The first thing that strikes Lucy is that the flat is very quiet. 'Are the girls asleep?'

In reply, Adele simply holds a finger to her lips.

The living room is untidier than it was the last time Lucy visited, and a large hole has been knocked in one wall. Chunks of plaster and brick are heaped on a dust sheet, and there are tools strewn around. Adele notices Lucy's eye being drawn to the half-finished work.

'The damp in this place is something terrible. It's one reason why Paige has all these problems with asthma.' She rolls her eyes, before pulling her phone out of her pocket and checking the screen. 'The bloody council don't want to know, of course, so a mate of my dad's supposed to be sorting out the wet wall. But, of course, he's pissed off and left it half-finished.' She's paces restlessly, glancing at the door and checking her phone repeatedly.

'Did you speak to Jamil? About Pauline's surname? Is that what you needed to tell me?'

'Kind of.' Adele sits on the sofa and indicates that Lucy should sit too, but her body is tensed and her eyes keep flicking to the door.

'So go on then…' Lucy experiences a curious sinking in her stomach; a realisation too late that agreeing to make this impromptu visit was probably not a good idea. 'What's so important that I had to drive all the way down from London?'

Adele doesn't answer, but gives her the strangest look. Heavy footsteps approach the door of the flat, and a key is inserted into the lock.

'Is that your boyfriend?'

Adele nods. 'My better half,' she says with pride, and the strange look morphs into one of outright infatuation.

The footsteps thump down the hall, not quite muffled by the carpet, and the light is drained from the room as a large shape obscures the door to the living room. Lucy's throat tightens, and all she can do is stare in horror.

'Hullo, Blondie,' says Denny Renard.

PART THREE

THIRTY-TWO

Lucy feels the air leave her lungs, as though she has been struck hard from behind. Both hands fly instinctively to her mouth.

'Is this…'

'My boyfriend,' Adele says with satisfaction.

'So you two…' Lucy's voice is a high-pitched croak she doesn't recognise.

'Seeing as you were always the class nerd, I'm surprised you didn't work that out for yourself.' Ever since Denny entered the room Adele's demeanour has changed, becoming simultaneously energised and hardened. He stands next to her, grinning his animal grin. In addition to the usual branded sportswear, he's carrying a large gym bag, which he drops at Adele's feet. The ominous clunking sound sends little ripples of panic through Lucy, making her stomach churn.

'So why am I here? What do you want?'

Even as she asks the question, the answers swarm into Lucy's brain. Because those answers are all so obvious now that these two pieces of the puzzle are joined together. Adele offered Denny's help because they were already a unit, and she must have intended to benefit financially along with her lover.

But Lucy can't afford to think about all of that now. With the instinct of the trapped, she lunges for the door, but Denny is too quick for her, grabbing her by the shoulder and sinking his huge fingers into her flesh.

'Oh no you don't, Mrs Wheedon. You're going nowhere.'

Still gripping her upper arm with one hand, he gestures to Adele to open the gym bag. She pulls out two lengths of steel chain and a heavy padlock. The first piece of chain is lassoed round Lucy's ankles and the second wrapped around the radiator on the wall opposite the window and the two are locked together. She lets out a strangled scream and starts tugging frantically at the brackets fixing the radiator to the wall, but Denny holds up a meaty paw. He gestures to the bag.

'I've got another bit of chain in there: if you don't pack that in, I'll use it on your wrists.'

'You can't do this,' she shouts, the panic now engulfing all of her, making her break into a sweat. She kicks furiously at the wall, then pounds at the radiator again with the flat of her hand, the movement mirroring the slamming of her heart against her ribs.

'Up to you,' Denny, quite unmoved, reaches into the bag. 'Let's do your hands too, then.'

'No,' Lucy mumbles, the fight evaporating from her. 'You don't need to.' She looks desperately in Adele's direction, but her face is turned away.

The length of chain fixed to the radiator is just long enough to allow Lucy to sit down. She sinks into a squat and covers her eyes for a few seconds, resigned.

The girls, she thinks suddenly. The girls are here, and Paige at least is old enough to be persuaded that this egregious behaviour is wrong.

'Help!' she screams, tipping back her head. Her voice still sounds thin and scratchy, but she inflates her lungs and makes as much noise as she can. 'Paige! Skye! Help me!'

Adele grins. 'Oh sorry, Luce… didn't I tell you? The girls are staying with my mum for a bit. Old Lois next door is ninety and as deaf as a post and the guy upstairs is a druggie who sleeps all day and parties all night.' Sure enough, the sound of grunge metal thumps through the ceiling. 'So no point screaming. Nobody's going to hear you.'

'Adele, you can't keep me here. Somebody's going to come looking for me.' She tries to remember if she mentioned Adele to DC Andrewes. She's pretty sure she didn't, but Adele and Denny don't know that. 'I've told the police where I was going.'

'Ah well, that was a stupid thing to do; going to the old Bill,' says Denny, with mock sadness. 'You shouldn't have done that, and then you wouldn't have wound up in this pickle.'

'If you'd just given Den the money when he asked, then you wouldn't be here now,' Adele says, sounding aggrieved, as though this was genuinely Lucy's fault. 'It would have all been very simple.' She goes to put her arm around Denny, but he steps away and avoids her gesture of affection. Adele shrugs and lights a cigarette.

'Anyway, don't worry. If you play along then you don't need to be here very long. Okay?' Denny grins at Lucy.

'You mean you're going to let me go?'

'As long as you obey certain rules: yes.' Denny looks around the room until he spots Lucy's handbag next to the sofa. 'First I'm going to need your keys and your phone.' He rummages through her bag until he finds them, slipping them into the pocket of his tracksuit bottoms. 'Right, all set then. I'll see you ladies later.' He raises a hand in salute and strides out of the room. Lucy gives an involuntary shiver as she wonders what he plans to do when he does see them again.

Adele makes Lucy a mug of tea and places it next to her on the floor, but she is reluctant to drink it; worried about needing to use the bathroom. Denny has been gone for what feels like around an hour, and she calculates it must now be around ten thirty.

'You'll get dehydrated,' Adele observes without much interest, kicking her legs up onto the sofa and blowing smoke at the ceiling.

Lucy is surprised by how calm she feels, putting this down to some primordial survival instinct. This is Adele, she tells herself. Adele has no reason to want to hurt her; she's just under Denny's spell. If anything is ever going to get her out of this horrible situation, it's the fact that she knows Adele a lot better than he does. That they have history. She has to exploit that, and not allow herself to get panicked.

'So whose idea was this?' she asks in a conversational tone, taking a small sip of the cooling tea.

'His.' Adele continues to keep her gaze directed at the ceiling. 'I told him about you coming down to the Dog and Fox that night. We'd just met then.' There is a smile in her voice when she mentions her beloved. 'I told him about how you'd married someone rich and moved to London and he said, "There's an opportunity there, babe."' Adele twists her body far enough to drop her cigarette butt in the ashtray. 'And in case you were wondering, it was him that chased me.'

'I wasn't,' says Lucy, though she was, a little. The dynamic she's briefly witnessed had painted a picture of neediness on Adele's side and lack of interest on Denny's.

'He saw me out and about and he came up to me. Said he'd fancied me as soon as he first saw me, and wanted to get to know me.'

'I see. So this Pauline Jennings… Jenkins. She doesn't exist either?'

Adele shakes her head. 'Made her up. I told Den you were looking for fake ID and he said he'd sort it. He reckoned he could make a bit of cash and also that it would get you trusting me again.' She rummages in the packet for a fresh cigarette, then lies back on the sofa again. 'Originally, Denny's idea was that we would threaten to tell your old man where you were unless you paid up.'

'But when I left Marcus and started over, I couldn't get my hands on any money. I literally left with just a couple of grand.'

Lucy feels obliged to point out this flaw in their plan. Relying on logic is helping her to focus.

Adele lifts her shoulders towards the ceiling. 'I know. So Den had to think again. And he decided he'd try and get your husband to pay to find out where you were. But the geezer found you somehow anyway. So that didn't work either.'

Lucy feels a hollow shiver of memory run through her. 'You're right,' she offers grimly, 'Marcus found me anyway. He managed to get a location through my secret phone. Turned out it wasn't so secret after all.'

'That was still a result for us though,' says Adele blithely. 'Because we stood a better chance of getting our hands on a decent sum of money if you were still with him. So it was better for us if you were back with him; didn't really matter how. And by then Den had come up with the idea of making it look like you'd killed your old man and getting you to pay to stay out of trouble.'

'I could never have killed Marcus,' Lucy says firmly. 'He made me unhappy… he made me very angry, but I just wanted to get my life back. I didn't want to harm him.'

'I know that.' Even though she can't see her face, Lucy can tell Adele is grinning. 'But Den was going to take care of it.'

A cold stab of shock runs up Lucy's spine. 'You mean to tell me he would really have gone ahead and killed Marcus?' Denny had outlined this plan to her of course, the one with the overdose and the carbon monoxide poisoning from the car's exhaust, but Lucy assumed it was just for the purpose of getting her to incriminate herself on audiotape.

'He didn't need to, did he though? Your husband went and killed himself. So all Den had to do was make it look like you'd done it and the cash would roll in.'

Except it hadn't, because Lucy had resisted. Called his bluff. But one thing has become clear from this exchange: Denny is clearly Adele's Achilles heel.

'I told you he's not really Denny Renard though. It's a fictitious name. Doesn't that worry you?'

'Why the fuck should it?' Adele, belligerent as ever. 'A lot of people who've been inside use a new name when they get out. Keep the heat off them.'

'So he was convicted of fraud?'

'And… other stuff.'

More serious stuff, presumably. GBH, or even murder.

'And how were you and he proposing to share the proceeds of your blackmail? What was the deal? Fifty-fifty?'

Adele simply scowls, but her discomfort at the question suggests this detail has not been nailed down.

'Adele…' Lucy draws in a long lungful of breath. Her back is starting to ache, and her bladder is uncomfortably full. 'You and I go way back. And as you pointed out yourself a few months ago, I did you a massive favour and kept quiet about Joanne Beckett's… accident. Why would you want to hurt me like this? If you needed money that badly, I'd have given you money.'

Adele sits up and turns to face her. 'You just don't get it do you?' Her expression is fierce. 'Ever since we were kids, you've thought you were better than me. Your mum and dad didn't want us being friends. They looked down on me, thought I was common because I came from Danemoor. And now we're gown up, I'm just some thieving lowlife with useful connections. Well, I'm showing you that I'm more than that. That you need to show me some respect.'

She stands up abruptly and disappears into the girls' bedroom, returning with something shiny in her right hand. As she gets closer, Lucy recognises her silver christening bangle. Bending down, Adele forces the metal over Lucy's left hand and up onto her wrist. Lucy's arms are slim, but the bangle is designed for a child under the age of eight and the metal cuts cruelly into her flesh, causing a stab of pain. She tries to tug it off with her right hand, but Adele yanks her wrist away.

'You leave that where it is, or I'll handcuff you.' The look she gives Lucy sears her like the pain in her wrist; a look of combined fury and disdain. 'You'll wear that to teach you that I'm better than just a common thief.'

THIRTY-THREE

SEPTEMBER 2002

'How are you getting on?' Felicity Gibson stands in the door of Lucy's bedroom and takes in the pile of belongings on the floor – two large suitcases, a duvet and pillows, piles of towels, a brand new kettle, toaster and microwave still in their boxes. 'Are you just about ready? Only we ought to get going soon.'

Lucy looks around the room she's slept in since she was three, a room that will soon be empty. 'As ready as I'll ever be.'

She and her parents load her things into the boot of Felicity's Volvo estate, filling it completely, then she hugs Jeffrey goodbye and pats the elderly Kibble, who wags his tail in farewell. She's leaving home for the first time in her life, heading for the fresh pastures of the University of East Anglia and a degree in Society, Culture and Media.

'Does it feel strange?' her mother asks as they head towards the ring road. 'Leaving Redgate for good?'

Lucy shrugs. 'I don't know. I won't really know until I'm not here any more. Oh, hold on… slow down.'

Felicity glances in her partially obscured rear mirror and changes down a gear as they pass the Dog and Fox. 'For heaven's sake, what is it?' she asks, not hiding her irritation.

'Look – it's Adele Watts.'

A group of teenagers are laughing and mock-brawling in the pub's car park, and Adele is at the centre of their group. Her olive skin is darkly tanned after the summer holidays and she's dressed in a tiny miniskirt, brandishing a cigarette.

'Can we stop, Mum? I ought to say goodbye.'

Felicity scrunches her shoulders. 'Really, darling? Is that necessary? It's not like you've seen her recently.'

'For old times' sake. It won't take a minute, I promise.'

The car is pulled up onto the kerb, with hazard lights flashing, and Lucy jumps out. Adele narrows her eyes as she approaches but says nothing. Her friends stare.

Lucy holds up a hand awkwardly. 'Hi Adele… I just thought I'd stop and say goodbye. Because, you know, I'm leaving.'

'Where you going?' Adele asks, without much interest.

'University,' Lucy says, smiling. 'In Norwich.'

'Norwich,' Adele repeats blankly. 'What you want to go there for?' She takes a swig of her drink, a pint glass of what looks like cider. Her friends snigger and nudge each other.

'It's a good university.'

'A good university? Very nice,' Adele drags on her cigarette. 'Very nice for those who can afford it, I suppose.'

Lucy nods, at a loss. She now feels as though she's showing off.

'Well, don't let us keep you. Off you toddle,' Adele waves a dismissive hand. 'Go and join all the other little posh kids being driven by their mummies and daddies.' She turns her back as Lucy walks away.

'Was she pleased to see you?' Felicity asks, as Lucy slams the car door and yanks at her seat belt.

'Sort of,' Lucy says disingenuously. Felicity raises her eyebrows but keeps her eyes on the road ahead.

'You never liked Adele, did you?' Lucy says, her tone matter-of-fact rather than accusatory.

Her mother fiddles with the radio controls, trying to find Classic FM. 'It's really not that simple, darling. When you're a parent, it's not about liking or not liking certain children, it's about...' Her voice trails off. 'Anyway, I regret that. I know I tended to be overprotective when you were younger. I am sorry.'

Her mother was to apologise to her again, fifteen years later when she lay in bed in the Royal Surrey Hospital at the end of her battle with terminal cancer. 'I'm so sorry I'm leaving you, darling.'

Lucy squeezed her hand. 'It's okay, Mum. I've got Dad.'

'But it's not the same. He doesn't feel the same way about him as I do.'

And she realised that her mother was referring to Marcus. To her fear about his treatment of her daughter. A tear leaked out of her half-closed eyes and ran down the paper-thin skin of her cheek.

'I'm sorry I won't be there to protect you.'

THIRTY-FOUR

Within thirty minutes the bangle has made an angry red weal on Lucy's wrist, causing her fingers to swell.

Her bladder is becoming uncomfortably full too, but Adele insists she has to wait until Denny returns before she can use the toilet. He appears after what feels like hours, and Lucy is unchained and guarded while she uses the small, windowless bathroom.

'This really isn't necessary,' she sighs, as she's chained to the radiator again. 'I'm not going to try and run off. That would be pretty pointless.'

'Won't be too long, Blondie, don't worry,' says Denny cheerfully. He holds up her iPad, presumably just fetched from the house in Barnes; a property he now has total control over. He shows Lucy that he has already opened the banking app and logged into her account. 'You shouldn't let your ID and password get saved to your keychain,' he tells her. 'Not on a bank account. Rookie error.' His pale eyes flit down the screen, checking the balance in both current and savings account. 'Sixty-seven grand? That's all you've got?'

He sounds both surprised and aggrieved.

'Obviously, most of my money is in investment funds, and Marcus's pension fund.'

'Fuck's sake. Can't you transfer it?' Adele asks angrily.

'I'd have to go and see my financial advisor in person to orga-nise it.' Lucy grits her teeth, trying to remain patient, trying to ignore the throbbing pain in her left wrist. 'It's not a question of just making an online transfer. There are penalty clauses for early withdrawal from that kind of investment bond. You have to sign a special waiver form.'

Denny and Adele exchange a look. 'I could go,' Adele says.

'You need official ID.'

'No worries there, darling.' Denny waggles Lucy's passport, which he must have found in the desk drawer. 'Easy enough to doctor the photo. You two are the same age after all.'

'My financial advisor has met me. He'd know it wasn't me. They check these things really carefully.'

As soon as she has spoken, Lucy regrets pointing this out. How better to raise the alarm than for Alan Bradbury to get a visit from Adele, posing as her? The more potential errors she allows the two of them to make, the better it will be for her.

'Good point,' Denny is still irritatingly cheerful. 'We've got the big prize to play for, right here.' He waggles the house keys at Lucy. 'But meanwhile you can transfer the sixty-seven grand into my account. I'll just make myself a payee…' He starts entering data on the screen. 'Says here I need to enter a passcode sent to your phone before it can be set up, but that's not a problem, is it?' He holds up Lucy's mobile. 'Because I've got it here.'

Adele fetches a can of lager from the fridge, and sits swigging it while she watches Denny. He stabs his huge thumbs on the screen, becoming increasingly frustrated.

'It won't let me do it. Fucking thing.' He slams the iPad roughly onto the table, cracking the screen. 'Well?' he snarls at Lucy. 'Why won't it transfer the cash?'

'There's a limit to how much I can transfer online. I think it's fifty thousand. Over that and I have to make a phone call to a manager.'

If he has any brains, Lucy thinks, he will take the fifty grand and leave it at that, rather than try and clear out the account. But Denny's already shoving the phone at her.

'Are they open?'

Lucy decides against lying. As one of the bank's gold account holders, she has access to customer service twenty-four hours a day. She nods.

'Phone them then. And no funny business. No trying to tell them the wrong security information or anything.' To reinforce his point, he pulls a flick knife from his pocket and opens it, holding the blade up to her face.

Lucy calls the bank's number and beckons to Denny to show her the iPad screen so that she can reel off his account number for the transfer as soon as she has cleared their security procedures. She comforts herself with the fact that the bank now has its own record of the destination account. That's evidence of sorts. And by insisting on her emptying her accounts completely, Denny's greed may have led to the raising of some sort of red flag. But she keeps these thoughts to herself. She had a chance to glimpse the time on the tablet screen briefly, before Denny snatched it away again. Ten minutes to midnight.

'The other thing's going to have to wait until first thing tomorrow,' Adele says, as though reading her thoughts. 'Come on.'

She and Denny retire to the bedroom. Lucy half crouches, half lies on the sitting room carpet, with her hands over hear ears to both block out the sound of noisy coitus and quell her rampant anxiety. Eventually, several hours later, she sleeps.

'Rise and shine, sleeping beauty!'

Lucy is prodded awake by a foot in a fluffy panda slipper. Adele stands there, wearing a towelling dressing gown and sipping on a cup of tea. There's a lit cigarette in her other hand.

'I need to use the bathroom,' Lucy croaks.

Adele fetches the padlock key and frees her. 'But if you were thinking of trying anything, don't bother. Denny's already awake.'

Once the door is closed behind her, Lucy sinks with relief onto the toilet seat. She splashes her face with cold water, then leans her face down to the tap and gulps awkwardly at the stream. The silver bracelet has sunk deeply into the flesh of her arm, which is now so swollen that the strip of metal is barely visible.

'Hurry up for Christ's sake!' Adele hammers on the door. 'We need you to make a phone call.'

Lucy strips off her T-shirt and washes her armpits, then smears toothpaste on her finger and rubs it round her teeth before swilling it out again into the basin. In the mirror, a puffy, grey face with greasy hair looks back at her. *Please let this end today.* She repeats the words like a silent mantra.

When she comes out of the bathroom, Denny is sitting with one elbow on the table in the living room, shovelling cereal noisily into his mouth with the other arm. Milk drips down his chin, and he uses a scarf of Adele's that's hanging over the back of the chair to wipe it off.

'Oi – don't do that!' Adele snatches the scarf from him, giving him a sour look. In response, Denny merely raises a forefinger in an aggressive gesture of warning. Clearly last night's passion has evaporated.

Denny explains to Lucy that she's to phone one of the prestigious estate agencies in Barnes and put her house on the market, priced for a quick sale. Then Adele will go to their office in person to sign the forms, with Denny's bank account the one nominated to receive the sale proceeds.

'Knightons: they're the poshest one,' Adele interjects.

Lucy keeps her expression neutral, but her mind is whirring. Knightons was the agency she consulted about putting the house on the market, only a couple of weeks ago. Just as she's calculating, with a fresh surge of hope that some quick-witted agent might remember speaking to her and think it's odd that she's phoning again about the same property, Adele says quickly: 'Hold on... if she's the one that phones them and then I show up, they'll spot the fact that we sound completely different. I'll have to phone them myself.'

She dials the number and puts on a faux middle-class voice, giving an almost comical impression of the way Lucy speaks when she requests a valuation of her property: 'Yes; I'll give you all the details when I come in… That would be terrific… I'll see you later on. Cheerio for now!'

'Tell 'em three million, okay?' Denny calls after her, as she hangs up and goes into the bedroom to change. 'We could probably put it on for higher, but we don't want to wait months for an offer.'

Adele comes back into the living room twenty minutes later, having applied a full face of make-up. She's wearing jeans with stiletto ankle boots, a plain white shirt and a black jacket. 'Do I look like one of them yummy mummies?' she crows.

Denny narrows his eyes but doesn't smile. 'It'll do, I suppose.'

After Adele has left to catch the train to Waterloo, Denny roams the flat, picking his teeth, performing pull-ups on the door frames and holding grunted, monosyllabic phone conversations with his shady associates.

Lucy leans back against the radiator, eyes half-closed, trying to slide the fingers of her right hand underneath the bracelet and relieve the pressure on her wrist. The pain is becoming unbearable.

Suddenly she is aware of Denny standing near her. She can smell the musk in his cheap aftershave, and glimpse the blinding white of his trainers through her dry, gritty eyelids. 'I can sort that for you if you like.'

When she opens her eyes, he's pointing at her wrist.

'I can get that off for you. That'd be cool, yeah?'

Lucy nods warily. Denny starts to rummage through the toolbox left behind by Adele's father's friend. He pulls out a large pair of pliers and sizes them up against Lucy's arm, but it's obvious that there isn't enough space between bracelet and flesh to get purchase on the metal. He eventually finds a fine hacksaw blade and, with difficulty and a lot of wincing on Lucy's part, inserts it under the bracelet and starts to work it to and fro. The metalwork is thin and malleable, and after a few minutes it snaps in two. Lucy touches the weal on her wrist tentatively. The skin is broken and it still hurts, but at least the insistent pressure has stopped.

'That better, princess?'

Lucy gives Denny a reluctant nod of assent. 'Thanks.'

'Only I reckon one favour deserves another, don't you?'

She stares blankly. 'What do you mean?'

He reaches for a lock of her hair, darkened with sweat and dirt but still luminously blonde. 'I've always fancied you, you know that don't you?'

She shakes her head vigorously, but Denny is undeterred.

'Always thought you were a classy bit of stuff. A cut above your slapper mate, Adele.' He lets his thick finger trail down her cheek and neck to her collarbone. 'No one would ever think the two of you were such good friends.'

Lucy's laugh is derisive. 'Yes, because friends keep one another prisoner.'

Denny's huge paw is now cupping her breast, rubbing his thumb over her nipple. 'No one in their right mind would choose her over you. Who would have thought you'd turn into such a looker?' The strangeness of these words doesn't have a chance to sink in, because he's now inserting his other hand into the waistband of her jeans. Lucy shrinks away from his touch, but he grips her firmly. 'Don't tell me you're not feeling a bit deprived of Vitamin F? Bit of the old in-out? Must have been a while since you had a seeing to.' He nips the side of her neck with his wolf's teeth. 'How long is it now since you broke up with that scruffy-looking geezer you were shagging?'

At the mention of Noah, Lucy's self-pity flares into blind fury. While she might have accepted that she and Noah can no longer see one another, she hasn't stopped thinking about him. She thinks about him all the time, and hearing Denny belittle him feels like a violation. She lunges at him, using her fingernails to leave scratch marks down his face. The raised setting of her engagement ring catches his cheek, leaving a half-centimetre cut.

'You little bitch!' he snarls, baring the long incisors that were nibbling her seconds earlier. He jumps away from her and pulls out his knife, exposing the blade. 'You'll regret doing that. I reckon it's time someone taught you a lesson. Taught you not to be so up yourself.'

Lucy can't run from him, but she continues to lash out at him wildly, so possessed by anger that she's even prepared to risk the knife. As the tip of the blade catches at the skin of her wrist, the flat door is unlocked and Adele stands there. Her eyes widen in shock. 'What the fuck's going on?'

'It's true what they say about posh birds. Bit of a witch, your mate, isn't she?' Denny's hand goes to the gash on his cheek and he holds up his bloodied fingers as proof. 'Me and her were having a bit of private time, but she got all psycho on me.'

'Oh, I get it,' Adele's slanting eyes flash at Lucy. 'The minute my back's turned, you make a move on my fella. Trying to sweet-talk him into letting you go, were you?'

Still fuelled by rage and frustration, Lucy laughs out loud. 'Come off it, Adele! He's hardly my type, and from what he's just told me, you're not really his type either.'

'What d'you mean by that?' Suddenly the old Adele is back, proud and prickly, but also strangely vulnerable. Her body shrinks down like a balloon losing air.

'Ask your "fella",' Lucy says, sliding down the wall again and onto the carpet with a clatter of her chains. 'You know: the one who hasn't even told you his real name.'

Adele kicks off her high heels and stalks off into the bedroom, beckoning aggressively to Denny. 'You and I need a bleedin' word. In private.'

A row ensues, and Lucy can piece together the gist of it from the raised voices. Adele claims that she has been disrespected, which prompts an indecipherable but jeering response from her beau.

Their arguing is interrupted by Adele's phone ringing. Lucy hears her snarled 'Hello!' as she answers. Then her voice changes abruptly. 'Yes, this is she… this is Lucy Wheedon… What? Oh.' After a few seconds she must have hung up, because in her normal voice she says to Denny. 'Christ. We've got a huge fucking problem.'

THIRTY-FIVE

'Why didn't you tell us that Knightons are already selling your house?' Adele spits, whirling into the living room again.

'You didn't ask,' Lucy replies mildly. 'Anyway, I only asked their advice. I haven't actually instructed them.'

'Well they remembered you. In fact, someone in the office remembered you very well, and when I came in using your name and address and my mobile number, it must have looked dodgy. They were very polite, of course, the guy who just phoned didn't come right out and say I was pretending to own the house. He just said "an issue has been flagged up" and started talking about lawyers, and money-laundering prevention, and me having to produce all sorts of documents before they could proceed with selling the place.'

'Well that's just fucking brilliant,' says Denny sourly. 'Well done. They'll probably have the police going over to the house now, or at least asking questions.'

'Hardly my fault,' Adele hisses. 'And anyway, we can't keep her here,' she points at Lucy – who seems to have dropped down their list of concerns – without even looking at her. 'We were going to have to get rid of her anyway: take her somewhere else. It takes weeks for a sale to go through. Apart from anything else, Mum'll be bringing the kids back soon. She can't hang on to them for ever.'

'And we can't exactly let Blondie go either,' Denny raises his voice. 'I mean, think about it. The second we let her go, she's going to go straight to the authorities and tell them what we've done.' Only now does he look in Lucy's direction. 'And don't pretend you wouldn't, because we all know that's exactly what you'll do.'

'So what was your fucking plan then, eh?' Adele shrieks, hands on hips, hair whirling round her head. 'Only you don't seem to have thought this through, do you?'

'My plan?' The tendons in Denny's neck bulge. 'My plan was the same as your plan, remember? To keep the merry widow here a couple of weeks while we forced through a quick sale, and as soon as the money had transferred, piss off abroad. Start a new life.'

'Well that's not going to work, is it?' Adele hurls herself onto the sofa and snatches up a packet of cigarettes. She places one between her lips but carries on speaking. 'Apart from anything else, what about Paige and Skye? Am I just supposed to take them away from the rest of their family?' She jabs at the wheel of her lighter, trying to spark a flame and shoots a furious look in Lucy's direction, as if this is somehow all her fault.

'I don't give a shit about your kids, okay?' Denny tells her with a curl of his lip. 'What did you think was going to happen? That you and me were going to play happy families? You're dreaming, love.'

He strides into the bedroom and comes back with a fistful of clothes, which he starts to cram into his sports bag.

'Den!' Adele whines. 'Don't do this.'

'You know what…' Denny snatches up Lucy's keys and tosses them onto the carpet at her feet. 'You may as well keep the bleedin' house, darling. It's too much bloody hassle. I've got sixty-seven K; that'll do me for two minutes' work.'

'Hang on,' Adele stabs her cigarette into the ashtray and wheels round to face him. 'You can't keep all the money. Half of that's supposed to be mine, remember?'

A strange look crosses Denny's face: an expression that sends a chill shiver through Lucy's insides. 'Oh no it's not. Never was, never will be.' He gives a hard, dry laugh. 'You're even more stupid than I gave you credit for if you thought you were ever going to see a penny from me.'

'But Den… you and me…' Adele's voice trails off.

'Why do you think I came after you? You surely didn't think I really fancied you?' His leer is mocking.

Adele stares, open-mouthed. 'So that's it then? You're leaving me?' Her voice trembles, and her eyes are suddenly glassy with tears.

'No,' says Denny, his voice low; deadly. 'Not yet. There's something I need to do first.'

He strides over to Lucy and unfastens the chains from her ankles, then, with the speed of a big cat, crosses the room and grabs Adele with a single swift, decisive movement. She's caught completely off guard and off balance, and within a few seconds he has her on the carpet with both hands pinioned above her head. Yanking the length of chain towards him, he twists it round her wrists. Adele screams and lashes out with her feet, but Denny has already darted over to his bag and pulled out a roll of duct tape. He slaps a length of it over Adele's mouth, although nobody would be able to hear her above the acid house from the flat upstairs. Then he winds a length tightly round her ankles. Trussed like an animal around her arms and legs, she's completely powerless. Denny tosses her onto the sofa like a bag of laundry.

'Denny, for God's sake, what are you doing?' Although she's now free, Lucy finds herself too shocked to even move. She stumbles towards Adele, but he holds up a huge hand in warning.

'Leave her,' he barks.

'But why?' Lucy strains to make her voice heard over the music. 'Why not just take the money and go? What has Adele ever done to you?'

He gives her a curious glance. 'Have you really not worked it out yet, princess?'

Lucy shakes her head.

'Two words,' says Denny, holding up a pair of thick fingers. His voice is slowed down, heavy. 'Joanne Beckett.'

THIRTY-SIX

'You really didn't catch on, did you?' Denny says, his voice gravelly with bile. 'Either of you. It never occurred to you, because you didn't give a shit about poor little Joanne, even though you were both there when she died.'

Lucy edges towards the door to the hallway, thinking that the best thing she can do now is to try and get help, but Denny is too quick for her. Blocking her path, he strides into the hall and locks the front door from the inside, pocketing the key.

'Oh no you don't, Mrs W, not yet. I need you to hear what I've got to say.'

Adele's eyes are rolling wildly in her face, trying to communicate something to Lucy. That she should scream for help? But the music's still thudding from upstairs, no one will hear her if she does. And besides, some perverse part of her wants to hear what Denny has to say. He has closed the living room door and is leaning against it, tattooed arms crossed.

'The thing is: I know exactly what happened to Joanne. I know, because I was there. Me and a bunch of my friends drove down there that afternoon.'

Lucy is suddenly back at the reservoir on that baking-hot day. She can hear the carefree shouts, the splashes as bodies hit the water. And the older boys who were there too. The vague sense of recognition when she first met him must have been because Denny was one of them, no longer recognisable as the skinny adolescent after countless hours in the gym and almost as many hours under the tattoo artist's needle.

'My real name's Jason Fox. Jason Dennis Fox. Ring any bells?'

'No,' Lucy says quietly, although the name is vaguely familiar.

'You?' He prods Adele's torso with his foot until she shakes her head. 'Renard is fox in French. An educated bird like you would know that, though, wouldn't you?' Denny grins at Lucy, clearly proud of this piece of cultured word play. 'But what you wouldn't know is that my mum's name before she married was Beckett. Sandra Beckett. Her younger sister is Sally Beckett. Joanne's mum.'

Lucy's hand goes to her mouth. 'So you're Joanne's cousin?'

He gives a slow, sarcastic hand clap. 'Give the girl a prize. Yes, she was my cousin. Except closer than a cousin, because after I got in trouble with the police, I fell out with my mum and dad and I lived round at my auntie's for a bit.'

Lucy suddenly remembers the bikes in the garage. One belonged to Jamie Beckett and the other to Joanne's cousin.

'And she lived in Chandler Drive. Joanne. Chandler. Does that ring a bell either?'

The name on the passport. Not randomly generated, but deliberately selected as part of Denny's twisted little game. How obvious it is now, with hindsight. And yet she'd dismissed the uncomfortable reminder of the dead Joanne as a coincidence.

'I knew she wasn't supposed to be down at Blackwater. But she went there with you,' He points at Lucy, 'You were the speccy four-eyed kid from the posh house, so I figured I'd let her get on with it and have a bit of fun. And then I see this piece of shit…' he jabs at Adele with a finger, '… pull the rope out of her hand so that she falls and cracks her head open.'

'It was an accident,' Lucy says quietly. 'A tragic accident.'

'Oh no,' Denny is shaking his head firmly. 'It was no accident. *She* did it on purpose. *She* was showing off, trying to impress the other lads. Broke my fucking family apart with the grief.' He gives

Adele a look of pure loathing. 'Oh, and I know it wasn't your fault, Blondie. But you knew exactly what she did and you kept quiet about it. You lied to the police.'

Lucy is pressing her fingers into her temples, trying to wrap her mind around this new perspective on a piece of her past. 'If you knew what happened, why didn't you speak to the police yourself?'

'Because I was out on parole from Young Offenders, and I was breaking the terms of my bail by being there. I was so terrified about the prospect of going back inside that I kept quiet. I didn't tell anyone what I knew. Not even after I carried Jo's coffin into the church.' A look of anguish passes over his face, and for a few seconds he looks human; vulnerable.

'I'm sorry,' says Lucy quietly.

Denny carries on as though he can't hear her. 'And I did come close to saying something. But then I thought, nah, her little bitch of a killer is a kid: she'll get punished as a kid. I wanted something much worse for her. I decided I would wait. Wait until the right moment.'

He extracts the knife from his pocket and holds the blade up towards the light bulb, making it flash. Lucy's gaze turns automatically to Adele, bound and helpless, and her heart begins to thump.

'Anyhow, the family ended up moving away,' Denny continues. 'They couldn't deal with the memories; needed a fresh start. And I fell in with some not very nice people and ended up inside again. After I got out last year I moved back to the area anyway; didn't know where else to go. Saw a girl I vaguely fancied on a night out and picked her up. It was only after I'd slept with her a couple of times that I realised who she was. That she was *that* Adele Watts. My first instinct was to dump her, but then I thought to myself "This is it. This is the chance I've been waiting for."'

There are tears on Adele's cheeks now. Lucy makes to move towards her, but Denny holds up a huge hand.

'So I made out I was really into her. Because why not: she was easy. Bit of a slag, your mate. Always up for it. And while I was stringing her along and trying to figure out how I was going to get my own back on her, just like magic, *you* appear looking for help getting away from an abusive husband. And I can't believe my luck. Another person who was down at Blackwater, and one who's done all right for herself. Got a load of fucking money.'

Lucy recalls, with dawning realisation, his earlier remark about her having 'turned into a looker'.

'And the fact that you're here now, darling…' Still holding his knife aloft, Denny chucks her playfully under the chin. 'Well, it couldn't be more perfect really, could it? You were there to witness what *she* did to Joanne twenty-four years ago, and you're going to witness what I'm going to do to her now.'

Lucy stares in horror, first at Adele, then at the knife blade. 'No. No! Please tell me you're not…'

'Oh, but I am. I'm going to slice her fucking neck.'

Under the length of duct tape, Adele gives a muffled scream and starts to kick her legs wildly, impotently.

'No!' Lucy cries. 'Denny… Jason, you can't! Please stop this.' She tries to pull the knife from his hand, but he swats her away like an insect with one huge arm.

'Squeamish are you? I'm not surprised you've not got the stomach for it, a posh bird like you. Tell you what…' He fishes in his pocket and pulls out the key to the front door of the flat. 'Seeing as you don't fancy watching, you can leave. Leave me to it and save yourself. After all, she's been a pretty shit friend to you, hasn't she? She's lied to you, tried to swindle money out of you, she's even tried to take your house. Not much of a friendship, is it?'

Dumbly, Lucy holds out her hand for the key. He's absolutely right about Adele not deserving loyalty from her. Adele has unilaterally destroyed what was left of their friendship. She has tormented Lucy, mocked her. It was she who sent Denny to pursue her, causing her to lose Noah and, potentially, her new job. Her knees shaking beneath her, she stumbles towards the front door. Out of the corner of her eye, there is a metallic flash, then a guttural groan from Adele that makes Lucy turn back, despite herself. Denny has clumps of Adele's hair in his left fist, and the knife blade is at her throat.

And then Lucy hears laughter in her head, peals of laughter from the twelve-year-old Adele as she bounces on the bed in front of the camcorder. She feels the ecstatic rush of icy water as they plunge themselves into Blackwater Pond. She hears the laughter mingled with screams at the Hot Box concert and remembers the joy of that night; the most intense happiness she has ever experienced. The most euphoric moments of her life have been spent with, and orchestrated by, Adele.

Hurling herself back into the living room, she snatches a lump hammer from the pile of tools left on the dust sheet. And then, at the exact moment Denny is pressing the blade of the knife into Adele's windpipe, she brings down the hammer. There is a horrible splintering sound as it makes contact with Denny's skull. Then silence.

THIRTY-SEVEN

When she looks back on that day, Lucy will never be quite sure how long she was standing there, the hammer still in her hand, staring down at the damage it has caused to Denny's skull.

But she will always remember the sight of it. The chasm that has appeared, like a bony sinkhole, falling in on itself. And the blood; some bright red splashed over her jeans and soaking into the carpet and some – more distressingly – black and clotted around the site of the wound, matting his hair.

Adele, unable to speak or move, is rolling her eyes wildly and making muffled sounds. There is a horizontal gash across her windpipe, and her white shirt is turning scarlet with a spreading stain. At the sight of it, Lucy is jolted out of her fugue state and hurries over to her, pulling the duct tape from Adele's mouth before fetching a tea towel from the kitchen and staunching the wound.

'Is he breathing?' Adele croaks.

'I… I don't know,' Lucy mutters. She pulls the cloth away and inspects the cut on Adele's neck. Fortunately, it seems to be shallow. 'But you very nearly had your throat cut.'

The shock catches up with her, turning her lips and her extremities numb and making her shake violently.

'We need to check,' Adele says with an impressive calm. 'But first you need to untie me.'

Lucy fetches scissors and cuts the duct tape from Adele's legs, helping her swing them round and sit up on the sofa. She somehow manages to keep her gaze averted from the large, hulking body at their feet while she does this. 'Where's the key for the padlock?' she asks.

'I don't fucking know!' Adele's face is white, and she's sweating profusely. 'Probably in his pocket. But I can't check while my hands are like this; you're going to have to.'

Swallowing down the saliva that has pooled in her mouth, Lucy drops to her knees.

But then immediately she recoils, and needs to breathe deeply and slowly for a few seconds before she can speak.

'I can't, Adele. I can't touch him.'

Adele closes her eyes briefly, her lips moving slightly as though praying. 'The key. Check his pockets,' she repeats. 'Come on! Quickly!'

'I'll have to turn him over,' Lucy hisses. 'You'll have to help me.'

With her wrists chained but her fingers free, Adele manages to grab hold of Denny's left shoulder while Lucy twists his legs. For the first time, she understands the meaning of the expression 'dead weight'. When the body is finally dragged into a supine position, both women gasp. Denny's eyes are opened wide and fixed in a furious stare, and blood is oozing from his mouth and nose.

'Oh Christ, I'm going to throw up.'

Adele stumbles into the bathroom, chains jangling, and Lucy hears her retching. Closing her own eyes, she fumbles inside first one, then the other of Denny's tracksuit bottoms until she finds the padlock key.

Once Adele's hands have been freed, she drops to her knees and touches her fingers to Denny's broad, tattooed wrist. His flesh looks cool and waxy. She shakes her head, gnawing her top lip with her teeth. 'No.'

'Are you sure?' Lucy croaks.

'He's dead, Luce. You killed him.'

Don't think about that now. You can't think about that now.

Lucy makes a sound that is half gasp, half shuddering sigh. Then she takes hold of Adele's arm and guides her back into the bathroom.

She makes her remove her shirt and sit down on the closed toilet seat while she soaks the tea towel with antiseptic and cleans her neck.

'I should be able to patch this up, I think,' Lucy says, inspecting the clean edges of the cut, forcing herself to focus on practicalities. 'Have you got any dressings?

'There's a first aid kit on top of the cabinet.'

Lucy has just finished fixing a series of Steri-Strips in place when there is the unmistakeable sound of a key turning in the front door. She freezes, staring at Adele in horror.

'My mum!' Adele whispers. 'Quick! You'll have to do something. She can't see me like this.' Bundling the blood-stained shirt and tea towel into the laundry hamper, Adele scuttles into her bedroom and slams the door. Lucy pulls the sitting room door shut and is poised awkwardly in the hallway when the door opens and Dawn Watts stands there, key aloft.

'Oh,' she says confused. 'Where's Adele?'

'She's lying down… migraine, well… bad headache. I came over to see her, but she wasn't feeling too good, so… I'm Lucy. You might remember me?… Lucy Gibson. From school.'

She's babbling so fast that it takes her a few seconds to realise that Dawn is not alone. Paige and Skye have followed her into the hallway.

'Oh yeah,' says Dawn, looking her up and down suspiciously. Lucy is grateful that her jeans are a deep-dyed denim and therefore the blood splatter isn't immediately visible. 'She did say something about that.'

'We know Lucy,' Skye says confidently. 'She took us to guinea pig land and brought us sweeties.'

'Girls!' Adele calls from the bedroom. 'Come in here!'

They trot off obediently, and Dawn follows them. From the doorway, Lucy can see that Adele has tugged the curtains across, making the room dark, and has covered her neck by pulling the duvet up to her chin.

'What's going on, Dell?' Dawn demands. 'I've never known you have a migraine.'

'I don't know what it is,' Adele says in a half-whisper. 'It could be flu. I feel like shit.' The sallow cast to her olive skin gives substance to the lie.

The girls dive onto the bed and snuggle up next to their mother.

'Mum, can you keep the girls a bit longer?'

'No, I can't, I'm going out.'

'Please!'

'I can't Dell, I've had 'em ages as it is. I've got to go to the doctor, and then I need to go down the town hall to sort out my council tax. I can't have the kids with me.'

'But Mum—'

'Lucy here can help look after them, can't she?'

Lucy somehow forces a smile. 'Sure.'

'And anyway, just bung 'em in front of the telly. They won't be any trouble.'

Adele and Lucy exchange a look of alarm, both picturing Denny's – now Jason's – corpse a few feet away from the television.

'Right, I'm off,' says Dawn briskly, turning on her heel and slamming the front door before she can be presented with any further argument.

'Shit!' Adele mouths to Lucy.

'Why don't you two show me your room?' Lucy says quickly, and the girls happily grab her hand and pull her into the tiny second bedroom. 'If you stay here and keep your eyes closed, and count to twenty, I'll have a surprise for you.'

She darts back into the sitting room and covers Jason's body with the dust sheet left by the builders, before retrieving her iPad from the coffee table where he left it. It hasn't been charged for at least twenty-four hours, but there is a modest amount of battery life remaining. Lucy shows it to the delighted girls, telling them they can chose a movie from the iTunes store. 'But you'll have to stay in here to watch it, okay? It won't work if you leave your bedroom.'

Adele emerges from her own room, dressed in sweatpants and a navy polo-neck sweater that covers her wound. She gestures silently towards the living room, and the two of them go in together, closing the door quickly behind them.

'I've bought us a bit of time with the girls,' Lucy whispers.

'We're going to have to get them out of here, like, immediately.' Adele looks down at the huge shrouded figure at her feet. 'Bloody hell, Luce, I can't believe you clipped him. I didn't think you had it in you.' Her tone is almost admiring.

'I didn't mean to,' Lucy pulls her arms around her body, still shivering with shock. 'I didn't really think; it was just instinctive. It just… happened.'

Adele takes a deep breath. From the girls' bedroom come the distant strains of Elsa in *Frozen* singing 'Let it Go'. 'Okay, so we have to sort this situation, and we have to be quick.'

The two of them look directly at one another, locking eyes. With this seismic event comes a new, unspoken pact and they both know that from now on they have no choice but to cooperate. To face what comes next together. Lucy gives a terse nod of agreement.

'First off, we have to get the girls away from here,' Adele goes on. Her voice is deadened, robotic. 'Is there anywhere you can take them where they'll be safe? Somebody who can look after them?'

'I don't know…' Lucy's gaze is drawn by the awful stillness of the shrouded corpse. 'Surely you must be able to ask someone round here? A neighbour? A friend?'

'It's too close to home.' Adele looks down at Jason's body. 'Literally. I can't risk people round here asking questions, or seeing something.'

'Okay,' sighs Lucy. 'I suppose I could try and find someone.'

'Great. And once they're out of the way…' Adele prods the lifeless shape with the toes of her left foot. 'We'll deal with him.'

THIRTY-EIGHT

'I'm thirsty,' whines Skye, as Lucy edges her car onto the Redgate bypass.

'Me too!' protests Paige.

Once they are on the dual carriageway, Lucy pulls into a petrol station and buys crisps, flapjacks and cartons of Ribena. She hands them the drinks and watches the girls in her rear-view mirror. They seize on the drinks like wanderers in the desert, their pink cheeks moving rhythmically in and out round the straws. Taking advantage of this moment of peace, Lucy pulls out her phone and scrolls through the list of contacts. She dials Rhea's number, then immediately cuts the call before it has a chance to ring out. Her cousin will probably be at work, and even if she is free, she's the type to ask far too many questions. The only choice is to head to London. She passes the packets of crisps to the girl, turns the radio up loud enough to drown out her nightmarish thoughts, and heads towards the A3.

Jane Standish is the obvious person to petition for help. She can be relied on to babysit a couple of strange children without asking too many awkward questions.

But when Lucy pulls up outside the house in Clapham, her heart sinks. The shutters are closed and the blinds drawn in the upstairs windows. She realises that the private schools attended by the Standish children will still be on summer holiday, and that the family must be away at their house in France. Jane's car is parked in the driveway, but there is no sign of Robin's.

The remains of the drink and snacks are now strewn across the back seat, and the girls are growing restless.

'I need a wee!' complains Paige.

'So do I,' Skye squirms under the seat belt.

Lucy considers driving to Helen's flat, but not only does she live on the far side of London, but she will probably be on her way home from work, having secured a job in Haringay Social Services after graduation. She needs to locate someone who doesn't work, or who works from home. Someone who won't ask too many awkward questions.

Someone like Noah Kenyon.

Smiling at the girls through clenched teeth she says, 'Not long now,' and heads round the South Circular towards Putney Bridge.

When she rings Noah's doorbell twenty minutes later, Lucy's heart is thumping and her palms are sweating. It strikes her as deeply ironic that Noah will probably attribute this to nervousness over seeing him again, when in reality she is still in severe shock after causing a fatal blow to Jason Fox's head. At least the bloodstains on her jeans have dried, making them a little less conspicuous.

'Hello there!' Noah answers the door in the rumpled T-shirt and jogging bottoms he wears when he's working. His reaction is one of mixed pleasure and surprise. Then he sees that she's not alone and blinks hard. 'Oh.'

'Noah, I'm really sorry…' Seeing him standing there, so solid and reassuring, Lucy feels her voice crack and tears surface from nowhere. She just wants to throw her arms round him, to be held; if only for a few seconds. 'This is Paige and Skye… they're daughters of a friend of mine.'

'Hi, Paige and Skye. I'm Noah.' He raises a hand in salute.

'I need a wee,' Skye tells him solemnly.

'And me,' Paige adds.

'In that case you'd better follow me…' Noah ushers the girls in the direction of the bathroom, then comes back to the hallway, where Lucy is hovering, car keys in hand.

'I take it you're not just here because you couldn't find any public toilets in the vicinity? Although if you are, that's fine.'

'The thing is, their mum's going through a bit of a crisis, and I've got to get back to her and help her sort something out… I know it's a huge ask, but could you mind the girls, just for a couple of hours or so?'

Noah rubs his chin, looking uncertain. 'I don't know, Luce, they're only little, and they don't know me from Adam…'

'Please,' Lucy is aware her voice is rising, aware of the clock ticking. 'They'll be fine, honestly.'

Noah glances over his shoulder at the girls and sighs. 'Okay, go on then,'

'They're easy enough kids, but if you want, you can take them over to my place. I'll pay for a taxi.' She holds up the house keys, then wonders if this is a good idea. The last person in the house was Jason Fox, and who knows what sort of evidence he might have left behind him. The last thing she can afford now is to reinforce a link between Fox and herself. Thank God she never got round to taking the phone he gave her to be fingerprinted. From what she now knows of his history, Fox's prints would definitely be on a police database.

'No, you're okay,' Noah tells her. 'I've got DVDs and stuff from when my sister's kids come over, and there's always the CBeebies channel. I can feed them if you like?'

'Thank you,' Lucy says. 'That's incredibly kind of you.' And then, because even now she can't quite help herself, 'Are you sure your girlfriend will be all right with this?'

'No girlfriend,' Noah says equably, refusing to rise to the bait. 'I've been on a couple of dates, but nobody has met my ridiculously high standards.' He gives her a meaningful look with his dark-fringed eyes.

Lucy gives a little shrug. 'Great. That you're free to mind them, I mean. I've got to dash back now, but I'll explain everything later, I promise.'

But she wouldn't be explaining, of course; how could she? She will end up having to give Noah a fabricated backstory, and this makes her a little sad. A second irony occurs to her as she walks back to the car. Noah finished with her because he thought she might have conspired with Jason Fox to cause her husband's death. He was wrong about that. And yet now she has killed a man: Fox himself.

By the time she gets back to the A3, it's rush hour and the traffic is moving at a frustrating crawl. Her mobile rings.

Rhea calling.

Perhaps she had not cut the call to her cousin after all, and Rhea was phoning to see what she wanted after getting a missed call notification. She picks up using Bluetooth. 'Hi, Rhea. Sorry, I didn't mean to call—'

'You called me?' Rhea sounds confused. 'I didn't notice that… why, were you phoning about your dad? Has someone already told you?'

'Told me what?'

'He's had a bad fall. Broken a hip. He's in the Royal Surrey, Ward 6. I've just been to see him now, and he's a bit confused. He's asking for you.'

Lucy slaps a palm against the steering wheel. *Why*, she asks herself. *Why now, today?*

'Okay thanks, Rhea… look, I'm a tiny bit tied up just now, but I'll get over there as soon as I can. Give me an hour or so.'

*

She parks as close as she can to Adele's flat, mindful of the fact that whatever happens next, they will need her car as a means of transport. Once she gets inside, she finds that Adele has been busy cutting up thick black bin liners and using them to wrap Jason's body. The resulting mummy-like package has been sealed with his own roll of duct tape.

'I've had a go at cleaning the carpet,' she points to a bucket of soapy water and a scrubbing brush. 'But it's effing impossible. I don't think I'll ever get the marks out.'

Lucy inspects the stains, brownish against the light grey carpet. 'You'll have to replace it, I think.'

'How am I supposed to afford that?' Adele grumbles. 'Easy for you to say… Anyway,' she points to a strange hump on top of the plastic clad body, 'I packed up his bag with him – with the fucking chains in it – and I put that hammer in too. The one you used to… you know. Thought we may as well use it to weight him, since we need to get rid of it anyway.'

Lucy simply nods, following Adele into the kitchen. Anything not to have to look at the huge black shiny cadaver. Adele takes two cans of lager from the fridge and hands one to her. Lucy, who doesn't normally drink beer, takes it gratefully.

'I'm bloody glad you're back, I can tell you. It's been freaking me out being all on my own here with… with him.' She takes a large mouthful of lager, then sets the can down on the worktop while she lights a cigarette. 'Girls okay?'

'Fine. They're with a friend of mine. I'll go back for them later.'

Adele glances out of the window. It's seven thirty, and just starting to go dark. 'Reckon it's safe to move him now?'

'Let's give it ten more minutes…' A thought occurs to Lucy. 'While we've got a bit of time to kill…' She winces at the unfortunate choice of word, '… I could pop over to the hospital quickly and see my dad. He's just been admitted.'

'No way!' Adele sucks on her cigarette and taps the ash into the sink. 'You're not leaving me alone here with *that* again. My nerves can't take it.' She extends her hand, palm facing down, to demonstrate the shaking. 'Anyway, I've just thought of something else.'

'What?' Lucy eyes her over her lager can.

'Well, there's a sensor that switches on the lights in the fire exit stairwell automatically once it's got fully dark. And they're really effing bright, you know? We can't exactly take him down in the lift, can we?'

'No,' Lucy agrees.

'So we're stuck with using the stairs, and it'll be a lot less risky before the lights come on. In terms of someone spotting us. So we should do it now, before it's fully dark out.'

'Okay…' Lucy exhales hard and tips the remains of the beer down the sink. 'In that case, let's get it over with. But I'm going to stop off and see my dad quickly on the way.'

'You're crazy. It's too risky.'

'Just for five minutes. Anyway, hospital visiting is a normal activity. The more normally we behave, the better it'll be. If I'm picked up on CCTV in the hospital, so much the better.'

'Like an alibi, you mean?'

'Yes, exactly.' Lucy wipes her damp palms on her blood-stained jeans. 'Shall we?'

Moving Jason's body down from the second floor is more difficult than either of them had anticipated, but they're forced to move as quickly as they can to avoid discovery. The stairwell is narrow, with tight turning spaces, and the PVC-bound package refuses to bend to accommodate their manoeuvring. It also weighs more than two hundred pounds.

On the first floor mezzanine, Lucy leans back against the wall, hands on her thighs and closes her eyes for a few seconds.

'I don't think I can do this. I think I'm going to pass out.'

She's picturing herself in the dock in the Crown Court, being sentenced to ten years in prison for manslaughter. And then it occurs to her that if they're caught trying to cover up the crime like this, it would be worse. It could be a life sentence. Perhaps they should take their chances and just own up, claiming self-defence or duress. And what about Adele's part in it? Adele was simply the victim of a vicious knife attack, but if she's caught trying to dispose of a corpse, she will face charges too. 'Look, maybe we should go back. Unwrap… him… and call the police. Take our chances. It's probably less risky.'

'How are we going to convince them it wasn't premeditated?' Adele demands.

Lucy points to her neck, still obscured by the polo neck. 'He tried to cut your throat.'

'Yeah, but I've already got a criminal record for fraud; no one's going to take my word for anything. They'll say I did it myself. Anyway, I'm not going back up them fucking stairs again. It'll kill me.'

Lucy closes her eyes again. 'I don't know, Adele…'

'Come on, it's only a bit further,' Adele tips up the baseball cap that's covering her hair, so that Lucy can see her face. 'We can do this.'

By the time they reach the tiny lobby on the ground floor, they're both red-faced and sweating with exertion. But so far, at least, no one has seen them.

Adele waits just inside the fire door while Lucy fetches her car and reverses it as close as she can to the doorway. With a final surge of energy and effort, they lift the body over the sill of the boot and Lucy pulls the retractable parcel shelf closed to hide it from view.

Once they're parked outside the hospital, she hands the car keys to Adele. 'You'd better hang on to these, just in case. But I promise I won't be long.'

Adele frowns at the stains on her jeans. 'Bit of a giveaway, isn't it? Haven't you got anything you can change into?'

Lucy grabs her gym bag from the back seat of the car and changes into workout leggings and a zipped top, shoving her bloody clothing into the bottom of the bag before heading through the main doors of the building. Upstairs on the ward, she finds Jeffrey drowsy from morphine but sufficiently aware to be pleased to see her.

'Sorry I haven't had chance to bring you anything,' she says, kissing him on the forehead. 'I can pop down to the shop in the foyer.'

He shakes his head. 'I'm nil by mouth… preparation for surgery tomorrow. I've got to have a hip replacement apparently.'

'I'll try and come back tomorrow then,' Lucy squeezes his hand, 'and I'll bring some cake, and something to drink.'

Tomorrow, she thinks. *How wonderful it will be to get to tomorrow and engage in a mundane task like shopping for my dad. To have this nightmare over with.*

She's relieved to have had the chance to see him, but nevertheless walks briskly out of the hospital with her head down, hoping not to draw attention to her bedraggled state. The place is alive with comings and goings, with the usual spectrum of medical triumphs and tragedies and nobody pays her any attention. When she emerges through the automatic doors into the car park, squinting at the darkness, her heart leaps in her chest. She swivels her head from one side to another, looking in every direction.

But the car is gone.

THIRTY-NINE

Yanking her phone from her pocket, she dials Adele's number.

No reply.

Her pulse pounding, she tries again: once, twice, three times. Still no response.

It occurs to her suddenly that she has been incredibly naïve. Adele has already set out to deceive her in a calculated and manipulative way, conspiring with a seasoned criminal not just to take her money but to frame her for Marcus's murder. So why on earth is she trusting her now? Who was to say that Adele hadn't just driven her car to the police and told them that Lucy has murdered Jason Fox? After all, it would be easy to prove that the hammer was the murder weapon, and the hammer is conveniently parcelled up with his body. It has her DNA on it.

Lucy starts walking quickly round the perimeter of the car park, searching every row in turn, but the car definitely isn't there. She leaves the car park and heads out on to the main road, passing the station and Redgate Lawn Tennis Club. Searching for a midnight blue car in the dark is a fool's errand and she ends up staggering along the pavement, half-blinded by oncoming headlights.

Then her phone buzzes in her pocket. *Adele calling*.

'Where the hell are you?' Lucy demands angrily. 'I'm going out of my mind here!'

'All right, all right, calm down. There was a security guard, okay, patrolling the car park and looking at all the number plates. He kept stopping by your car and it was freaking me out, so I decided it was best I moved.'

'Where? I can't see you.'

Adele tells her she's in Maidwell Lane, a narrow track running down the western extremity of the tennis club. It's banked on both sides by tall hedges and devoid of either street light or security cameras.

As she trudges down the lane, at first Lucy can only see the car. There's no sign of Adele. Once again her mind starts working overtime. Is this some sort of a trap? Drawing nearer, she catches sight of a pale flash of colour near the rear tyre of the car, and realises it's Adele's pink trainer. She's crouched down on her haunches with her hands gripped round a cylindrical dark object. After a few seconds Lucy realises it's the snow shovel from the car's winter emergency kit. Adele has the tip of the shovel blade inserted inside the number plate, and is using force to try and jemmy it off its fixings.

'Adele, what the—'

'I'm removing the reg plates,' Adele tells her through gritted teeth. She doesn't have enough purchase from the shovel and ends up falling backwards onto the gravel. 'I swear that security guy was taking a note of the number.'

'Why would he do that? We were legally parked.' Lucy steps forward and pulls the shovel from Adele's grasp.

'Ideally we'd cover the plates with that stuff you can use to stop the number being picked up on camera, but since we haven't got any of that, then this is the next best thing. If we're got no licence plate then our movements can't be traced,' Adele insists gruffly, snatching the shovel back from her.

Lucy glances around her before lowering her voice. 'Have you any idea how suspicious a car with no plates is going to look? If we're spotted by the police – or anyone who then decides they should report us to the police – we're going to be pulled over, and they're going to search the car. And how are we going to explain

why we've got…' Lucy feels bile rising in her throat at the image…
'why we've got what we've got in the boot.'

Adele sinks back onto her heels, loosening her grip on the
shovel. 'Yeah, I suppose so. I didn't really see it like that. But then
you always were the clever one, weren't you?' She uses the word
as an insult.

'We just need to concentrate on driving legally and not draw
attention to ourselves.' Lucy prises the shovel from Adele's hand
and tosses it onto the rear seat. 'Come on, we need to go.'

On the main carriageway again, she takes the turning for the
heath road, and stays on it until they reach the track down to
the reservoir. Only then does she switch off the headlights. They
haven't discussed or even mentioned Blackwater Pond, and yet
they both knew instinctively that this is where they would go.
There's an inevitable logic about it. It could only be Blackwater.

Even with the car as near as possible to the reservoir's edge,
they still have to carry the body some distance in the dark, and
over uneven ground. The plastic sheeting slips from Adele's hand
at one point and she stumbles backwards, with the remains of her
former lover landing on top of her. She yelps with alarm, before
letting off a volley of swear words.

'Thank God you've already weighted it and we don't have to
waste time looking for something to do the job with,' Lucy says,
once they reach the dark, glassy expanse of water. A slight breeze
ripples its surface and makes the leaves of the overhanging trees
give a sighing sound. A solitary owl calls from the far bank.

'If we dump it at the edge, it's not going to be deep enough,'
Adele says quietly. 'Bits of it might be visible.' She's looking to her
right, to the flat rock that acted as their diving platform twenty-four
years ago. It projects several yards into the pond, to the deeper
water that's required.

'Yes,' Lucy says simply, and they drag their burden through the
long grass and out to the edge of the rock.

'Now?' asks Adele.

'Now.'

Adele hesitates a beat, laying down her end of the body long enough to cross herself, before they slide it into the water with one coordinated movement. It sinks without a splash, without a sound, into the same expanse that swallowed up Joanne Beckett.

'I wish I hadn't killed Joanne,' Adele says suddenly. 'I think about her all the time. He was right, Denny... I mean, Jason... what I did was a terrible thing. I never meant her to die, though. I know you know that.'

Lucy simply nods.

'Anyway, I guess we're one for one now.'

'What do you mean?' Lucy asks, although she fears she already knows the answer.

'I've killed someone, and now you've killed someone. You kept my secret, and now I'll keep yours.'

They turn and face one another in the dark. The expression on Adele's face is unreadable, her slanting eyes just glittering specks. She holds out her hand, palm upwards, and Lucy realises she is expected to lay hers flat on top, just like they did all those years ago.

'To seal the pact,' Adele says, and for a few brief seconds their hands connect.

FORTY

'Rough day?'

Lucy looks down at herself. She may have changed into her workout gear but is still in her mud-splashed shoes and her fingernails are filthy. She knows that if there was a mirror in front of her, she would see dirty hair plastered to her scalp, pale skin and haunted eyes; just as Noah was seeing them now. On a normal day she wouldn't dream of appearing in front of him in such a state. But today was not a normal day.

'It's been a very long one,' she says honestly, then realises she has no idea what time it is. A glance at the clock on the wall of Noah's flat tell her it's now five past nine.

'I've got a nice white Burgundy on the go…' Noah walks over to the kitchenette and picks up a half empty wine bottle. 'Want a glass?'

Lucy does. She wants to drink the wine, and soak in the bathtub until she's thoroughly clean and then – in bed in the dark – tell Noah exactly what has happened that day. But she can't even risk the wine; not least because she is barely holding back a torrent of tears. She shakes her head with a feigned decisiveness. 'I'd better get the girls back,' she tells him, beckoning to them. They're lolling on the sofa in front of *Ratatouille*, eyes half-closed. 'They're usually in bed by now.'

'No problem; they've been good as gold.' He lowers his voice slightly. 'Is everything going to be okay with them… you know, back at home. Only, you said there were problems?'

Lucy nods. 'Their mum's been the victim of domestic violence.'

This was not a lie: Adele had been in a relationship with Fox, and he had attacked her. He had chained her up and threatened her life. But it was far from the whole truth, and much as she longed to, Lucy knew she could never tell Noah the whole truth.

'Everything's been sorted out now though.' She forces a smile. 'They'll be quite safe.'

'Good.' Noah holds up the wine bottle. 'This will have to wait for another time. Or maybe we could go out for a drink somewhere? It would be good to catch up properly.'

'Yes,' Lucy smiles again, though it takes every ounce of energy left in her body to do so. 'I'd like that.'

She and Adele mutually agreed that it would be safest if Lucy's car wasn't seen anywhere near the Danemoor estate again, so she drops off Paige and Skye in an unlit layby on the Redgate ring road.

Both girls have been asleep all the way back from London, and when they're woken, Skye whimpers and Paige stares around her, confused.

'Will you manage to get them home okay?' Lucy asks, handing over their sweaters and the backpack containing a selection of their toys.

'I've got a taxi waiting,' Adele nods in the direction of the convenience store a couple of hundred yards away. 'They're not going to want to walk there, but that's just too bad. It's for the best.'

'Sure,' Lucy reaches into her purse and pulls out a fold of twenty-pound notes. 'Put this towards a new carpet,' she mutters, then sticks her hands into the pockets of her sweatpants and looks down at her feet. 'Well, I guess I'll say goodbye. I hope things, you know…'

Adele juts her chin, proud to the end. 'We'll be fine.' She moves as if to embrace her friend, but then thinks better of it and wraps an arm around the shoulders of each daughter instead. She looks back as she walks away, and Lucy watches her go. And both women know with absolute certainty that they will never see one another again.

EPILOGUE

FEBRUARY, 2019

'Name please?'

Lucy blinks, startled. Even now she's taken aback by the question. 'Um, Lucy. Lucy Gibson.'

The barista smiles and scribbles 'Lucy' on the side of her coffee cup, leaving her to queue at the collection point at the far end of the station coffee bar. A few minutes later, coffee cup clutched in her gloved hand, Lucy moves out onto the platform to wait for her train. It's a sharp, frosty day, and her breath makes clouds, which mingle with the steam from her latte.

She makes this fifteen-minute journey between Bath and Bristol every weekday morning. Taking the car would be more convenient in some ways, but ever since the previous September, Lucy has disliked driving. She sold her large blue SUV at the same time that she sold the house in Barnes, and now owns a modest hatchback that she uses for the occasional trip to the supermarket and to visit her father.

Home is now a flat-fronted Georgian town house on a hilly, honey-coloured terrace in Bath. Vicky is nearby, and through her, Lucy is slowly starting to meet like-minded people. She's volunteering at Umbrella, the refugee charity in Bristol that caught her eye nearly a year ago, when she was first planning to leave Marcus.

It's an unpaid position, but she has been assured that she will be considered for the next suitable permanent vacancy. Megan, at Pink Square, has generously agreed to give her a reference, even though Lucy's employment with them was short-lived and fraught with problems. Problems caused by Jason Fox.

Fox's body was discovered by anglers a few weeks after Lucy and Adele dropped it into Blackwater Pond. The discovery warranted a small piece in the local news but did not become a national story. He had made plenty of enemies during his time in prison and was on the wrong side of a local gang after drug deals he was involved in turned sour. So there was neither shock nor surprise when he was killed. Although the article mentioned briefly that Adele ('a local woman known to Fox') was questioned by police, she was not arrested or charged. Nor did she ever mention Lucy's name in connection with Jason Fox. She kept her pact of silence, and so did Lucy. Just as she had all those years ago.

In November, DC Andrewes followed up with Lucy, wanting to know if she was still being harassed by whoever was passing themselves off as Denny Renard. She wasn't, Lucy told him truthfully: it had stopped. But she let him know that she had put her house on the market anyway, and was planning to leave London. Given the absence of recoverable DNA from the paper fire bomb, Dale Andrewes said that he would mark the case as inactive for now. But, of course, she was welcome to get in touch if there was any further trouble.

Lucy has not returned to Redgate since that night in early September and knows now that she never will. After his discharge from hospital, Jeffrey Gibson sold his bungalow and moved into a care home near East Grinstead, thus ending Lucy's final link with the place. But with some of the proceeds from the Barnes house sale, she has set up two trust accounts; one for Paige Watts and one for Skye Watts. Her solicitor forwarded all the relevant paperwork to Adele, along with the instruction that she did not expect or want any communication in return.

*

Lucy gets off the train at Temple Meads, buys a second coffee to fuel her walk and sets off due east to the Umbrella headquarters in the suburb of Barton Hill. It takes her fifteen minutes, across railway tracks and major roads, but she relishes the contrast between this gritty, urban landscape and the sedate Jane Austen gentility of Bath.

'Morning, my lover!' crows Lilian, who mans the front desk and always addresses her with this Bristolian endearment. 'You're looking very bonny today. Roses in your cheeks.'

'It's the cold,' Lucy smiles, brandishing her coffee cup. 'And the exercise.'

She sits down briefly at a free desk and logs onto a terminal to check the day's agenda, before heading to the public access area to man the help desk. This is her main responsibility on most mornings, and dealing with problems fresh off the street has been a steep learning curve for her.

'Morning, Lucy.' Dougie, her line manager and closest work friend raises a hand in greeting. He's a bald, ascetic-looking man with an unexpectedly dry wit and a kind heart. She waves back. 'A group of us are doing a pub quiz tomorrow night, at the Barley Mow. Fancy lending us your brain? We need someone to cover the mysterious world of pop culture, and I thought you might fit the bill.'

'Maybe,' Lucy says with a grin. 'As long as I've got time to binge-watch the back catalogue of *Real Housewives* between now and then.'

She checks the facilities in the visitor room – tissues, water, information leaflets in a variety of languages – then goes to sit behind the help desk with a book to read while it's quiet. It's still only nine thirty and few clients with enquiries come in much before eleven.

Lilian appears a few minutes later.

'Lucy, my love, there's a man at the main reception desk asking to see you.'

Lucy frowns. 'Not a client?'

'No, definitely not a client. English. Big bloke. Asking for you by name.'

Lucy's heart lurches in her chest. She has a sudden, dizzying flashback to 'Denny' appearing in the offices of Pink Square. Her fingers start to tingle, and her heart races so hard that she feels as though she will pass out. She tries to draw air into her lungs, but her body won't comply. It's as though she's suffocating.

'You all right, sweetheart?' Lilian looks worried.

Lucy nods dumbly. 'Just give me a minute,' she says in a strangled gasp and heads outside through the fire door. The rush of wintry air acts like a slap in the face, and she manages to inhale, with gulping breaths at first, but then more slowly and regularly. She leans against the wall of the building and braces her arms on her thighs. *Breathe*, she instructs herself. *In for three counts, out for three counts.*

Her heart rate steadies, but her mind is racing. The black plastic sacks wrapped around Jason Fox obscured his identity. And it was Adele who did the wrapping, when she was on her own in the flat, with Lucy conveniently out of the way dropping off the girls. So she only had Adele's word that it was Jason Fox that they threw into Blackwater. If that really was his name. Even that could have been a bluff for her benefit.

You're being ridiculous, her rational self protests. *You saw his body. You saw the blood.*

But it was Adele who felt his pulse, who said he was dead. What if he had still been alive?

The fire door opens and Lilian sticks her head out. 'Okay there, Luce?'

Lucy straightens up slowly. 'Yes. Just needed some air… listen, Lilian, do me a favour and go and ask the man his name, will you?'

She has gathered herself sufficiently to return to the desk, smoothing her hair and rearranging her skirt.

Lilian reappears thirty seconds later.

'He says he's called Noah Kenyon.'

Noah. Giddy with relief, Lucy heads to the lobby.

'How on earth did you find me?' She greets him with a brief but warm embrace.

'Google, I'm afraid.' He throws up his hands. 'Go ahead and call me a stalker, but I saw the For Sale sign outside your house, and when I didn't hear any more from you…'

Lucy steers Noah out of the front door of the building, conscious of Lilian's curious surveillance. 'I've got five minutes, but then I need to get back, I'm afraid.'

They walk along the bank of the canal and sit down on a bench. Lucy is shivering in her thin wool dress, and he takes off his coat and drapes it over her shoulders.

'When I googled you, I found a picture of you at some Umbrella PR initiative or other. And I remembered you'd once been thinking about a move down here… I'm in Bristol to meet with a client, by the way.' He grins. 'I'm not just stalking you.'

Lucy turns and looks at him, at the familiar angle of his jaw, the curve of his dark lashes against his cheek. She has missed him so much. She likes him so much. But she also knows that she can't be with Noah, and not just because of geographical distance. Jason Fox's death is an insurmountable barrier between them, and it always will be. She can't engage in a relationship founded on dishonesty, and she cares too much about him to be lying by omission for ever more. And in any future relationships, she'll never again experience the heady euphoria of those early days with Noah. She will always be more circumspect, metaphorically looking over her shoulder.

She stands up abruptly, handing Noah's coat back to him. 'Look, I'm supposed to be on the help desk; I'd better go.'

'That's a shame. Are you maybe free for a drink later? This evening? I don't have to hurry back to London.'

Lucy shakes her head. 'I'm sorry, Noah, I can't.'

He shrugs. 'Okay, well… maybe another time then.'

She manages a bright smile. 'Sure.'

'Well…' Noah shoves his hands into his back pockets in an attempt to cover his awkwardness. 'Goodbye then.'

Lucy raises a hand in salute, and before heading back into the building she stands and watches him walk away, until he has completely disappeared from view.

The sun is low in the sky when she returns home that evening, casting a warm glow onto the amber stone buildings. As she trudges up the steep hill to her house, she notices she has two unread texts on her phone. The first is from Trisha, one of her neighbours.

A group of us are heading out to a live music night at that new bar in Camden. Fancy joining us? 6.30 onwards. T

The second is from Noah.

It was so lovely to see you today, however briefly. Promise me you'll get in touch when you're next in London? I miss you xxx

Lucy lets herself into her house and, after dropping her work bag in the hall, heads straight upstairs to change into jeans and reapply her make-up. Sitting on the edge of the bed, she types a quick reply to the first text.

See you there in 10. L

After reading and re-reading the second text, she deletes it without replying. This is, she reflects, the price of her pact with Adele. Then she sets off to the bar; to music and new friends and the beginning of the rest of her life.

A LETTER FROM ALISON

Thank you so much for choosing to read *The School Friend*. If you enjoyed it and want to keep up to date with all my latest releases, just sign up at the following link. Your email address will never be shared and you can unsubscribe at any time.

www.bookouture.com/alison-james

When I decided to create a standalone domestic thriller, there were two threads that intrigued me: dysfunctional marriages and friendships that take a dark turn. I always like to start a book with a 'what if?', and with *The School Friend* it was this: what if a dysfunctional marriage and a troubled friendship collide? What if the secrets from one were to infect the other? I hope you agree that the answers are intriguing, and they take Lucy and Adele on a journey full of shocks and betrayals.

I really hope you loved *The School Friend*, and if you did I would be so grateful if you could write a review. I'd love to hear what you think, and it makes such a difference helping new readers to discover one of my books for the first time.

I love hearing from my readers – you can get in touch on my Facebook page, through Twitter, Goodreads or my website.

Thanks,
Alison James

 17361567.Alison_James

@AlisonJbooks

 Alison James books

ACKNOWLEDGEMENTS

With huge thanks to all the team at Bookouture for their support and dedication, especially Natasha, Peta, Ellen, Kim and Noelle.